PRAISE FOR TURNAROUND

FROM FRANKLIN WHITE; BEST SELLING AUTHOR OF
Fed Up With The Fanny, Potentially Yours, and *Money For Good*:
"Carved from the same block as Elmore Leonard and Carl Hiassen,
Jimmy Hurd has created an emotional combination of mystery and
suspense; introducing a most colorful cast of characters and a very
believable story line… In an unprecedented debut, this author fashions
his fiction from today's own reality. A must-read."

FROM ZANE; NEW YORK TIMES BEST SELLING AUTHOR OF
Afterburn, Addicted, and *Nervous*:
"*Turnaround* will have readers trying to guess what will happen next but
they never will. A true master of suspense, Jimmy Hurd has spun an
exhilarating tale of a young woman who ends up biting off way more than
she can chew."

FROM DENISE PUTMAN; PRESIDENT AND CEO, PUTMAN APPRAISALS,
ATLANTA, GEORGIA
"Wow! What a storyteller. *Turnaround* kept me on the edge…
quite more than the story I expected…"

TURNAROUND

TURNAROUND
By JIMMY HURD

STREBOR BOOKS

NEW YORK   LONDON   TORONTO   SYDNEY

Strebor Books
P.O. Box 6505
Largo, MD 20792
http://www.streborbooks.com

Cover design: www.mariondesigns.com

ISBN-13 978-1-59309-045-6

LCCN 2004118414

First Strebor Books trade paperback edition October 2005

10 9 8 7 6 5 4 3 2 1

Manufactured in the United States of America

For information regarding special discounts for bulk purchases, please contact Simon & Schuster Special Sales at 1-800-456-6798 or business@simonandschuster.com

DEDICATION

For Sarah and Madison
Daddy loves you

ACKNOWLEDGMENTS

As this book goes to press, I wish to acknowledge those people who have influenced the process in manners both large and small. This list, however, could never include everyone.

Many thanks to: Zane, for the faith she has in others. To Franklin White; author and publisher, for getting the whole ball rolling. To Charmaine and Margaret for their guidance in getting things done, thank you ladies. Much love and thanks to Buster and Jill Johnson, your friendship and encouragement have and always will be so very important. James and Rhonda Green, who told me long ago to live by example and everything else will fall into place. Special thanks to Denise and Sharon Greene, for among other things, allowing me to use the island home. Much gratitude goes also to Tabitha Floyd, who believes that love never stops. To Cassie Wrye, my harshest and most honest critic, many thanks. To the cast of characters at Starbucks in Fayetteville, Georgia, all my love. To Mia Allen, whose smile makes even the worst day wonderful. Thanks also to Wayne Martin of the Baton Rouge Louisiana Police Department. And last but not least, eternal gratitude to my wife, Patricia, for her patience and understanding throughout the process.

CHAPTER ONE

Breaux Bridge was a slow-moving town of ancient Acadian culture and beauty about forty miles east of Lafayette, Louisiana; perhaps best known for its annual Crawfish Festival and its abundance of beautiful women. Jerzy Rabideaux was such a woman. At least most folks who made her acquaintance thought she was a woman. In reality, Jerzy wasn't quite sixteen.

While most girls her age were involved in the things of childhood, playing sports or practicing their cheers, planning shopping trips or parties, Jerzy was trying to find a better life for herself. Considered freakish at school and often taunted by the other girls, she preferred to be alone. For a child, that's not a comfortable place to be, but Jerzy made the best of it. She whiled away her time playing music in her room while she mixed and matched her clothing, playing dress-up, and modeling her dreamy fashions for no one. She lay awake some nights wishing she had at least one good friend that wasn't furry and stuffed.

Raised poor by most standards, Jerzy was never able to enjoy the finer things in life. But girls want things, and Jerzy was no exception. So she learned early in life that she could use her beauty and charm, along with her body, to get the things she wanted from the seemingly ever-present men in her life. She had never actually had intercourse with a man, but she had fondled a few to climax with her soft hands. Her sexual jousting was only a means to an end, and she manipulated many men into thinking they were well on their way to full-blown sexual bliss. In Jerzy's limited experience, most men worked into a sexual frenzy would go deep into their wallets for her, anticipating more.

In material terms, Jerzy had almost everything she wanted. The only thing she lacked, the one thing she truly wanted more than anything, was perhaps the only thing she couldn't get using her learned tactics. Jerzy wanted a family. What every little girl needs and wants; a wholly functioning, bonafide family. Ironically, it was her beauty and her natural ability to unwittingly draw men to her that had kept her family from ever developing. Jerzy coped the best that she could, attempting to heal her subconscious hurt with superficial affections from the male gender and the material items they could provide her.

Jerzy knew it was pointless to approach her mother whenever new fashions in clothing arrived in her little town, or one of her favorite recording artists released a new CD. More often than not, the young girl purchased the food in the house. Shopping trips with Mom for clothing were unthinkable. Jerzy's methods were simple but effective, and born of necessity. She would hitch a ride with someone going to Lafayette and hang out in the side room of the Ragin' Cajun, a poorly lit watering hole that boasted the only two pool tables in Breaux Bridge. Scantily clad in little more than a camisole and short skirt, Jerzy mingled with the crowd as an adult, shooting pool and making conversation until the first proposition came along. The propositions always came. Jerzy had her choice of many. If she didn't like the looks of the first, she would flirt with him and play a little pool, all the time waiting for something more promising to walk in the door. Men were suckers for big breasts and shapely asses, and already Jerzy knew how to press herself against a man just enough to up the ante for the night. A rub here, a little pressure there, a toss of her long black hair at the right moment, allowing it to trail over her shoulders and hide just enough of her swollen cleavage to entice a man to touch. But touching Jerzy was costly. No one ever got away without paying some price. Unfortunately for the men who would encounter this young Southern prize, the prices were going up every day.

Whether for clothing or cash or a dozen other things teenage girls wanted or needed, Jerzy seductively manipulated weak-minded men to secure her needs. When he lived at home, her father wasn't an ambitious wage earner. Since his disappearance, life for Jerzy had become a day-to-day disaster.

The relationship between Jerzy and her father was a good one while he was still around. The two of them talked almost every night about running off and starting a new life in a different town. Jerzy believed in her father's ideas. If given a chance, she knew in her heart he could provide a good home for the two of them. When it became apparent that Parlee had left town without her, Jerzy was devastated. She vowed that she would find him and make him live up to his promises.

Parlee Rabideaux left town to escape the embarrassment brought on by his continued string of failures and the drunken wretch his wife had evolved into. Parlee thought that his dreams could come true in a place where people didn't know him. He had not been seen or heard from in several months, but Jerzy felt sure someone in Breaux Bridge knew where he was living.

Every small town in America has a Parlee Rabideaux. Part town drunk and part town clown, Jerzy's dad had become the falling down source of laughter for the high-minded side of the community. Parlee fancied himself as an entrepreneur, pitching ideas like knuckleballs, with none of them ever finding the zone. He was a schemer and a fantasist with most of his ideas generated by the cloudy gray genius of alcohol. Parlee had decided to make one last attempt to pitch a hair-brained idea about something or another to Abner Ralieau, the janitor at St. Patrick's Catholic Church. If Abner couldn't see the genius of Parlee's plan, then it was off to Atlanta, where true genius was recognized.

Shortly after realizing her father was gone for good, Jerzy decided she'd put up with enough of her mother's drunken abuse and ran away from home. She'd stayed long enough with the mean old bitch, she thought. She treated her mother with respect, unlike most others in their small town. She pretended not to remember the previous night's beating whenever her mother came to and was sober enough to talk to her.

Marlene Rabideaux had at one time been as beautiful and shapely as her daughter. Those days were long in the past, washed away by an enormous ocean of alcohol and lip-dangling cigarettes. Marlene blamed her declining figure and wrinkled features not on liquor and nicotine, but on the child she'd birthed. The poor diet and long nights had less to do with her appearance than the daughter who was stealing her life. Whatever life Marlene had left became increasingly irritating as Jerzy aged and began to develop physically. Men were paying more attention to Jerzy than to Marlene. Out of frustration or retaliation, Marlene would drink herself into a violent stupor and attempt to beat the beauty and poise out of the young girl. Somewhere in Marlene's inebriated mind, she was certain this would somehow make her prettier, or at least make Jerzy less pleasing to the eyes of the men who were supposed to be looking at Marlene. As the days of Marlene's youth drifted into nothingness, the beatings for Jerzy were becoming more frequent and severe.

When she reached the point where she'd tolerated enough of the mean-spirited woman—suffering one too many beatings—Jerzy packed a small duffle and left one night after her mother had passed out on the sofa. Earlier that evening, Marlene had used a broomstick on the young girl, beating her severely. Crying in the darkness of her shabby little bedroom, Jerzy heard her mother lower her sagging body onto the couch. Minutes later she heard the bottle hit the floor as Marlene slipped into unconsciousness. Jerzy retrieved her bag from its hiding place and walked to the front door. As she was leaving the house, she stopped to bend down and kiss her mother goodbye, avoiding the slimy sputum Marlene had vomited on herself.

Jerzy spent a week hiding in the basement of the old Parish church while she surreptitiously questioned some of the local residents of her father's whereabouts. Picking through a garbage can in the church kitchen after Wednesday's Potluck Supper and Bingo night, Jerzy didn't hear Abner Ralieau approach her from behind. Abner's scabby right hand was already on her shoulder when she realized he was there. Startled, Jerzy pulled away and turned to face him.

"I 'pologize for scarin' ya, missy. Did you lose something in that can?" Abner asked. He knew Jerzy was living in the church basement. He also knew that she'd been sneaking around, questioning some of the parishioners.

Like most others in Breaux Bridge, Abner found the Rabideaux family an odd lot. Jerzy—with her good looks and womanly features—was beyond a doubt the oddest of them all.

"Yes, I... Well, no; not really. No, I didn't lose anything in there," she stammered. "I'm looking for something. Some... Well, I haven't eaten in days, and I was looking for something to eat."

Abner let go of her shoulder and began to walk away, toward the darkened corridor that led to the church storage rooms. Looking back over his shoulder, he called to Jerzy.

"If ya want somethin' to eat, I have some stuff back here you can have."

Jerzy didn't hesitate to follow. Not simply because she was hungry, but also because she knew her father often talked to Abner. She remembered seeing them together at Hilo's bar a few nights before her father went missing. The way Abner approached her tonight, and the way he was acting, said that he had something to tell her. Hopefully it would be information about her father that he wanted to share, and not what most of the other men had in mind.

At the end of the corridor, steel double doors opened into a room full of discarded pews and kneeboards. Christmas and other holiday decorations were stacked neatly in boxes lining one wall. The big crucifix that stood in the church courtyard over Easter was leaning against the wall in the near corner of the room. In the far corner of the large room, a smaller room had been built. Abner was fumbling with the lock on the heavy steel mesh door, trying to get it open. Jerzy walked up behind him and—taking the keys from his huge hands—unlocked the door for him. When she returned the keys to him, she let her fingers trail upward to his wrist.

"I really appreciate your hospitality, Mr. Abner. Really, I do. I can't go back home no more. My mama's got so bad about drinking and coming home mad. I can't stand to be around there."

Abner opened a can of potted meat and handed Jerzy a pack of saltines while he searched a nearby basket for a knife. "I know she was beatin' ya pretty bad for a while there," Abner said. "I remember your daddy sayin' she was plum jealous of you, seeing how you were so much prettier than her and all." Still searching the storage cabinets, Abner produced another can of something—no label attached—and announced to Jerzy that it was probably Beanie-Weenies.

Jerzy declined the offering. "This is enough right here, Mr. Abner. I'll get sick if I eat too much at once, after being hungry for so long." As she spoke, she rubbed Abner's arm, and decided then was the time to ask.

Still rubbing Abner's arm, Jerzy stepped closer to him and smiled. She sat the potted meat and crackers down on the cot in the makeshift room. Abner shuffled uncomfortably, struggling to keep from looking at her large breasts, one of which was now partially exposed.

"Mr. Abner, I need something from you. Something I'm sure nobody else but you can help me with." She slathered her words like hot butter on warm crabmeat. "I've got to find my daddy, Mr. Abner. I know he talked to you right before he left. He told you where he was going, didn't he?"

Abner reached up and took Jerzy's hand from his shoulder. "It ain't right for you to touch me like that, Miss Jerzy. And you ain't supposed to be uncoverin' yourself in front of people. You're a little girl." He took a step back and Jerzy pulled at her blouse.

Conscious now of Abner's discomfort, she apologized. "I'm sorry, Mr. Abner. I only want to know where my daddy is, and I'd do just about anything to find him. I figured you wanted what everyone else does; especially if you were going to tell me anything."

The more she talked, the more withdrawn Abner became. "I can't tell you where your daddy is, Miss Jerzy. I know where he said he was goin', but you know how he made things up. He was always gonna do somethin' or go someplace. This time he said he was headed east, but we both know Atlanta ain't no place for Parlee Rabideaux."

Jerzy agreed with Abner, already knowing what she would do next. Abner offered her the cot in the little room, telling her that he knew she had been sleeping in the stairway broom closet. Jerzy accepted the cot, making more apologies to Abner for her behavior. With a warning to make sure that only the two of them knew she was in the basement, Abner was gone.

Jerzy waited several minutes after Abner left before moving. She gathered her thoughts as she slowly spread potted meat on several saltines. She plotted her route from Breaux Bridge to Atlanta, and reckoned she could make it within two days if the wrong person didn't pick her up. Even if someone bad did pick her up, she thought, maybe it wouldn't be so bad. She looked at the little wristwatch in her duffel bag and saw that it was ten-thirty. Anyone worth worrying about was already getting good and soaked over at Hilo's or had made their way south to one of Lafayette's many watering holes.

She could walk from the church to at least Poydras Street, or maybe even Grandpointe. She was fit, and who knew what or who might come along as she made her way toward highway 347 and the long road to Atlanta. She knew he was there. Once she found him, she could help him and they could live together and life would be good again. Daddy didn't have to be afraid to be nice to her if Mama wasn't around. Life could be good. She could go back to school and finish her education. Excited at the thought of finding her father and starting over in a new city, Jerzy inhaled her dinner and left the basement. She ran all the way from Van Buren Street and made her way across a corner lot to East Bridge Street before she slowed down to a fast walk.

After walking less than a mile on Poydras Street, a car with an older couple inside pulled alongside her and asked if she needed help.

"I had a flat tire a few miles back," she lied. "I need to get over to the Quick Sak on 347 before my shift starts at midnight. If ya'll could give me a ride, I'd really appreciate it."

The woman in the passenger seat of the old Buick got out and opened the rear door. "Come on, child. You ain't got much time. We ain't goin' that way, but we'll give you a ride."

Jerzy Rabideaux had a way with people. Innate charm and charisma—or perhaps the gift of gab—allowed her to communicate clearly with anyone. Or maybe the sight of her physical presence stunned people out of rational thought. Big black eyes in a beautiful childlike face affixed to a head full of flowing, deep rich, blue-black hair that fell to her waist in a flood of thick curls. These attributes were perched atop the body of a full-grown goddess that most men would die for. People meeting her for the first time loved her instantly without ever knowing why. Whatever Jerzy had, it was working for her that night. She was on her way to Atlanta and—hopefully—to her daddy.

CHAPTER TWO

December in Atlanta could be warm at times. This particular December found temperatures in the seventies throughout the month. Residents washing their cars one day were scraping frost from the windshield the next. Judge Caine sat at the table in the breakfast nook of his home reading the morning paper and drinking coffee. With an hour to go before he would arrive in his chambers and address the morning's calendar, he thought about calling the clerk and postponing the day's work until tomorrow. At seven in the morning the temperature was already fifty-five and was forecast to reach seventy-two. Perfect winter golf weather, the judge thought. He wondered briefly if Ralph Light would be willing to cancel his day as well. As his thoughts grew more seriously toward a day of golf, his wife, Beatrice, walked into the kitchen and took the seat next to him.

"What does your day look like today?" she asked him as he folded his newspaper.

"Honestly, I was thinking about calling Ralph and seeing if he wanted to run up to the club for eighteen," he said. "Of course, it's simply a thought. My calendar is full, as I recall. With the Christmas holidays coming, postponement will only aggravate people. Besides, everyone would know where I was. Why do you ask?"

Beatrice smiled at him, remembering her question. "You know, we have that Christmas party at the Knowles' house this Friday. I have a green dress at Jester's cleaners that's ready to be picked up. I'd like to have it this evening, but I won't be able to make it into town today. I was wondering if you'd stop by on your way home and get it for me."

The judge looked at his wife for a moment, pretending to mentally picture his day. He wondered what made this woman tick. He'd loved her once, when they were both happy doing the same things. Beatrice had once loved to play golf with him, and he'd loved for her to be with him. They'd compete against each other for dinner or drinks and sometimes—in their younger years—even sex.

A lot of things had changed over the past fifteen years. It had been at least that long since they'd been intimate, but that was to be expected with old age and all. The most troublesome changes were Beatrice's lack of interest in anything the judge championed. She seemed preoccupied with her bridge club, or the Tour of Homes Association. Her constant worry over William's well-being was yet another thing he found aggravating. He'd long since given up on bailing young William out of the trouble he got himself into. At one time, he'd suspended William's allowance, promising to restore it if William completed one year of junior college. On the other hand, Beatrice insisted the allowance be restored and that the judge refrain from putting so much pressure on the boy. She moped around the house for days until he finally relented.

"Certainly," he answered. "I can stop by there on my way to the package store. I need to pick up a few bottles for the DA's party Saturday night."

"Thank you, dear. Have you seen William this morning?" Beatrice asked this often. It was her way of gauging his mood regarding their son.

"I haven't seen him this entire week," he scoffed. "Probably out getting an early start on a holiday drunk."

"Oh really, Carter. Why can't you have at least one good thing to say about our son?"

Taking the question as completely rhetorical, he didn't respond.

\

Arriving at the courthouse, Caine pulled his Lincoln LS into his reserved parking space. As he walked around the front of the building, he noticed a young woman crouched on the sidewalk at the side of the courthouse. She appeared to be looking for something on the concrete. As he approached her to offer assistance, he noticed she was picking up coins that had spilled from a broken parking meter.

"Excuse me, Miss," he said.

Startled, the woman rose to her feet and began to stammer. "I have a... I want to get... I mean, someone broke this meter and I need to turn this money in to the proper authorities."

Caine examined the meter. Someone had pried it with a tool, trying to get it open.

"I can help you with that. It's not often that a person finds money in this city and offers to return it."

He couldn't help but stare at the woman in front of him. She was like no other he had ever seen; not even in the skin magazines. He was certain he was looking at the largest, most perfectly shaped breasts on earth. Draped across both of them—although not enough to hide them from view—was luxuriously thick black hair.

"I... Uh... Can help you get this to the proper people. Right this way, Miss."

He put his hand on the back of her shoulder, guiding her toward the satellite police precinct on the first floor of the courthouse. As she walked slightly in front of him, he glanced at her backside. It was also draped with that beautiful blue-black hair.

At fifty-five, Caine wasn't without sexual desires. Surely they hadn't been stirred to this degree in some time. He couldn't remember ever having been this aroused in the presence of a fully clothed woman.

But damn! Aroused he was, and plenty at that. He led her to the precinct door, and allowed her to walk in first. As he walked in behind her, Caine met a police officer he knew through his troubles with William.

"Judge Caine. How are you, Sir?" the officer asked.

"Fine, Dan, and you?"

The cop looked quickly at the woman with Judge Caine, and responded, "I'm great, Sir. Getting ready for the holidays and all. Say, how's young William getting on these days?"

Caine had become quite proficient at hiding his disgust and disappointment with his son. "He's well, Dan. But here, meet Miss... Uh, I'm sorry, dear. I didn't even get your name."

"Jerzy. Jerzy Rabideaux. I was walking on the sidewalk and saw all this change under a busted parking meter. I thought I better pick it up and find out where it belongs before someone came along and stole it."

Everything about this woman was titillating to Judge Caine. Even the way she spoke soaked into him like a healing salve. He wondered about the accent. Deep South mixed with broken English, perhaps. Whatever it was, he could listen to her for hours. Assuming, of course, that she wanted to talk to him.

As the police officer held out a canvas bag he'd retrieved from a drawer in the desk, he began asking questions. "So, how did you say the meter got opened?"

"I don't know," Jerzy said. "I was just walking up the street and saw the coins laying on the ground. I didn't notice the meter at first, until I looked up."

"It's like she said, Dan," Caine interjected. "I was parking my car when I noticed her down on the sidewalk, picking up the money. That's when I walked over and offered to help her find the police precinct."

Dan appeared satisfied with this explanation. "Okay, Judge. I'll check around outside and look at the other meters. Maybe someone needed a little cash." Dan turned to Jerzy. "Thank you, Miss. It's not often that someone turns in found money. We get a lot of wallets and purses, but they've mostly been gone through and picked clean by the time someone turns them in."

Looking at his watch, Caine said, "I better get going. I have court in fifteen minutes. May I walk you somewhere, Miss?"

Jerzy blushed at the offer and spoke softly. "That's mighty nice of you, Sir, but I was just out walking. I'm not going anywhere in particular. I really don't know my way around here that well."

"Really?" queried the judge. "Are you not from around here?"

He hoped he could learn a little more about her, like where she was from, or where she was staying in Atlanta.

Jerzy played the moment the way she always did, never knowing where it was going to take her.

"No, Sir. I'm from a tiny little place in Louisiana. This is the first time I've ever been in Atlanta. I came up here because my daddy went missing, and I have to find him. I thought I'd check a few shelters; maybe cheap motels. He has to be stayin' someplace, and he didn't have much money. My mother's dead, and he's all I've got left. So it's important that I find him."

Caine looked at his watch again and sighed. At least he had a way in, an opening that could offer another—perhaps lengthier—encounter with this beautiful creature.

"I've an idea," Caine said, reaching into his briefcase. "Take my card. Call me this evening around four-thirty. I have a few friends in the police department who may be able to help us locate your father. It's worth a try anyway."

Jerzy inspected his business card. "Wow, you're a judge? Like in court and all?"

This time Caine smiled openly as she spoke. A grown woman, impressed as if she were a child.

"Yes," he answered. "Just like that. Please call me. I'd like to help you."

At that, he turned toward the courthouse and the calendar he cared even less about now that he'd met Jerzy Rabideaux.

"I will!" she shouted at his back. "I'll call you! Thank you!"

She ran across the street happily, and set out to find another parking meter to pry open.

⸙

The day in court was probably one of the longest the judge had ever endured. Every part of him was consumed by thoughts of the young woman he'd met earlier. During the first recess, he called an eager young bailiff named Christian into his chambers.

"Christian, I need you to investigate something for me." Caine appeared more serious than usual, as though this undertaking was very important, and could further the young man's career. He took a piece of notepaper from his desk and wrote down several names.

"There's a man I need to locate. He may or may not be in the Atlanta area. The name is Rabideaux; although I'm not sure if the spelling is correct. Check with your buddies at the Sheriff's Department. See if they've turned up a man by this name. You may want to check out any other sources you have as well. Anything you can do will be appreciated and remembered."

Christian took the paper from the judge's hand. "Any idea of the first name, Judge?" Christian asked.

"No, not yet, but I may know more later. I'll let you know if I do."

"All right, Sir. I'll see what I can turn up for you. Thanks for asking me to help."

The young bailiff retreated back into the courtroom to restore order for the judge's reentry.

Caine had just returned from the washroom in his chambers when his telephone rang. Olivia, his clerk, was on the other end.

"Judge Caine, I have a call from a young woman outside the building. Should I put her through?"

"Yes, dear," Caine said, "and go ahead and finish up. I'm leaving at five today. I have some errands to run for Beatrice before I go home."

He sat back in his studded leather chair and picked up the phone. "Judge Caine here," he said. The voice on the other end made him smile again, and he began to feel the adrenaline seeping into his veins.

"Judge Carter Caine?" Her voice dripped honey as she spoke into the telephone. "This is Jerzy Rabideaux, Judge. We met this morning."

It was a question as much as a statement, and Caine felt a pang of guilt over his less than virtuous thoughts and feelings. This woman couldn't be older than twenty-one, and a man his age... Well, a man his age and legal stature should refer this person to the appropriate authorities for help locating her father.

"Yes, Miss Rabideaux, I remember. Have you found your father yet?"

"No, Sir. I think it may take a while. I never thought a city could be as big as this. Are you still offering to help me?"

"Yes, I am, Miss Rabideaux," Caine said. "The courthouse is getting ready to close. Can we meet in the coffee shop across the street?

"That's fine with me, Sir. I'll see you over there."

She turned from the telephone and looked into the blue glass of the half-booth. She checked her hair and ran a finger across her teeth. As she crossed the street to the coffee shop, she pushed her breasts up out of her bra as far as she could without exposing her nipples.

CHAPTER THREE

At five o'clock in the afternoon, three days before the Christmas break, the coffee shop was nearly deserted. A panhandler was right inside the door, working the incoming patrons for spare change. Jerzy was already seated near the front windows in a plush leather sofa, watching for the judge to arrive. As she watched her new friend waiting for the crosswalk light to change, the panhandler approached her.

"Wasn't you at the shelter over by the park last night?" the bum asked.

"No, you must be mistaking me for someone else," Jerzy replied. "Now please, go away. I'm waiting for someone."

"I ain't mistakin' you for anyone else. I remember you good. I may be down on my luck, but I ain't stupid. I never saw anyone who looks like you. I remember thinkin' that when you came in."

Jerzy fidgeted with the hem of her too-short skirt, afraid to look up.

"Okay, yes, it was me, and I'll be there again tonight. Please leave now. My friend's crossing the street right there." She pointed out the window as she spoke.

The man moved away from Jerzy and opened the door for Caine to enter the coffee shop.

"Got any spare change, bud?" the bum asked Caine as he entered.

Caine reached into his pocket and pulled out a one-dollar bill. "Here you go, Sir. I'm sorry I can't help you more."

"Thank you, Sir, and Merry Christmas to you."

With that, the panhandler turned and walked out of the door, winking at Jerzy as he passed her.

"Well, Miss Rabideaux. I mean... it is Miss, is it not?" Caine looked at Jerzy over the rim of his glasses, smiling.

"Uh, yes, Sir. Miss is right. I ain't married or nothing. Only please call me Jerzy. I like that better than Miss or anything."

"Alright then, Jerzy. May I get you something to drink? It isn't nearly cold enough for it, but they make a great hot cocoa here."

"That would be really nice of you, Sir. Thank you very much." She smiled and looked down at her hands, allowing her hair to fall forward in a seductive fashion. "I'm not used to people being as kind as you; offering to help me and all."

She blushed, and Caine's temperature soared.

"Not at all, my dear. Not at all. Just wait right here while I get those drinks."

He soon returned from the counter carrying two steaming mugs. "Here you go, Jerzy. You may want to let it cool a bit before drinking it."

He leaned over her and inhaled her scent as he placed the mug on the table beside her. Rather than sit in the open seat on the sofa next to Jerzy, he pulled a chair away from the window and sat directly in front of her.

After an awkward moment of silence—during which they both looked out at the street—Caine spoke.

"I spoke with a deputy friend of mine today, and asked him to check with his sources. You mentioned looking at motels in the area; maybe a homeless shelter. I asked him to check around a few of those places for anyone named Rabideaux. I feel certain we'll know something in a day or two. Maybe we can get you two back together in time for Christmas. How'd that be?"

Jerzy didn't hear the last of what he was saying. His earlier words had taken her by surprise, and she'd immediately gone into panic mode. She'd been using her own name at the shelter across from Woodruff Park. If the judge had his police friends looking for a person named Rabideaux, her name would surely turn up. She'd placed her name on a job search list. She didn't really want the old man to know that she had no money herself and no place to live while in town. If he had to know, she wanted to be the one to tell him; not his police friends.

"Jerzy? Did you hear me, darling?" "Darling" may have been a bit presumptuous that early on, but Caine had thrown it out there before he could catch himself.

"I'm sorry, Sir. What were you saying? My mind kinda wandered there for a spell."

"I was saying, maybe with some luck, we could get you and your father back together in time for a Christmas reunion. Wouldn't that be great?"

"Oh yes, Sir. That would be fine. Christmas ain't but three or four days away. That would be just wonderful, Judge."

Jerzy used the momentary silence that passed between the two of them to process her thoughts regarding this new information. She had to be honest with him. She couldn't stand the embarrassment of him finding out from someone else that she was homeless. He'd know then about the parking meter too, she thought. Being a judge, he'd probably have her locked up. There were several other meters as well, so she'd be blamed for all of them.

But what if she told him, and it wasn't a big deal to him? What if he still wanted to help her? He seemed like a nice old man. He really wasn't that old at all, she thought. Maybe he still had those thoughts. Maybe those thoughts did to him what they did to every other man she knew; every other man except the old janitor at the church. Mr. Abner didn't want anything like that from Jerzy. That encounter had haunted her all the way to Atlanta, and she still thought about it sometimes.

She glanced up at Caine and they both laughed.

"You looked like you were about to cry there for a minute, Jerzy. Are you all right?" he asked.

"I'm fine, Sir. Except I can't be lying to you; after you've been so kind and all."

"Well, Jerzy, relax a bit. You don't have to lie to me about anything. I only want to help you. I can't do that very well if you're not one hundred percent honest with me."

"It's just that I... Well, I haven't told you much; except that I'm from Louisiana and I came here looking for my father." She looked into the judge's eyes this time; cold, steel blue eyes; clear and bright. They must've been beautiful years ago. Then she saw the look. They all have the look, she thought. Or at least, sooner or later, they all get the look.

"What else is there to tell me, Jerzy? Are you in any trouble? Did you do something, or did someone do something to you?"

"No, nothing like that, Judge. Do you like being called Judge, or is there something else people call you?" She needed to get closer to the man; make him easier to get to. Now that she had recognized the look of lust in his eyes, she was sure she could get anything she wanted. She always did.

"I suppose you could call me what my friends call me; if that's comfortable for you. My name's Carter. You could call me that, if you'd like."

"Yes, I think I'd like that just fine," she said. "Anyway, uh... Carter, I better tell you something before your police friend finds out and tells you. You should hear this from me first. I'm not in trouble or anything; at least not yet." Once again she lowered her head and let her hair drape over her ample breasts. She focused on her hands in her lap, as if in deep thought, watching her fingers roll the hem of her skirt up and down. When she once again raised her head, she moved her hair aside with her hands. As she made this motion, she stealthily opened her shirt a little further. The front clasp of her bra was now in full view, along with two perfect half orbs of creamy white skin. When she looked up at Caine to speak to him, she knew she was right about the look. He was staring directly into her blouse, open-mouthed.

"If you're checking the homeless shelters in town for the name Rabideaux, you may get my name on your list. I've been staying at the Sisters Mission over by the big park downtown for about a month now; as long as I've been in Atlanta. The uh... the parking meter that was broken wasn't really broken, either. I... Well, I pried it open with a screwdriver I stole from the kitchen at the shelter." She didn't know if she should continue, but so far, he hadn't made any gesture or movement that let her know what he was thinking.

"I pried open some others, too," she added. "And I done a few other things that ain't really a big deal, but I don't feel real good about them right now."

Caine still showed no sign of what he was thinking. His eyes were alternating between her face and her chest, until at last he finally spoke.

"I guess I should've known about the parking meter," he said. "And I guess I would do the same thing, were it me in a strange place with no friends or family." He needed to make her feel safe; he didn't want her to run. "These other things, the things you don't feel so good about, what were they?" If she came clean about the rest, then he had her trust, and more than likely had her also, he thought.

"I got real hungry a time or two and didn't have any money; not even meter change. So I took a few things from a little store out by the express-way. Chips and candy; that kind of stuff. I also took a quart of milk from another store near there. Nobody saw me and I never got caught."

This was all the truth, and Judge Caine knew it. She seemed so innocent, so eager to confess. At that moment, he thought about asking her age, but the manager of the coffee shop approached, wiping his hands on his dirty apron.

"I'm sorry to bother ya'll, but we're closing now, and I'd like to lock these doors up so I can count the drawer." He waited for a response.

"Yes, of course, I'm sorry," Caine said as he stood. He took Jerzy's empty cup from the coffee table and handed both of them to the apron. "Sorry we've kept you," he said again as he led Jerzy toward the door and the sidewalk.

Once outside, Caine looked at his watch. He looked up the street in thought for a moment, and then turned to Jerzy. "I'll tell you what." He pointed to a tall glass tube towering over the city skyline. "That's the Peachtree Plaza. Inside is the Westin Hotel. Have you ever been to a Westin?" He was feeling good now, comfortable that he had something to hold over her head.

"I don't really know what a Westin is, Carter. Is that a hotel or something?"

"Yes, a very nice hotel. A girl as beautiful as you shouldn't be staying on the street. Do you mind if I put you up there until we get this mess with your father sorted out?"

Jerzy was ecstatic. That was almost the biggest, tallest building in the whole city of Atlanta. And she was going to be living there. She smiled as she looked at the judge.

"I don't think so, Judge… Uh, Carter. I couldn't ever pay you back for something so expensive. That place must cost hundreds; just for a night."

"I think it's probably much less than that, Jerzy. Besides, you wouldn't owe me a thing. I'm glad I can help you; that's all. You probably won't have to be there long. We should know something about your father soon."

With this, he reached into his jacket pocket and took out his wallet. He reached inside and took out five hundred dollar bills.

"Here, take this money and get the room. Buy yourself something nice to wear. Call me in my office again tomorrow afternoon. It's the last day of work for me, so we can start looking for your father together."

Jerzy looked at the money he was holding out in front of her. She wasn't sure she'd ever seen five hundred dollars all at one time.

"Could you please walk me over there? To the hotel, I mean?" She pouted. "I'm not sure I know what to do."

Again Caine looked up the street. He walked over to the corner and looked around it, spotting a taxi on the curb. He didn't need to be seen in his own car with a strange woman.

"There's a taxi right here. Let's ride over there together, and I'll help you get checked in. Then I really must be going. I still have a few errands to run before I go home."

Inside the hotel room, Jerzy yanked the drapes open wide, looking out over Centennial Park and the city's west side.

"Oh my goodness!" she exclaimed. "What a wonderful place. Sixty-seven floors up in the air. I never imagined anything like this." She turned and ran to Caine, grabbing him in a great hug. "Thank you, Carter! This is going to be fun!"

The old man smiled and realized at that moment, he was being held by a woman forty years younger than him, and as beautiful as any he'd ever seen. He was dizzy and giddy, feeling young and virile for the first time in many years.

"You can order anything you want from the room service menu. They wouldn't take the cash, so they have my credit card number. Simply sign for anything you want. There's also a pool and a gym on the third floor. Have a good time, and call me tomorrow afternoon. I'll be waiting to hear from you."

"Oh, you'll hear from me, alright. I'll call you right at four-thirty, and thanks again for being so nice to me." With this, she stood on her tiptoes and kissed the old man on the cheek.

As he drove into Jester's Cleaners, his thoughts were still on the young girl high up in the hotel room above the city. Waiting for him. Even Beatrice had never waited for him. Lawyers waited for him, and convicts. Filth and stink waited for him every day. They all stood when he walked into the room, and waited while he gathered his thoughts. But women like Jerzy Rabideaux had never waited for him.

The orange sign on Jester's front door indicated they were closed. But Caine knew this was the time when the cleaning was actually done, so he walked around to the rear of the building and knocked on the door. An ancient Asian woman slowly opened the door a crack and looked out.

"Yes? What you want, Sir?"

"Li Ming, it's me. Carter Caine. My wife asked me to pick up a dress for her, and I absolutely forgot. Can I please get it now, so I'll be alive for Christmas?"

"You have ticket, Judge?" Li Ming asked.

"No, I don't. I think I left it on my desk at work. I'm certain she said it is a green formal. You should have a number in your computer under her name. Beatrice Caine."

"No computer. Don't do. I know dress. Miss Caine. Green dress. Be right back."

Soon Li Ming opened the door and pushed the dress out to the judge. He handed her a twenty-dollar bill and wished her a Merry Christmas. Walking around to the front of the building, he checked his watch. Nine o'clock. Beatrice wouldn't care that he was late when she saw he remembered to get her dress. The liquor for the DA's party could be purchased tomorrow.

CHAPTER FOUR

E arly morning, two days before Christmas Eve, and Beatrice was just getting around to putting the Christmas decorations up. Judge Caine walked down the stairs quickly, whistling as he went. Beatrice looked over her shoulder as he whisked by her and playfully slapped her butt on his way to the kitchen.

"What's got you in such good spirits this morning?" she called to him from the foyer.

Whistling louder now, he couldn't hear his wife's question. Beatrice hurriedly finished hanging the antique Santa face on the foyer wall and curiously walked into the kitchen. Caine was toasting a bagel and dancing a one-sided waltz as he waited for his breakfast.

Standing in the doorway unnoticed by the judge, Beatrice laughed silently at his silly behavior.

"Well, Mr. Astaire, may I have the next dance?"

He turned and reached for her outstretched arms and waltzed her the length of the kitchen. "You may at that, my dear, and the next as well, if you choose."

He didn't notice the tears that graced her eyes at the first sincere touch from her husband in many years.

The toaster ejected the bagel, ending the fantasy music much too soon for Beatrice's liking. She held on to him for a moment longer; looking not at him, but into him. Suddenly uncomfortable, he pulled away.

"Don't want my breakfast to get cold," he said as he walked to the toaster.

As he began to butter the hot dough, he turned to Beatrice. "I have a long one again today, dear. Finishing up before the Christmas holidays is always so tiresome. I also forgot to get the liquor for the DA's party tomorrow night, so I may be later than usual getting in tonight."

"Well, I'm glad you made time to get my dress for me. That was thoughtful of you."

She smiled at him and returned to her decorations.

The day in court was spent mostly on jury selection for an important trial set to begin in early January. Again the judge found himself immersed in thoughts of Jerzy Rabideaux. He wondered how she must've felt sleeping in such luxury at the Westin while he lay sleepless, trying to develop a plan that would accelerate their relationship into intimacy. The old man had reserved a place in the back of his mind where he and Jerzy lay naked and spent. He could practically feel the perspiration and smell the young woman's panted breath. This behavior was completely out of character for him, and he was barely aware of his irrational thinking.

During the lunch recess, he sat in the courthouse cafeteria eating a Caesar salad and reading the newspaper. He glanced up between bites and noticed Ralph Light exiting the cashier's station.

He raised his hand and shouted lightly across the room. "Ralph! Over here!" He gestured to his friend.

"Carter, good to see you," Ralph said as he pulled out a chair and placed his tray of food on the table.

"Still on for the party tomorrow night?" Caine asked.

"Yes, with a minor adjustment," Ralph said. "Carney hired a limo to pick me up at the house and take me to the party and then home. She's afraid I may get a bit shit-faced, I think."

"You? Shit-faced? I can't imagine," Caine said jokingly. "How's Carney these days anyway? I haven't seen her in years."

"She's good," Ralph said. "She's still working for Wrye Cameras over at Lenox Mall, and she does some volunteer work here in the city a couple days a week. Keeps herself busy. We have dinner together every Friday night at the house."

"Any thoughts about returning to the world of law?" Caine asked. He was aware of the ire raised in Ralph when Carney finished law school and decided not to take the bar exams.

"No, not that she's let me in on. No men in her life; no real career path. She spends a month in Destin every winter and a month every summer. Walks the beach, fishes with the locals. Never asks me for a dime, so she must be doing all right for herself."

"Yes, well, she always was a good girl. Tell her hello for me the next time you see her." Caine rose to return to court. "I'll see you tomorrow night."

"Without a doubt, arriving in regal style."

Ralph laughed as the judge walked away.

In his chambers with a sleazy defense attorney from Cobb County, Caine sat back in his chair with his eyes closed; rubbing his temples with his fingers. He looked over his glasses at the attorney and spoke.

"The best thing for you to do now, Mr. Beaker, is stop whining and accept the jury as is. You've been through the selection process before, and you know how it works. The trial will begin on January 5th, and I'd advise you to be ready." Caine was becoming more irritated the longer the diminutive parasite sat in his chambers. "Now get the hell out of here and see what you can do about growing a spine over the holidays." With this, he pressed a button on his desk phone and Bailiff Christian walked in. "Christian, please escort Mr. Beaker to the elevators, and come back as soon as you see him on. I need to speak with you."

When Christian returned to the judge's chambers, the old man was in a much better humor.

"Thank you, Christian. My apologies for being rude. I can't stand that little bastard. A worthless oxygen thief is all that man will ever amount to."

Christian smiled as he spoke to the judge. "I think I have something that'll please you, Sir. Some information on Rabideaux."

Caine tried to hide his pleasure. "That's exactly what I wanted to speak to you about. What information do you have, officer?" He reached for his pen and a sheet of notepaper.

"Well, Sir, there are two names actually. One is Parlee, apparently a male, forty to fifty years old. He's signed on as a day laborer with a group that runs into town every day from Doraville. Group runs a framing crew, I think. He listed his address as the Urban Shelter of Atlanta, over near Georgia State. Listed a Cordell Anthony as a reference. Anthony is a trustee over at the county lockup."

The judge nodded as Christian spoke.

"And the second name, is it the same person using an alias? Listing a criminal as a reference, that would figure."

"No sir, Judge. The second name is female. Jerzy Rabideaux. She's at the Salvation Sisters over near Five Points. I spoke with a Jesse Sims over there. Got her name as Miss Rabideaux's reference on a job application over at the Dunkin Diner. This one may be trouble for sure. Mrs. Sims says the girl is about twenty to twenty-five, and a real good-looking girl."

"So what's the trouble with that, Christian?" Caine asked.

Christian looked confused. "Oh no, not that, Sir. Mrs. Sims says she's seen the girl stealing things from other women at the shelter. You know, woman-type things."

"That's great work, Christian. Fast, too. Tell you what. Get Olivia out front to get you a package from her desk. Tell her I told you to ask for it. There'll be two dinner theatre tickets and a voucher for limo service. I think there are also coupons for that little Bohemian place over in Buckhead, the uh... Oh yes, the Café Intermezzo. Great coffee; great dessert; nice ambience. You'll absolutely love the place. Take your wife or your favorite girl and have a good time on me. I really appreciate your help with this matter."

Christian was impressed. "Will there be anything else you'll need on these two, Your Honor?"

"I'm not certain yet. If I need you again, may I feel free to ask?"

"Any time I can help, Sir. My pleasure." Pride swelled in the young man's chest.

As soon as the clock struck four-thirty, Caine heard the phone. He pretended to be busy when Olivia entered the room.

"You have a call from an outside line, Sir. Do you wish to take it?" Olivia smiled as Caine looked up from his papers.

"Yes, of course, dear. It's probably Beatrice's niece again. Coming in from Ireland for the holidays. She wants to surprise her aunt. Are you not leaving tonight? It's later than usual and you're still here."

"Yes. Just finishing up a load of work I agreed to help the clerk with. I'll put this call through and be on my way. Good night, Sir."

"Good night, Olivia, and thank you, dear."

He watched as she pulled the door closed behind her. She closed the outer office door as Jerzy's voice came on the line.

"Carter? Is that you?"

Jerzy's voice seemed to awaken him from some functional coma. He put on his sweetest, youngest voice. "Of course it is, silly. Who'd you expect?"

"Oh, Carter, can you come and see me right this minute? Please? Pretty please?" She poured it on. Like new varnish on an old dresser, her voice made him shine inside and out. "I planned on having you meet me some-where... discreet. Will that work for you?"

He hesitated in uncomfortable silence.

"I... Uh, I'm married, and I have an important position. There's a chance I could be seen... And I... that could be seen as inappro..."

Jerzy interrupted him in mid-sentence. "I know that, but didn't you tell them at the front desk that I was your niece?"

He could hear her pouting through the phone; her lips curling into a seductive arch.

"Well, yes," he answered. "I had to tell them something when they refused to take cash and asked for my credit card. That was the quickest lie I could think of, and I've told it again this afternoon."

Jerzy persisted. "Then what's the harm of a girl's uncle visiting her in her hotel room? I've bought some things downstairs and I want you to tell me if they look good on me."

†

He pulled his car into the underground garage and tossed the keys to the valet.

"Room six seventy-two," he said as he walked through the door into the hotel. He rode the elevator up from the garage level, smoothing himself in the brass panels of the elevator door.

"Who is it?" Jerzy played as he knocked on the door. He didn't answer, and stepped aside so as not to be seen through the peephole. When she opened the door, she didn't see him at first, and he surprised her by grabbing her from behind.

"Oh!" she exclaimed. "What a dirty old man!"

She turned and pressed herself into him.

"It's entirely your fault, young lady; egging me on like that. You could cost an old man his family, his career, and everything else."

He dodged the truth of the statement, looking into her big, black eyes.

"Oh, Carter, you're not old. You're just… mature. That's it; mature. Besides, I kinda like older fellas. A lot of girls do, you know."

He almost blushed. He hadn't felt this much alive in years. He could easily lose control, if he let himself.

"Be that as it may, we better get out of this hallway. Even uncles don't hold their nieces like this."

Once inside the room, Jerzy pirouetted in front of him. The dress she wore was red silk, and the slit up the side gave away more of her thighs than it would have on any other woman.

"So what about this dress? Do you like it?" She knew she didn't have to ask this question.

"I think it looks great on you. Felt good, too, when I grabbed you in the hall. Is it silk?"

"Yes, but not expensive, if that's what you're asking." She needed a response to this. She needed to know how much was too much.

"That's not what I meant." He faked indignation. "As far as I'm concerned, nothing's too expensive for you. I mean that, Jerzy."

"Okay, well, I have another one to show you. It's more like a dinner dress, I think."

She pulled the thin red dress up over her thighs and buttocks, then raised it up over her head and flung it to the bed.

Caine almost exploded. "Jerzy, I… don't you want to… uh… do that in the other room?"

"I got these new undies, too, and I wanted you to see what you've bought for me! Don't worry, I won't bite." She giggled through a sheepish grin.

This was a vision Caine had conjured in his mind since he'd first seen her on the street, and never imagined he'd see it for real. She probably weighed one-fifteen and stood five feet even. The underwear was red satin or an equally reflective material. The bra was mostly lace and left nothing to the imagination. The panties were the t-back variety and as she pirouetted once more, he nearly fainted at the sight of her perfectly shaped bottom.

He had to speak or else he would faint for sure. But the gravel in his throat made speech almost impossible.

"I don't think I've ever seen a more beautiful woman than you, Jerzy. You're perfect in every way. That's for sure."

She smiled, silent as she put the new dress on and spun around in front of him one more time.

"I've got an idea!" Caine shouted.

"What?" Jerzy asked. "Want to go out tonight? I can wear this and..."

He cut her off. "No, better than that. I've a party to attend tomorrow night. A real shindig, as they say around here. You could come as if you were on your own, and we could pretend to have just met each other. That way, we can spend some time together and have a few drinks. It'll be fun, I promise."

She feigned concern. "Well, are you sure? I mean, will your wife be there and all?"

"No, she doesn't make this particular function. It's a party for the members of the DA's, uh, the District Attorney's staff. A few others and myself are also invited every year. Would you be comfortable going?"

Jerzy sat on the bed next to him and stared at the floor.

"I don't know, Carter. I can't even figure out what we are doing here. First, you offer to help me find my daddy; then all of a sudden, I feel like I really like you, and it's like I..."

He reached out and took her hand. Her skin was soft and warm. He could feel his heart pulse through his fingers.

"I know, Jerzy. I was thinking the same thing on the way over here. We're going to find your father. I've gotten so wrapped up in who and what you are, and how happy and alive you make me feel. I don't know. It's not real;

I guess. A young girl like you and an old man like me, there's really no chance..." He let his words trail off. Jerzy stood up and turned to face him. She pulled his face into her stomach and he inhaled her once again.

"Don't be saying things like that, Carter. Anything can happen. You're not so old that you can't be loved."

His insides were boiling. If the heat and pressure had been unable to escape through his pores, he would've exploded. Passionately, he reached his hands up under the material of the dress and squeezed her bare buttocks.

Jerzy stiffened for an instant, imperceptible to the judge. *Oh God*, she thought. *Too far. Mama always said some day I'd go too far. Oh God.* She thought about her actions then, exposing her half-naked body to an almost perfect stranger. She thought about the men back home and how they'd barter with her to get her to expose herself. A quick review of her short past ran through her mind.

Several men in Breaux Bridge had been exactly where Caine was with Jerzy. Not in a hotel or motel, but in little out-of-the-way places like the women's room at Hilo's Bar and Grill, or in the old disused kitchen at the VFW Hall. With promises of money, clothing, or jewelry in exchange for a quick peek, they'd watched with gaped mouths and swollen glands as she removed a skimpy blouse and skirt to expose the curvaceous flesh beneath. She felt good knowing that there was something about her that actually had value. Jerzy also knew that someday, when the time was right and the right person came along, she would end the game.

Jerzy had never had to tell them not to touch. She teased and taunted men to the very edge of sanity, but not one of them had ever put his hands on those intimate parts of her.

To her relief, Caine let her go and stood up. He looked down at her and smiled. He tried to be as cheery as possible.

"So, is it a date? The party starts at seven, but most folks arrive around eight. Would you like to try it?"

Jerzy was still thinking about his hands on her naked bottom. *Just got a little overheated*, she thought. *They all get that way sooner or later. Just a little too much for the old guy and just a little too soon.*

"Well, how do we do it? I mean, do I simply walk in and start mixing it up with folks?" she asked.

"Yes, that's it exactly. You come in around eight. I'll show you the way tonight, and I'll already be there. After a little while, walk over to me and start a conversation. It's that easy. After drinks and dancing, we'll leave and come back here."

"I guess it might be fun."

She was a little concerned about the "coming back here" part, but she could handle him, she thought.

Caine smiled. "It'll be great fun. Don't worry; I'll have everything under control. Show up around eight. Now, let's go downstairs and get a cab. Right now, I'll show you where to go. Tomorrow night, I'll have a cab here for you at seven-thirty."

Jerzy smiled and nodded her head. She leaned up and kissed his cheek, just to remind herself of who was really in control.

After the trip around the city, Caine had the cab driver pull into the underground garage. He paid the fare as he and Jerzy exited the cab, and gave his name to the garage valet. He walked Jerzy to the hotel entrance and kissed her as an uncle would, promising her that tomorrow night would be great fun. When he climbed into his car and made the turn toward home, he regretted buying the Lincoln, and wished instead that it were a Mustang. Hell, at this point, he didn't even need a car. He could fly home.

CHAPTER FIVE

Jerzy cried in the elevator up to her room. She wasn't sure why, but she knew she always felt better afterward, so she didn't hold back her tears. When she opened the door to her room and sat on the bed, she noticed a round red light blinking on the telephone. She picked up the receiver and spoke.

"Hello?"

No one answered her.

She dialed the zero and waited. After four rings, a voice came on the line.

"Front desk. How can I help you, Miss Caine?"

Jerzy was confused. "Miss who?"

The voice again. "I'm sorry, this is the front desk. How can we help you this evening, ma'am?"

"I called 'cause I got a little light blinking on my phone. How do I turn it off?" Simple things; very simple things.

"That's your message light, ma'am." The voice chuckled ever so slightly. "You have a message to retrieve."

Jerzy laughed at her own ignorance.

"Well, how do I get it then?"

"You can dial in yourself, or I can get that for you, if you'd like." Another slight chuckle.

"Well, I'm pretty tired. Can you get that for me?"

Too much, too soon.

"Glad to help, ma'am. Hold for your message."

Such a helpful voice; always willing to help.

Jerzy held the phone for a few seconds before she heard Carter's voice.

"Jerzy, in all the excitement of tonight I forgot to tell you the most important thing of all. I have some information concerning your father. Call me on this phone."

She scrambled in the drawer for a pen and some paper, barely able to get them in time to write down the number. She dialed and waited until he answered.

"Carter Caine," he said, just in case someone else was calling.

"Hi, Carter. I got your message. What did you find out?" She was feeling better already. The night had been full of emotions, and now one more. Good news, she hoped, about her daddy.

Caine sounded excited as he explained what he had learned earlier in the day.

"Well, baby, he's in one of the shelters in the city, and he's working a construction job west of town. From that, he shouldn't be too hard to find."

The word "baby" bothered her a bit, but she pretended not to notice.

"How many shelters are in Atlanta, Carter? Are there a lot of them?"

He heard the urgency in her voice. He felt a momentary twinge of guilt, but justified the feeling by assuring himself he was really going to find her father.

"Not a great many. Not for a city this size. I'll have the name of the place tomorrow in the late afternoon. There's only a few more to look into. I have a good man on it. He'll find him."

Jerzy was about to ask something else when the judge broke in.

"I think we may even be able to leave the party around ten and go wake him. If you'd like, you can bring him back to the Westin to stay the night with you."

This last comment sent Jerzy into euphoria. "Oh my God! Are you pulling my leg, Carter? Are you sure?" She thought of her father there on the sixty-seventh floor. He'd probably be very impressed with her and the connections she'd made in order to find him.

Caine smiled into the phone. "I think I'm pretty sure, Jerzy. Like I said, I've got a good man on it."

She was completely overwhelmed, having experienced more emotions in one day than most fifteen-year-old girls encounter at that point in their young lives. She felt compelled to speak, to say something that would make him remember his promise until the next day. So many promises had gone unremembered. She spoke the words before she realized they were present in her mind.

"Oh, Carter, I love you so much. I'd do anything for you; you've been so good to me. No one would ever have done this for me but you. Whatever it is you want, sweetheart, you just ask. Anything."

After the conversation ended, the young girl realized the commitment she'd made. She couldn't possibly have understood how much Caine had taken her words to heart, and would hold her to them. He was intelligent, well-educated, and held in high esteem by the legal community. But Carter Caine was drunk on an elixir more potent than any other. The young girl had played many games with many people, but Jerzy had never before played on this level. Now she was going to learn the rules of the game, whether she liked them or not.

†

The District Attorney for the state held his Christmas party every Christmas Eve in a large multipurpose room on the second floor of the courthouse building. As the room's main entrance was actually at street level, one could see those coming and going.

Just after seven-thirty Judge Caine was in the foyer discussing college football with Randy Dumas, one of the assistant DA's.

"Georgia this and Georgia that," he was saying. "That's all I've heard since the new coach arrived last spring. They had a new coach last season, and a damn good one. What happened to him? I think I'd rather..."

He interrupted himself as he watched a long Lincoln Navigator limousine pull up to the curb in front of the building.

"Damn, Randy, how many people do you think they have in that bus?"

Dumas shook his head and turned to leave. "Gotta get another drink. See you inside later on."

The limo driver exited and walked around to the rear door of the car and opened it. The first person to exit the car was a plump, exceptionally beautiful blonde wearing a long black coat. *Classy girl*, the judge thought. *Wonder who she came with.* The man still inside the limo stepped out onto the sidewalk and straightened up, speaking to the driver.

Caine walked out into the night to greet the new arrivals, carrying his drink with him.

"Ralph!" the judge exclaimed. "You said you were coming in a limo. I didn't expect to see you in a bus."

"It is huge, isn't it? Nice ride though." Clumsily, Ralph acknowledged the presence of his daughter. "Carter, you remember my daughter, Carney, don't you?"

"It's been many years since I last saw you, my dear." The judge took her hand and held it.

Carney smiled and allowed a handshake. "I remember you, Judge Caine. I spent a lot of time around your office years ago. Dad was always talking about you when I was younger."

"Yes, well, I hope you didn't believe all those awful things." Caine chuckled.

Carney smiled back at him. "No, I only remember you two once worked together."

"That we did, Carney. That we did. We had some really great years together, before I left the firm for the public sector. But Ralph here has done fine without me, in spite of himself."

"I need a drink," Ralph interrupted. "Let's go inside, shall we?"

Carney walked back to the rear door of the limo and climbed inside.

"Are you not staying for the party?" Caine asked.

"No, Sir. I'm meeting some friends over at Tech for dinner. The limo's coming back for Dad. I'll get a cab home later. Good to see you again, Sir, and Merry Christmas."

"Merry Christmas to you, Carney. Come and see us sometime."

He waved as he turned and walked back inside the building with Ralph.

With enough liquor in him to realize he had enough courage to spar with the old judge, Randy Dumas made his way over to Judge Caine and Ralph Light to continue the Georgia football argument. A third man standing with the two friends was Albert Sparks, the only defense attorney in Atlanta ever invited to the party. Sparks was finishing a joke as Dumas approached. "...And the guy said; my chicken died, too!" The three of them were laughing when Dumas walked up.

"Well, Randall, my good man, where have you been?" Caine asked.

He was about to make introductions when he looked beyond Dumas to the petite brunette in a tight red dress walking in the main entrance. Seeing his distraction, the others turned in the direction he was looking and watched as Jerzy walked in and began to survey the room.

Dumas was the first to speak, slurring his words. "Fuck me runnin'..."

"Backward up a hill wearin' a pointy hat..." Albert Sparks was equally impressed.

"Carter, let's leave these youngsters to the chase and go freshen our drinks." Ralph took the judge's elbow and steered him toward the bar.

Caine stole every discreet opportunity he could to watch Jerzy as she mingled with the crowd. Pangs of jealousy arced through him as first one and then another man approached her. Finally, Ralph excused himself to go to the men's room. Seizing the opportunity, Caine sauntered over to Jerzy.

"Good evening, young lady," he said as he approached her. "You look particularly wonderful tonight. Red is definitely your color."

Jerzy liked this game. "Thank you, kind sir. A wonderful friend bought this dress for me yesterday and he said the same thing."

"Do you have a date for this evening, or are you all alone?" He smiled, looking forward to how she'd participate in this childish role-playing.

"Oh no, Sir. I certainly do have a date tonight, but he's picking me up later. We're going to a wonderful place."

She blushed and turned her face away, feeling the red approach.

"I do hope you and your friend have a splendid evening, Miss. Can I get you a drink?"

They walked together to the large bar. The judge spoke in a whispered tone only Jerzy could hear.

"I'll be ready to leave in about an hour," he said. "Will that be good for you?"

"Yes, if that's what you want. Where do you want me to meet you?"

"I'll be with the man you saw me with earlier. Walk over to us and say your date hasn't yet arrived, and you want to leave. Ask if we know where you can use a phone to call a cab. I'll take it from there. Just be sincere."

With that, he winked and turned to find Ralph.

Standing at the bar an hour later, Caine and Ralph were talking. With his mind rushing forward to the rest of the night with Jerzy, he could barely stay focused on the conversation. The old man was thriving on the mixture of adrenaline and alcoholic lust.

Both men turned at the sound of the soft voice behind them.

"Excuse me, gentlemen. I was supposed to meet my boyfriend here at eight, and he has yet to show up. I need to leave now, and I can't find a phone to call a cab. Can one of you tell me where I might find a telephone?"

"The offices are all locked for the evening," Ralph said. "Perhaps we can get someone to unlock one for you."

"I was about to leave myself. I could give you a lift. Where do you need to go?" Caine hoped he was only appearing to be helpful.

"I don't live here in Atlanta," Jerzy said. "I flew in from Denver and I'm staying at the Westin on Peachtree."

"Yes, I know where that is. It's a bit out of my way, but I suppose I can get you there. Get your things. I'll be ready to go as soon as I say a few goodbyes."

Ralph looked at his friend; surprised. "Are you sure you're not too drunk to drive?" he asked quietly.

"No, I'm fine. I'll call you tomorrow and we'll see if we can get in eighteen before the weather changes. Have a good holiday, and tell Carney it was great to see her again."

Ralph smiled. "Alright then. Give Beatrice my love and don't do anything I wouldn't do."

Caine raised his eyebrows and turned to leave.

CHAPTER SIX

"I love these leather seats. They're so comfortable," Jerzy said as she lowered herself into the judge's car. She threw her head back against the plush headrest and closed her eyes. "I may have had a few too many drinks tonight. I feel like I could go to sleep right here."

She squirmed her body into the leather upholstery, allowing it to absorb her weight and embrace her.

"No, you have a wonderful place to sleep tonight, and I'll have you there in a few minutes," Caine said. "If you fall asleep now, I'll have to carry you into the hotel, and how would that look?"

A few moments of silence passed as the judge negotiated Atlanta's one-way maze to Peachtree Street. Finally he spoke.

"I'll let you out at the main entrance and you go on up. Then I'll follow in a few minutes, after I park my car. I can hardly wait to be alone with you. I've thought about you all day."

Jerzy began to feel uncomfortable again. She was aware of the crescendo building within him, and knew she was the cause of it. She didn't quite know how to tell him that what he had in mind wasn't going to happen. She thought of an attempt to anger him, to start an argument that would leave them stranded apart. The relationship would become strained, but at least she could postpone an even more painful moment.

"I guess I should tell you now, I charged some more stuff on your credit card today, at that store inside the hotel lobby." Spending too much money always made men mad, she thought.

"Well, then, I suppose there'll be another fashion show tonight." Caine smiled, feeling the surge again.

Shit. That didn't work at all like it was supposed to.

"Not unless you want me to model men's clothes for you." She peeked at him from the corner of her eye, gauging his reaction.

"Oh, I see. Did you go shopping for me today?" He swelled up, wondering what she could have bought him, not knowing his tastes.

"Not exactly. Since you said we were likely going to find my daddy tonight, and him being in a shelter and all, I thought it would be nice to get him some new clothes. He's probably still wearin' what he left home with."

No response from the judge. The air seemed to chill a bit.

"All I got was pants and a shirt; one of those nice silky-looking ones with short sleeves. Oh, and I found a pair of shoes that looked like his size, so I got them also."

Caine listened and waited for her to continue. When she finished talking, he began to speak.

"I've told the officers to call me on my cell phone when they have his exact location. So this'll work out fine. We'll stay together until we get the call, then we'll go and pick him up." With this he reached over and eased her dress up slightly, caressing her tightly muscled thigh.

Jerzy stared out the window, making no attempt to move his hand until he pulled up in front of the hotel.

"Okay, sweetheart, go on up and I'll be there in a minute. Leave the door unlocked and I'll let myself in."

With this, he reached over her and opened the door.

As Jerzy walked unsteadily into the hotel lobby, the thought of running away occurred to her. *Don't even go up there*, she thought. *But where can I go? He'd find me anyway; just a quick call to his police friends, and then what? He'd probably find a way to put me and Daddy both in jail. He'd probably say we stole clothes and broke into parking meters.* The elevator stopped on the sixty-seventh floor and Jerzy stepped out, making her way to her room. She was sitting on the bed, trying to think of a way out of all this when the door opened and Caine walked in.

Caine bent to kiss her on the cheek, then walked to the small bar in the room and made them both a drink. He sat down on the bed next to her and handed her the glass.

"You'll like this; it's very good," he said. Jerzy took the drink and swallowed it down. "I never thought it was quite that good," the old man said, watching her drink the liquid without stopping for breath. "Would you like another?" he asked. Jerzy nodded.

After an hour passed and more drinks were consumed, the judge stood up and removed his tuxedo jacket. He pulled his shirt from his pants and sat in the chair to remove his shoes.

"What do you want me to do?" Jerzy asked, not certain she wanted to know the answer.

The question stunned him. "What do you mean?"

"Is there anything you want me to do?"

"Why, yes, there is. I want you to get as comfortable as you'd like. It'll probably be a while before the call comes in about your father, so we may as well settle in for a bit."

Jerzy went into the bathroom and pulled an old pair of sweatpants from her duffel. Shedding the dress and letting it drop to the floor, she pulled the pants on and took a long men's tank top from the towel hook on the door. When she walked out of the bathroom, the judge was lying naked under the covers in her bed.

"Sit here," he said and patted the bed next to him.

She walked timidly to the side of the bed and sat where directed. He pulled her down onto him.

"Jerzy, thank you so much for this time together. You'll never know what you mean to me."

His eyes fixed on her nipples through the ribbing of the opaque white cotton as his hand began to snake its way under her shirt. She quivered and was almost sick. Forcing a light smile, she rose from the bed and walked to the bar for another drink. Her mind was spinning wildly in thought as she poured the topaz-colored liquid into her glass. Her heart beat rapidly as she stared briefly through the window at the city so far below. *Mama told me,* she scolded herself. *Mama said someday I'd do this; someday I'd go too far.* She suppressed the urge to cry and returned to her place on the bed.

She finished her drink and placed her glass on the nightstand, turning to face the judge. "I've never been with a man before; not like this. I mean, not like having sex or anything. I don't know what to do... I wish we could..."

Caine was more than a little drunk on the liquor. He was more than drunk with the lust he'd been building within himself for this girl. In his mind she was telling him what some men want to hear. She wanted him to think that she was a virgin, and had decided he was the one she wanted to end that with. He was touched by her eagerness to please him in every way she could.

So the little girl that lived her short life in so much emotional pain was going to grow into a woman tonight. At the hands of a callous old man who knew so little about pain, Jerzy Rabideaux was about to experience a great deal more. No call was going to come about Daddy at all. She knew that now. If he did know anything about her daddy, it wouldn't be revealed until after the deed was done. The alcohol collided with the emotions and shattered hopes. The victim of the tragic accident lay on the bed in a trance of morbid acceptance. Thoughts of home and her daddy, Mr. Abner and the can of potted meat. These things and more filled her head and heart as the little girl lay staring at the ceiling, oblivious to the wrinkled old man who climbed atop her.

Jerzy made no attempt to stop him as he fumbled with her new red panties, fresh washed in the bathroom sink. She only wanted to not be there, to be somewhere safe with her daddy, someplace where she wouldn't be beaten or cursed.

The judge winced once and Jerzy felt intense pain dart from her groin and chase itself up and down the length of her lithe young body. Almost instantly his wrinkled face twisted into a grotesque mask of satisfied relief. She screamed into her fists as the old man stared at her in horrified disbelief.

Tears spilled from her beautiful black eyes, falling into thick wavy puddles in her lustrous black hair. He looked away from her face then, and saw the blood. Not much of course, but enough to effect an immediate education. She'd been telling him the truth. She'd never known intercourse, and she wasn't in her twenties. He was vomiting into his hand before he made it to the bathroom door.

CHAPTER SEVEN

J erzy ran from the room and careened down the long carpeted hall. She cowered against the wall in the mirrored elevator, hoping the ugly old man wouldn't come after her. She reached the lobby floor, running breathlessly to the front entrance and across Peachtree Street. Suddenly, she realized she was wearing only her tank top and sweatpants. The old man was hunkered over the commode, preventing her from grabbing her duffel on the way out. He didn't even know she'd fled the room.

She stopped briefly to catch her breath and slowly became aware of something warm and moist tickling the inside of her thigh. Jerzy looked down at herself and saw the blood that had seeped through the front of her sweats.

"Damn!" she exclaimed out loud. Looking around in a panic, she began to run toward Centennial Park. Slowing her pace as she passed the park, she surveyed the area carefully for the judge or any sign of his friends. Jerzy pushed her weakened body, willing the strength into her legs and feet to keep moving forward. At last, she reached the arena where she crossed the street, running down the ramp into the lower parking decks of the CNN Center. A known place; a safe place. A corner stairwell she lived under for two days when first arriving in Atlanta, before she learned of the Sisters Shelter. She made her way past the unattended booth and began running toward the stairwell.

Off-duty Atlanta police office Charlie Puckett had just climbed into his wife's beat up Taurus wagon. Having finished his job moonlighting as a security officer in Philips Arena, Charlie had to call Kim to pick him up because he couldn't coax his truck into starting. It was two in the morning on Christmas day, and Kim was in a hurry to get home and get back to bed.

Rounding the corner to begin the ascent up to Spring Street, Kim nearly ran over the young girl running through the parking lot. As she brought the wagon to a screeching stop, Jerzy fell haphazardly across the hood.

"What the hell is this?" Charlie yelled, climbing out of the car, still in uniform.

Jerzy stood up and froze. Seeing Charlie in uniform scared the young girl and she turned as if to bolt. This had to be one of the judge's police friends, she thought, and then noticed the woman in the driver's seat. Kim saw the fear in Jerzy's eyes and the blood at the front of her pants, and opened the door to get out of the car.

"Don't be afraid, girl," Kim said. "Look there, Charlie, she's bleeding." Kim showed genuine concern and noticed that Jerzy loosened up ever so slightly.

"What happened to you? What are you running from?" Charlie began shooting questions at the frightened child.

"Ease up, Charlie. Can't you see she's hurt? Damn, let the cop stuff go for a minute. Come here, baby."

Kim walked to Jerzy and took her into her arms. The child recoiled slightly from Kim's touch and then allowed herself to be comforted by the policeman's wife. She looked up into Kim's eyes and fell limp as the events of the evening careened through her brain and overwhelmed her consciousness. Charlie took Jerzy's limp and damaged body from Kim's grasp and lowered her onto the pavement. He turned to speak to his wife, now crying into the sleeve of her overcoat.

"Now what?" Charlie asked.

"I think she's been raped, Charlie. It doesn't look like she's been hurt badly, but I do think someone's had their way with her. Either that or she's pregnant and has tried to abort the baby on her own. Whatever the case, she needs our help."

"Do I need to get some of the guys from the precinct over here and make a report? Get an investigation started?" Charlie was becoming angry at the thought of this young girl being brutalized by some street beast. This was Christmas, for God's sake.

"I know a place we can take her. I've seen it on my way to work. It's over in Midtown, but it'll be better for her than a hospital. You can call the precinct from there, if you want to, or let them take care of calling the police. Here, help me get her into the back seat."

"Just get in the car. I'll get her." Charlie bent to lift the young body. He spoke to her as he gathered her wilted mass into his arms. "Come on, baby girl," the gruff man said. "Into the car with you. You're safe now."

Jerzy showed no sign of waking.

Myrna Blake normally didn't work holidays at the center she founded, but was still at work late in the afternoon on Christmas Eve. With no husband or immediate family to go home to, Myrna decided to stay overnight at the center and celebrate Christmas with some of her guests and the rare volunteers who came in on Christmas Day. It was nearly three in the morning when Myrna heard loud footsteps thumping up the front steps, and an even louder knocking on the large wooden doors to the old Victorian home. She ran to investigate the knocking before the noise could disturb any of the women sleeping in the building.

As she peeked through the curtains, Myrna saw a uniform and a badge. This wasn't unusual for the Midtown Women's Center. The police often brought women here seeking shelter. As Myrna swung the big door inward to acknowledge the officer, he pushed himself and the bundle he carried past her and into the foyer. As a flustered Myrna began to close the door, a woman walked in behind the policeman and smiled as she reached for the blanket the officer carried in his arms.

Kim Puckett pulled the blanket back from the face of the still unconscious girl in her husband's arms.

"We almost ran over this girl running through a parking deck downtown..." she began to explain to Myrna.

"Tell me about it later," Myrna said in a hurried tone as she led them down a hallway. "Right now, let's get her into an exam room and make her comfortable. I don't have a nurse scheduled for tonight; it being Christmas and all. Does she need any medical attention, that you know of?"

Charlie looked at his wife and then back at Myrna.

"We know she has some blood on her sweatpants, and that's about it. Like my wife said, we were leaving the parking deck trying to get home when this kid runs out in front of us looking all scared. We don't know what she needs."

Myrna led them into a small makeshift examination room at the end of the hall. She pulled the bedspread back on the bed and Charlie laid the young girl down and began to remove the blanket from around her.

Jerzy awakened, slowly opening her eyes and looking at the three figures hovering over her.

"Where am I?" she asked, trying to adjust her eyes to the bright light and bring her surroundings into focus. "Who are you people? Did the judge send you for me? Am I...?"

Myrna patted the child's leg. "Slow down, baby. You're safe now. My name's Myrna Blake, and this is Officer..."

"Puckett. Charlie Puckett, and this is my wife, Kim. We almost ran over you in the parking deck. Are you okay?" Charlie was beginning to feel physically drained. He'd worked his regular shift at the precinct and then his after-hours shift at the arena. He winced as Jerzy struggled to pull herself up to a sitting position, dragging the bedspread up around her.

Kim Puckett pushed between Charlie and Myrna and helped the girl up, looking around the room.

"Do you have something else she can put on? She's freezing in these clothes."

Myrna opened the drawer of a small chest and took out a pair of too-large pajamas. She turned to Charlie.

"You leave so we can get her cleaned up and into something warm. We'll call for you when she's finished. If you need to question her, I'd recommend you hold off for a day or two, if that's alright with you."

"That's fine with me, once we find out that everything's okay with her. If there's a crime involved, I'll call somebody from the precinct over. This is my day off."

Myrna closed the door on Charlie's back and turned to Kim. "I've some hot tea in the kitchen and a serving tray on the dining room table. Why don't you get us all a cup while I help her get washed up and dressed? Oh, there's some instant coffee on the serving tray, if your husband wants a cup. Should be plenty of hot water in the teakettle."

Kim left the room to get the tea and Myrna continued to chatter on with Jerzy about nothing in particular. Once the young girl had stripped out of her tank top and sweatpants, Myrna led her behind a white folding screen to a small porcelain basin and Jerzy began to scrub herself.

After she removed what she could of the night's degradation, she dressed in the big flannel pajamas that Myrna gave her and returned to the bed.

As Kim returned to the examination room she found Myrna in the hall pulling the door closed behind her.

"I guess she won't be needing the tea after all," Myrna said.

Kim smiled at Myrna. "You're so kind to take these women in like this. That girl probably has no place else to go. Did she tell you anything before she went to sleep?"

Myrna looked troubled. "Yes, she said her name is Jerzy, and that she's from Louisiana. She claimed she simply had a bad night, and then she fell off to sleep. There seems to be much more hidden behind those black eyes though. At least, that's been my experience with these younger ones."

The two women found Charlie in the large family room staring at several framed photographs of various women, past residents of the center.

"Are you ready to go now?" Kim asked her husband as she entered the room.

"I'm ready. Do I need to call one of the guys over before we leave?"

Kim turned to Myrna. "You can answer that better than me."

"Let us get her settled in first. I need to do an intake interview on her. She may want to leave without telling us anything. She has that right, you know."

Charlie thought for a moment before responding.

"Yes, I suppose you're right, Ms. Blake. But if there's anything we can do, either Kim or I, please call us." He turned to Kim. "Do you have one of your cards with you?"

Kim went through her purse and came up with her business card. She wrote her cell phone and home phone numbers on the back. She handed the card to Myrna.

"Like Charlie said, if there's anything we can do, call us. Please."

CHAPTER EIGHT

The Midtown Women's Center became Jerzy's home for the next two weeks. The only home she'd known for some time, she found the old Victorian structure to be comfortable and safe. She'd awakened in the afternoon on Christmas Day to find a rather pretty blonde woman putting clothes in a chest across the room from the large overstuffed bed where she lay. A small decorated Christmas tree stood in a corner. Sunlight crowded into the room from a large bay window draped with lace curtains. Small crystal butterflies clung to the center window and cast tiny prisms of light on the adjacent wall.

Jerzy lay still, silently studying the room and its contents. She was afraid to speak to the woman for fear of startling her. When the woman turned to leave the room, she saw that Jerzy was awake.

The stranger smiled and spoke. "I'm glad to see you've finally come around. I've put some clean clothes in the drawer there that should be close to your size." She pointed to the other side of the room. "There's a shower in the bathroom and some toiletries, if you'd like to get dressed so you can get up and look around."

"Where am I?" Jerzy inquired.

"You're at the Midtown Women's Center. We take care of women in crisis. You've been here since early this morning."

Jerzy was confused. "Am I still in Atlanta?"

"Of course. You're in Midtown, but it's still Atlanta." The woman smiled at the child-like question.

"Is today Christmas?" the child spoke again, in anticipation.

The woman smiled as she responded to Jerzy's question. "Why yes, come to think of it. Today is Christmas. Merry Christmas, young lady."

"Did the police bring me here?"

"No. Well, actually a policeman and his wife did bring you in, but he was off-duty. Not knowing exactly what happened to you, there hasn't been an issue with the law or anything."

"Oh, I see. I remember he was in a uniform. I didn't know if I was in trouble or anything. Do you work here?"

"I do volunteer work here a few days a week, but my paying job is over at Lenox Mall. Have you ever been there?"

Jerzy thought for a moment before answering. "No, I've never been anywhere in Atlanta except right in town. I'd like to go there sometime though, to the mall I mean." She smiled shyly at the woman.

The small talk continued as the woman and the child built a rapport. There existed a contradictory nature about the new arrival, slipping back and forth from woman to child so that one couldn't anticipate what was coming out of her mouth next. Jerzy learned much about the stocky blonde as they went through the social motions of familiarity. She learned that her new friend had graduated from law school in Nashville, Tennessee, that her father was a lawyer in Atlanta, and that she had no brothers or sisters. She also learned that the woman's mother died when she was a little girl. Jerzy watched the excitement grow within the woman as she shared her love of the ocean and the beach that encircled the clear blue water. Jerzy smiled dreamily as she listened to the stories of the sugar-white sand and big oceans in places she'd never heard of.

Jerzy shared her brief history as well. Her modest home in the tiny town of Breaux Bridge, the Sego palms that her father had planted in the back-yard and how they pricked her legs when she walked past them. She told the woman about the blood-red mandevilla that grew up the trellis her father had placed beneath her bedroom window, and the gardenia that smelled like sweet perfume in late spring and early summer.

She didn't share any specific facts about her father and mother, but she did say that her father had traveled to Atlanta to seek employment, and that her reason for coming to Atlanta was to find him.

It wasn't until later in the evening when the woman returned to Jerzy's room with a tray of food that they formally introduced themselves to one another.

Jerzy jumped, startled at the knock on the door.

"Yes? Come in." Jerzy watched as the door eased open and the stocky blonde pushed a small cart into the room.

"I thought you might be hungry by now, so I brought you a few things. We have some pork roast, new potatoes, and some overcooked greens. Oh, and sweet tea as well. Are you hungry?"

Jerzy had been listening to her stomach growl for the past hour. She couldn't remember the last time she'd eaten. "Oh God, yes. I'm starved. Thank you so much."

The woman arranged the plate and tea glass on a table near the bay window in the small room. She watched as Jerzy sat and grabbed at the meat, ignoring the utensils.

After a few bites, the young girl reached for her napkin and smiled sheepishly. "Dang, I'm so sorry. I do know better than to eat with my fingers. I'm just so hungry." With this, she reached for her fork and began shoveling the soggy greens into her mouth.

After she finished eating, she sat back in her chair and sipped her tea. "That was great... Uh... Well, I don't even know your name. We've talked and talked, and we never even got each other's names."

She stood and walked to where the woman sat on the edge of the bed. The woman watched as the beautiful girl extended her hand to her and smiled as she spoke.

"I'm Jerzy Rabideaux. Thank you so much for all you've done for me. The dinner was delicious."

She dropped her head, acknowledging the kindness of a complete stranger; awash with joy that nothing was expected of her in return.

"I'm glad to finally know your name, Jerzy. I'm Carney Light and it's a pleasure to meet you."

Jerzy felt safe with Carney. There was a natural calmness about her that seemed to draw Jerzy closer and closer. She smiled at the thought of all she'd said to this woman without even knowing her name. Overwhelmed with emotion, she walked back to her chair at the table and began crying as she tidied up her plate and utensils, returning them to the cart. She reached for her napkin and began drying the tears from her angelic face.

Carney watched as Jerzy nervously cleared the table of the dinnerware. When she noticed that the girl was crying, she rose from the bed and went to her, wrapping an arm around her shoulder. "Come on, baby, sit over here and get it all out. It's okay, really it is."

"Oh, Carney, I've messed up really bad this time." Jerzy sobbed harder now; unashamedly letting the tears fall with no effort to dry them.

"It's okay, Jerzy. I'm sure whatever it is, it can't be that bad." Carney tried to reassure her.

"Oh God, if you only knew, you wouldn't say that. I've really pushed my luck this time, and I'm probably in big trouble. I just know I am." She sobbed even harder, pressing her face into Carney's shoulder, wetting her blouse.

"Is it something you want to talk about, or would it be better to wait a day or two?" Carney asked.

"I don't... I want to tell... I can trust you, Carney, right?" She looked up and searched the older woman's eyes and face for an answer, as if unable to wait for her words.

"Yes, Jerzy, you can trust me with anything you tell me. I can only imagine why you're here, and what has happened to you. Believe me, whatever it is, I'll do whatever I can to help you."

The long night and the extended conversation began with Jerzy's mother, Marlene, the beauty queen of Breaux Bridge, Louisiana; and ended with Charlie and Kim Puckett in the parking deck at the CNN Center in Atlanta. Jerzy spared no details, speaking at times through tears that flowed freely down her face, and at other times through laughter that accentuated the lines of her shapely lips.

Carney listened with a combination of interest and disbelief at the courage and blatant insanity of such a young girl exposing herself to so many dangerous situations. She made no judgments and offered no convictions as Jerzy chattered on and on. The night rolled on into morning with no regard to time.

At some point, the two lay back on the bed with the large down-filled pillows under their heads. As Jerzy droned on, Carney began drifting in and out of sleep. Catching herself dozing at one point, she was about to suggest they finish the conversation later when a familiar name slipped into her consciousness. As Jerzy began to recount the relationship she had formed with Judge Carter Caine, Carney came awake. The plump woman suddenly jumped up from the bed and sat back down cross-legged in front of Jerzy. Startled by Carney's sudden movement, Jerzy sat up on the bed and assumed the same position, face to face with her new friend.

Carney appeared stunned. "Whoa... Wait a minute. Did you say what I think you said?" Carney stared at Jerzy in amazed disbelief. "Did you say the man's name is Carter Caine?"

Jerzy saw the look on Carney's face. Her mouth was wide open, as were her beautiful blue eyes. The almost white curls of her bangs draped across her brow. Jerzy watched as the older woman's hand moved up to her face to cover her gaping mouth.

"Yes, he's a judge here in Atlanta. Have you heard of him?"

Carney searched Jerzy's face and couldn't doubt the girl's honesty.

"Do I know him?" Carney drew a loud hissing breath. "Yes, I know him. I spoke to him the very night you said this happened, not two hours before. He was at the DA's party in the state building. He and my father have known each other for years. They're best friends and former law partners." Carney laughed. "Hell, yes, I know him. This is unbelievable. This is insane."

Jerzy dropped her head and stared at her hands for a time before she spoke. She looked up at Carney, who was still staring at her in complete shock.

"I know this is hard to believe, Carney. You don't have to believe me, if you don't want to. It all happened so fast. He caught me picking up change from a broken parking meter, and the next thing I know, I'm staying in a fancy hotel and he's fumbling with my underwear. I can't believe it myself.

But I know I ain't making none of this stuff up. It happened, and I'm so ashamed of myself I can't stand it." She began crying again, picking up the soft pillow and burying her face.

Carney sat speechless and continued to stare at the crying girl for what seemed like an eternity. She tried to picture the judge years earlier, when she'd spent her summer mornings at Ralph's office. She found it easy to remember the judge as she'd last seen him, standing on the sidewalk in front of the big limousine, holding a drink in his hand and seeming to not have a care in the world. The difficulty came in trying to imagine the old man seducing a fifteen-year-old girl. She reached her hands out and placed them over Jerzy's.

"I'm sure it all happened just as you say it did, Jerzy. It's simply hard for me to imagine the judge involved with someone so young. Hell, it's hard for me to see him seducing anyone at all. It seems so...impossible."

Jerzy looked at Carney through teary eyes. She shook her head as she spoke.

"You don't understand, Carney. It wasn't his doing at all. It was me who seduced him. I led him on; that's why he did what he did. It ain't his fault. He was helping me find my daddy and I really appreciated that. I felt like if I showed him my...apprec...well... you know, my..." She struggled to find the right words.

"I guess I don't know, Jerzy. If you showed him what?" Carney responded.

"All my life, I got the things I wanted by doing the same thing. I let my breasts show, or I wear something that shows my butt real good. It's usually harmless. I tease men, and sometimes promise them things... You know, sex and stuff. A couple of times, I took off all my clothes but my undies and let them look at me. I even went as far as getting one or two of them off with my hand, or rubbing them up against my chest. But I never did it. I always made sure I stopped before they got under my panties or bra."

Carney broke in. "So that's what you meant when you said you went too far? You were saying that in your sleep when I first came into your room."

Jerzy knew Carney was struggling to understand all she was being told.

"Yes, that's what I meant. He took me to the Westin. Did you ever stay there? It's really nice. And he let me buy things on his credit card. I even got some clothes for Daddy, and he didn't care. Then, when he let me out of his car in front of the hotel the night of the party, I almost ran away 'cause I knew what he expected. But I couldn't run; in case they found Daddy. I had to stay with him, and I knew that meant I had to let him have his way."

Carney caught a point of reference that could prove if Jerzy was being completely honest. She knew what the judge drove because her father always laughed at his frivolous spending habits when it came to basic needs.

"What time did the two of you leave the party?"

This was something she could verify with her father later, if she felt the need.

Jerzy thought for a moment before speaking. She knew that Carney was having difficulty believing her. She remembered seeing the big limousine pulling away from the curb.

"I got there about seven-thirty. There was a big black station wagon-lookin' car pulling away from the front door when I was walking down the street. It was still early and I saw the judge and another man standing on the sidewalk, then I watched them walk inside together. They were dressed the same, in fancy black suits. I think they were tuxedo suits. The other man was tall and skinny, even skinnier than the judge."

That was Ralph, Carney thought.

"But, Jerzy, what time did you leave the party?"

"I guess about ten; maybe. I went inside a little after the two of them did. Then I walked around and met a few people. I had a few drinks and danced some. So, yes, it was probably ten before we finally left."

"And what kind of car was he driving?" Carney knew the answer and was now almost sure that Jerzy did also.

Jerzy didn't have to think about it. Where she grew up, the kind of car you drove meant a lot to people.

"One of them really nice cars, with the fat leather seats, a Lincoln LS. Really nice. There are only two of them in Breaux Bridge. The funeral home guy owns both of them, though. Why?"

"I wanted to make sure we are talking about the same man. Apparently we are, as hard as that is to believe."

"I don't have any reason to lie to you, Carney. I messed up and there's nothing I can do about it."

"I don't think you messed up bad enough to have a man rape you, Jerzy. No woman messes up that bad. That man is a lawyer and a judge. He knows the law, and he knew you were not at the age of consent. He might not have wanted to admit it or acknowledge it, but he damn sure knew." Carney was growing angrier as she spoke. "Just because you flashed your tits or your ass at him doesn't give him the right to abuse you. The question is, what are you going to do about it?"

Jerzy thought about this for a moment, her furrowed brow bringing yet another dimension to her already beautiful face. She looked at Carney and saw the anger burning in her eyes.

"Really, Carney, don't get mad. I should've stayed at the shelter and never gone to that hotel. That way, nothing would've ever happened."

"Hotel or not, Jerzy, it would've happened. It's happened to me before. At least listening to you now makes me think it did. The only difference is that I'm older, and I always took my own clothes off. Either out of need of companionship or out of loneliness, or some other pitifully rationalized reason. It all amounts to the same thing. No, we're not doing the right thing by teasing or leading men on. And we're not doing the right thing by giving them something so intimately personal just to get something to make us feel better in return, but the things they do to us..."

Her sentence trailed off as she stepped deeper into thought. Jerzy could hear the pain in Carney's voice as she continued speaking. "I was always the fat girl. Everyone's best friend; no competition when it came to the boyfriends. But I was the one the boys would come to for sex when their beautiful, skinny girlfriends wouldn't put out. Then they'd end up marrying those same girls, and coming back to me years later, looking for what? And worse, I was always available and I always made time for them. So, in reality, there's not much difference between the two of us."

Jerzy was frightened at Carney's outburst. *This is probably why she works at a place like this,* the young girl thought. *She tries to help women like herself, so she'll become strong enough to do something about her own life, whether she will admit it or not. Like those recovering addicts that always loitered around the Beanery in Breaux Bridge. Always trying to get back part of his or her own wasted life by saving someone else.* The youngster was thinking as a much older woman would. She leaned over the bed and pulled Carney into a hug. They held each other for a time, crying as they stroked and patted and consoled one another.

Finally, Carney looked at her watch. She gently pushed away from Jerzy and looked into her eyes.

"It's late, Jerzy. Tomorrow, I want you to talk with Myrna Blake. She's the lady who started this place. She can help you with what you need to do next. I mean, in reference to the judge. If it were left up to me, I'd see to it that he fries. Or, at least, spend the rest of his life in jail. He raped you, Jerzy, no matter what you think you may have done to deserve it."

Jerzy nodded. "Will you stay with me when I talk with this lady? I'd like to have you there; now that you know everything."

"Yes, I guess I can stay here in an empty room tonight. But after you speak with Myrna, if you decide to press charges against the judge, I can't help with anything. I can already see what will happen. He'll ask my dad to represent him in court, and there'll be a conflict. It's best I stay a volunteer and not a woman's rights advocate."

Jerzy didn't like this. "But I just met you, and I'd like to keep you as my friend. I've told you things that I've never told anyone; not even my mama."

Carney smiled and hugged her again.

"Don't worry, Jerzy. I'll still be your friend. I'll be around the center during all of this, and when it's over we'll do something together. Hey, how does Florida sound to you? Maybe you can make the trip to Destin with me in April. That's not too far away. I might even be able to help you get a job at the mall, who knows?"

They parted after another long hug, with Carney reassuring the worried Jerzy that everything was going to turn out for the best. Jerzy crawled into bed, said goodnight to Carney, and watched as she closed the door.

CHAPTER NINE

Early the following day Jerzy awakened to a knock on her door. As she raised her head from the pillow to answer, Myrna Blake walked into the room.

"I've brought you some breakfast and a clean change of clothes. I hope these fit better than those pajamas."

She placed a pair of jeans and a pullover sweater on the foot of the bed, and walked back to the hall to retrieve the same small cart that Carney had brought in the night before.

"Carney left a note for me before she went to bed. She mentioned you wanted to speak to me. Sounds like you two were up most of the night."

Jerzy raised herself up and struggled to bring herself awake. Myrna continued to speak as Jerzy brought the woman's face into focus.

"Seems like you've hit a rough patch here lately. Tell you what. You eat breakfast and get yourself tidied up. Everything you need is right here. I think Carney put some other things in the bureau for you, if you'd like to wear something else. It'll be chilly today, and this old house is hard to heat, so dress warm. I'll be downstairs in my office when you're ready. Oh, please bring the cart to the kitchen when you come down."

After Myrna left the room, Jerzy pulled the cart to the bed and began to eat. Scrambled eggs, sausage, and grits were crowded on a large plate. Two oversize biscuits with real butter still steaming under a linen napkin disappeared in short order. Ice-cold orange juice with heavy pulp seemed to taste better than any she'd ever drunk. She sat and surveyed the room as she ate.

Myrna Blake had gone a long way to make sure everything in her center seemed like home. She wanted the women visiting there to be as comfortable as they'd be at home. This was even better than home to Jerzy. Her own bedroom was furnished with the necessities. This room was furnished with beautiful antiques, down to the heavy lace curtains that adorned the large windows. Jerzy thought that she'd never slept in a bed so big; except her few nights at the Westin. As her mind drifted back to the king-sized bed at the hotel, she began to feel sick. She stood suddenly and sharply pushed the cart away from the bed as if it carried her thoughts along with the dishes and biscuit crumbs.

After showering, Jerzy dressed and made her way downstairs, struggling with the cart and its burden of tableware. As she left the kitchen to find Myrna's office, she ran into Carney.

"Good Morning, Jerzy! I'm glad to see you're up and about. Myrna was right about your size. Those jeans fit you perfectly."

"I really appreciate the clothes. I can't imagine having to go back and find my own. Who knows what the judge will do with them. Probably throw them away," Jerzy said.

Carney put an arm around the young girl as they walked down the long hallway leading to the front of the house.

"Don't worry about any of that. We have clothes here, and you're welcome to use whatever you want. Have you talked with Myrna yet?"

"No, she came by this morning and brought me breakfast. I'm on my way to see her now. Can you come with me?"

Carney thought for a moment before answering.

"No, well, I could but it'd be best not to. Remember what I said last night? It's best I be your friend from a distance until this is all over. Judge Caine and my father are close friends. Well, they are until my father finds out what happened between you two. I don't know how my dad will handle this. He thinks the world of that old geezer."

Jerzy looked at Carney and was almost afraid to ask, "Will your dad be the judge's lawyer?"

"I don't even know Caine will ask of him, but let's not worry about all that right now. Go see Myrna, and the two of you decide what to do next. I'll be leaving this morning to go to my regular job, but I'll come back and visit you tonight. Here, Myrna's office is right down this hall."

Myrna Blake had heard a thousand heartbreaking stories in the years since she'd opened her center. Some were worse than others, but most followed the same theme. The women who came to Myrna's place were usually used and abused by a husband or live-in boyfriend. Some were pregnant; others had brought their children with them. Myrna herself had a story, one that she never shared with a single soul, but one that she thought was somehow much more tragic than the others. As she sat and listened to the young girl in front of her, she struggled to maintain her calm. Stifling her anger. Myrna patiently listened, passing tissues to Jerzy intermittently as the tears ebbed and flowed.

When Jerzy finished her story, Myrna sat up in her chair and looked directly into the young girl's eyes.

"So, what is it that you want to do about all of this?" she asked.

Jerzy looked confused. This was something she and Carney had discussed the night before, until the early morning. Jerzy had given considerable thought to letting it all go. She'd almost convinced herself that the entire ordeal was her fault, and didn't know what to do.

"What can I do? I'm not sure the judge is guilty of anything. I led him on, and it wouldn't be right to get him into trouble, would it?"

She waited for a response from Myrna. After a long silence, Myrna finally spoke.

"Yes, I guess it would be fair to say you led the man on. I'd even go so far as to say you implied you wanted to have sex with him. The thing for us to sort out is whether or not the old bastard had any idea of your age. Actually, I think that would be left up to a jury to decide; if you choose to go to the police, that is."

"What'll happen if I go to the police?"

Jerzy was more concerned about her father than anything else. What if he found out about her behavior? How would he react to his little girl having sex with an older, married man? How would he treat her, knowing she had instigated the whole thing? *He'd probably never even find out about all this,* she thought. *Caine said Daddy was living in a shelter himself, so how would he ever know...?*

Myrna Blake interrupted Jerzy's thoughts. "Listen, Jerzy."

The older woman reached and turned Jerzy's face toward her and began speaking in a soothing tone.

"Listen to me carefully. Nothing will happen to you. Nothing, that is, that you can't get over. But you have to pursue an ending to all this madness somehow. Believe me, something like this can haunt you for an eternity and beyond. Did you or didn't you? Was it your fault or his fault? Are you destined to a life of misery, living like a slut? Will all men treat you good, only until they get something from you?"

Jerzy stared into the woman's eyes and didn't move. Myrna's words were simple repeats of the questions the girl had already been asking herself over and over again.

Feeling that she was getting through to Jerzy, Myrna continued on, pushing her point into the young girl's mind.

"I know you probably won't believe this, Jerzy, but I was young once."

Jerzy smiled sheepishly and waved the statement off.

"You're still young, Miss Blake. At least, you don't look very old."

Myrna smiled and leaned back in her chair.

"Yeah, well, I'm pretty old. My point is, I was about seventeen years old when one of my dad's friends took advantage of me. He was really handsome and friendly, and was always hanging with my dad. He'd help my dad with his car; go fishing with him and things like that. I thought he was simply to die for and I'd always get spiffed up whenever I knew he was coming over."

The years began showing in Myrna's face as she recollected her story to Jerzy. She reached for the box of tissue as her eyes clouded over with tears. She struggled to continue, watching Jerzy as she spoke.

"One summer afternoon, when my mom had gone shopping, this friend was coming over to help my dad with an old boat that someone had given him. Before he arrived, my dad got called in to work and had to leave right away. When I answered the door I told him that my dad had to go to work, but he came inside anyway. He told me that he noticed how I looked at him. He told me he also knew that I always made a special effort to dress up for him. I don't know for certain what happened next. All I really remember is that I struggled for a moment and then stopped. I don't know why. I've run those few minutes through my mind every day for over twenty years, Jerzy. I still can't say why I didn't fight him off... I... I just..."

Myrna began to stutter as she finally broke down. Her body shuddered as she tried to control her sobbing. Jerzy could only reach out and pat the hurting woman on the leg. Silence consumed the room for several minutes before Myrna became still and tried to compose herself.

"A lot of different thoughts went through my head, Jerzy. I knew my dad really liked the guy. They were pals, you know? I didn't know what he'd do if he found out. I didn't know if he'd kill the guy and then my dad would be in jail, or if he'd beat the guy up... I just didn't know. I also thought for certain their friendship would end and then my dad would end up resenting me for it. Who knows why we have the thoughts we do? All I know for sure is that I did nothing. I was afraid of what it would do to our family, so I did nothing."

Myrna became quiet again and Jerzy sat still, waiting to hear the end of the story. When the anticipation overcame her, the youngster pressed Myrna to continue.

"So what happened, Myrna? Did your dad find out?"

"Nothing happened, Jerzy. No one ever found out. I think you're the first person I've ever told about all of that. The one thing I do know, and what I want you to know, is that I've hurt over that few minutes for twenty years, and it's a hurt I can't accurately describe. I've buried myself in my job. I opened this center and tried to find my own closure through the women we serve. I've been successful professionally, and never felt like I deserved it. Believe me, life has been awful at times. This is why it's so important for you to make a decision here. You'll never be able to go forward because you'll always be looking back. That has been my experience. I'd like to think I could help you avoid that same miserable life."

Jerzy watched as Myrna dabbed at her eyes with tissue.

"I think I know what I need to do, but I'm afraid. What will people think of me when this is all over? What will my family think? My daddy? How will they treat me when they find out?"

"Nobody will ever know the specifics, Jerzy. If the media is made aware of all this, they cannot use your name because you are a minor. Given the judge's standing in the community, this will surely be a big deal for the press around here. But I doubt that headlines will be made in Louisiana. It'll be up to you to tell your family what happened, if that is what you choose to do."

"Who'll call the police?" Jerzy asked. "Will I do that, or can you do that for me?"

"We should probably call the policeman who brought you in. Puckett, I think his name was. I have his card around here somewhere." Myrna began shuffling through some papers on her desk.

"Will I be able to stay here as long as I need to, or should I go back over to the shelter?"

Leaving the center was an idea that didn't appeal to Jerzy at all. She was comfortable knowing she had Myrna and Carney there for her support.

"Because you're a minor with no parents in the state and no legal guardians, more than likely the state will place you in foster care until this is over. Let's worry about long term when the time comes. It'll be easier for you that way. Carney has ideas of you staying around. She seems to have really taken a liking to you in the short time you've known each other."

"I really like her also. She seems to be really nice." Jerzy smiled and once again lowered her head.

CHAPTER TEN

The conversation with Myrna did more than give Jerzy the confidence she needed to bring closure to her issues with Judge Caine. She wasn't the only woman in the world who made mistakes regarding men and refused to look at their motivation. Myrna could no more explain her caving in to the man who'd taken advantage of her than Jerzy could. Carney said that she'd also let men take advantage of her. At the time, she'd felt that was the best she could do. So Jerzy wasn't the only one. She wasn't alone after all.

That afternoon Officer Puckett arrived at the center with his partner, Sarah Yeakle. Moments later, Kim Puckett arrived. After introductions were made, Myrna led everyone into the center's large family room. The female officer began asking questions, with Puckett answering for Jerzy when she couldn't recall the events which had brought her to the Midtown Women's Center.

"So, you didn't regain consciousness until you arrived here in the examination room. Is that correct?" the uniformed woman asked.

"Yes, I think that's right," Jerzy responded. "I remember waking up in the back of a station wagon, and a woman was driving. I didn't know her, and I was scared for a second. But then I saw the policeman in the passenger seat and I remembered what happened. Then I must've gone back to sleep or something, 'cause I don't remember anything until I woke up here."

"I think She was in shock, and just kept fainting," Puckett added. "She seemed to be really scared when we first saw her. She never even saw our car. She ran right out in front of us."

Officer Yeakle was writing notes in a leather binder as she continued to question both Jerzy and Puckett. "Were you in shock, Miss Rabideaux? From the rape?" She stopped writing for a moment and looked up from her notebook.

Jerzy hesitated before answering. "I didn't think... I mean, I don't think I was raped. That's not what I'm telling you. I thought that..." She stopped, trying to find the words to describe what happened.

Sarah Yeakle looked from Jerzy to Officer Puckett and then at Myrna Blake. She sat upright and laid her notes in her lap.

"You did say he put his penis inside you. Is that correct, Miss Rabideaux?"

"Please, call me Jerzy. Yes, he did put his penis inside me. But I guess I let him. He didn't hurt me or anything. I only wanted him to help me find my daddy."

Officer Yeakle smiled and tried to loosen up. Tact was not one of the young officer's strong points. "Okay, Jerzy, you didn't fight him, and you didn't struggle. I remember you said you took off all your clothes, except for your panties and a tank top, and then laid on the bed next to him. Rape may be too strong a word, but the fact remains, he's an adult and you're a minor. Even if we assume you consented to having sex with him, he'll still be charged with statutory rape. That's the law. Fair or unfair, that's the way it is."

The room fell silent as the four adults watched Jerzy process this information. Carney had explained the same thing to her in a much kinder fashion. This all sounded so harsh coming from Officer Yeakle.

Jerzy kept her head down as she responded, "I understand. I'm just afraid of what'll happen next. I've already caused enough trouble. Can we forget this ever happened? Somehow, I'll be the one that gets in trouble over all this."

Kim Puckett was becoming agitated at Sarah Yeakle's coarseness. She rose from her seat and walked across the room to where Jerzy sat next to the center's large Christmas tree. She lowered herself to the floor and sat cross-legged next to her. She placed her hand on the young girl's leg and looked up into her face.

"You haven't caused any trouble, Jerzy. You made a mistake and chose to play a very dangerous game. Now, the man was married and he knew it.

That fact alone says a lot about his integrity. He also knew you were many years younger than him, so why didn't he ask your age? Don't you think he would've been at least a little curious to know how old you are? See what I mean? He didn't ask because he already knew the answer. You understand what I'm saying, don't you?"

"Yes, I understand. If he'd asked me, then he wouldn't have an excuse if anyone found out. I've heard guys whispering things about me before. Sometimes they're not nice things either, you know?"

"Yes, I know. Men can be real assholes sometimes. Then again, I guess we can all be assholes sometimes." With this, Kim turned and looked directly at Officer Sarah Yeakle.

Nonplussed, Officer Yeakle stood and closed her notebook.

"We have all the information we need, Miss Rabideaux. I'll arrange for you to be examined by a medical doctor and the DA will need a report. We'll have to call Children's Services and try to find a home for you until this is all over…"

Kim Puckett stepped forward. "She can stay with Charlie and me, if that's alright with everybody. I mean, if she wants to." Kim turned and looked at Jerzy for a response.

"Can I stay here?" the girl asked, looking at Myrna Blake.

"You can, Jerzy, but you may have to share your room if someone else comes in. Besides, it might be better for you to be with a family during all of this commotion."

Jerzy looked first at Kim and then at Charlie. "Are you sure I wouldn't be in the way? I…"

"Not at all, Jerzy. We'll have fun," Kim said.

"You won't be in my way at all. I'm working two jobs, so I'm hardly ever home," Charlie responded.

After all the arrangements were discussed, the two police officers returned to their car and sped off with Sarah Yeakle at the wheel.

Kim left as well. She'd return in a day or so to take Jerzy to the doctor's appointment and they'd go to the Pucketts' house from there. *I am finally going to have a family,* Jerzy thought. *Sure it's only temporary, but it's a family.*

✝

Later that evening, the only other woman staying at the center joined Jerzy and Myrna in the family room. Jerzy was peaceful at last, having reconciled her mixed feelings about the impending events. Shortly, Carney arrived at the Center and found the three women in the large room.

"There you all are. I thought I'd stop by and see how our newest client is doing." She smiled at Jerzy.

"I'm fine, thanks. Guess what? I'll be leaving in a day or so to go stay with the people who brought me here; the Pucketts. I've got their number so you can call me whenever you want."

"Wow, Jerzy, that's terrific. Will I be able to visit you there?"

"I'm sure it will be alright. Mrs. Puckett's really nice. I told her that we might go to Florida. She said that would be great."

"Well, remember what I said. I usually don't go until April, and I hope this thing is over with by then. I don't want there to be any conflict because we are friends."

"There won't be any conflict, Carney. I've spent a lot of time talking with Myrna and Mrs. Puckett. I know what I'm doing now. I feel like I'll be happy with whatever the outcome is. I didn't commit a crime, but I did do bad things. I think I've learned a lot from all of you. I realize what I've done is wrong. I've been hurting people; mostly men. Some of them are probably good men, and I messed with them. That's not right. I won't do it again though; not after this. I can't say I'm sorry to all the people I've hurt, but I can try and live my life a little differently from now on. Others may never know it, but I'll know. That's what matters most right now."

CHAPTER ELEVEN

Judge Caine sat watching his wife weeping into a monogrammed pink handkerchief. Her eyes were red and swollen; only tiny slits remained for her to see through. Her voice sounded more like the croaking of a frog than that of a human.

"Why, Carter? You're the epitome of right. You hate our son because he's so… Well, because you think he's so bad. So why did you find it necessary to do something like this?"

She snorted and began to cough; gagging on the mucous lodged in a tight mass at the back of her throat.

"Beatrice, please try and understand. I wasn't in my right mind. I was… Well… I wasn't in my right mind. The woman seduced me. She touched me and she…"

"She what, Carter? She touched you and what? I touch you and you pull away. You've done that for years. No warmth, no intimacy, nothing. So what did she do to you?"

The judge looked away, knowing anything he said at that point couldn't be helpful.

"That's not important, Beatrice. What's important is I've done something unimaginable. I've hurt you and our family and I had to tell you. I needed to clear my conscience, to be honest with you as I always have. I couldn't live with myself otherwise. What I've done is inexcusable and unforgivable. I can only ask for your forgiveness and hope that you'll find it in your heart to…"

The doorbell interrupted the judge mid-sentence. "I'll get it," he said as he rose from his chair and turned toward the front door. He felt an acidic sickness rise into his throat from the pit of his stomach as he entered the foyer and saw the two police officers through the side glass at the front door. Opening the door, he was greeted with a cold breeze he was sure they'd brought with them.

"Good morning, officers. What can I do for you?" He clung desperately to the hope this was about another William problem. Those were comparatively easy to resolve.

The female officer spoke first. "Judge Caine, may we come in, Sir?"

"Certainly. My, it's freezing out there this morning." As he stepped back to let the officers in, he saw Beatrice walking into the foyer. "It's alright, dear, go back to your breakfast. I'm sure everything's fine." He hoped Beatrice would walk back to the kitchen, or for that matter, to Hahira. *Anywhere but right here*, he thought, as he closed the heavy door behind the two officers.

"Please, come in and have a seat. Would either of you care for something warm to drink? Coffee or tea?" he asked, trying to stall them, trying to give Beatrice something to do to get her out of this.

The male officer spoke this time, a deep voice that seemed to last forever in the hollowness of the wide marble foyer. "I'm terribly sorry, Judge. We... Uh... We have a warrant for your arrest. I'm afraid you're going to have to come with us."

The female began taking handcuffs from a round leather pouch on her utility belt. "Please turn around and put your hands behind your back, Sir."

The old man felt lightheaded and dizzy, barely recognizing Beatrice's voice as she babbled out questions to the police.

"What is this about, officers? Why are you arresting my husband? He's a... He's a judge. You can't... You can get in big trouble for this. Is there a problem?"

Pulling a folded paper from his uniform pocket, the male officer ignored Beatrice's prattle. "Judge Carter Caine, you're under arrest for the rape of a minor child at the Westin Hotel, Atlanta, Georgia, on December twenty-fourth of this year. You have the..."

"Stop!" Caine shouted. "I know my rights. Stop, please. Now take these handcuffs off so I can go upstairs and get dressed."

Both officers stared coldly at the old man. He was still wearing pajamas and a bathrobe; brown leather house slippers finishing off his ensemble.

"One of us will have to go up with you, Sir. Either that, or you come with us dressed as you are."

"Fine then. Come with me; both of you. One inside, one outside. Just let me get dressed so we can get the hell out of here. My wife doesn't need to see all this."

Beatrice stepped in front of the officer reading from the paper. His words seemed to have finally reached her ears.

"Rape?" she asked. "What do you mean, rape? Did he rape someone?"

Charlie Puckett wanted to scream at the odd-looking woman in front of him. She too was in sleepwear and had diamonds bigger than golf balls hanging from her fleshy earlobes. He wanted to scream, "Yes, hell yes. He raped a little girl. Your goody-two-shoes prick of a husband raped a fifteen-year-old girl. He did some nice things for her so she'd feel obligated to let him run his wrinkled pink hands over her naked body. Then he shoved his..." *No, let it go, Charlie,* he thought, *getting himself under control. Let it go now, or you'll end up shooting this skinny bastard right in the...*

Charlie's thoughts were shattered by Beatrice's voice, raised an octave higher now as the rest of the story finally arrived at her thought processing center.

"Minor?" She seemed to be appalled. "What do you mean by minor? He raped a minor? A child? Are you saying my husband raped a child? This is impossible. A child?"

Charlie began to calm himself. He looked at Sarah Yeakle and then back at Beatrice Caine.

"Mrs. Caine, we're taking your husband to the county jail. You can meet him there later and ask him what this is about, but right now we have to go."

Officer Yeakle had the judge by the arm and was leading him upstairs so he could get dressed. Caine stopped and spoke to his wife before he ascended the stairs.

"Beatrice, call Ralph Light and tell him to meet me at the jail, and then call William to come and stay with you. I'll try and get this straightened out. It shouldn't take too long. If anyone other than the police come here asking questions, close the door in their faces."

"Carter, what did you do?" Beatrice looked at her husband as if she was seeing him for the first time. The old man saw the confusion and fear in her eyes. She was already off balance when the police arrived, having just learned of his infidelity. He didn't have words to comfort her. Such words didn't exist.

"Just call Ralph and tell him I need his help. Please, Beatrice. Do that for me, will you? Call William and tell him you need him to come home right now. You don't need to be here alone."

The judge knew what was coming next. Someone inside the police department would've already called a friend in the media. Soon reporters and photographers would be appearing at the door. The satellite trucks would line their quiet street and every resident coming and going would be stopped for a potential interview. Beatrice would be alone at the house and who knew what she might say. Better to get William over here to at least do the "no comment" thing. He hoped the boy had at least that much sense.

After allowing Caine to change into a pair of slacks and a clean shirt, the two officers led him out of the house and across the lawn to the patrol car waiting at the curb. Beatrice followed them outside as far as the sidewalk, continuing to ask questions with no apparent answers. She looked frantically up and down the street, as if in search of someone who could answer her endless stream of inane questions.

Not even the common decency to come in an unmarked unit, the old man thought as Charlie Puckett pushed the lanky old man into the rear seat of the car headfirst. Once he was seated, he pulled his legs up into the floor-board and watched as the officer slammed the door behind him. He mouthed the words "I love you" to Beatrice as the patrol car pulled away from the curb, headed for the Fulton County Jail. As the car made a left onto Old Alabama for the southern journey into downtown, a large white network news satellite truck turned right, in the direction of the Caine home. *Just like clockwork,* he thought. No more than forty minutes had elapsed since the doorbell rang and interrupted his conversation with Beatrice.

ϯ

Carter Caine had never seen the inside of a jail cell. Years before, as a defense attorney, he'd discussed legal strategy with clients in rooms provided for that purpose. He'd walked to and from these rooms through hallways that led to the actual prisoner's cells, but had no idea of what the cages looked like.

Now inside his own cell, he surveyed his surroundings. A metal bunk seemingly bolted to the floor with a mattress rolled up on one end would take the place of his king-sized bed at home. A stainless steel toilet sat in one corner with a small washbasin attached. That would replace his private bath, a sanctum that even Beatrice didn't invade. The single bulb recessed into the ceiling was covered by heavy acrylic and steel mesh, diminishing the amount of intended light. This wouldn't do for reading. Then again, he didn't have anything to read anyway, so what the hell. *It's only a matter of time*, he thought. Soon the cavalry would come and rescue him. Ralph Light would arrive momentarily and post his bond, and then he could talk to the right people about getting this situation over with. The only thing to do right then was to sit back and try to calm down; try to sort this entire thing out.

CHAPTER TWELVE

J udge Carter Caine and his son, William, sat in the visitor's room in Atlanta's Fulton County Jail, each man silently assessing the events of the past two months. At fifty-five years old, the judge had four hours earlier been convicted and sentenced for the statutory rape of a minor. At one time considered the harshest judge on the State Superior Court bench, Carter Caine was now facing a life sentence in a Georgia prison. It wasn't yet clear which one he would reside in, but even the best prison in the state was no place for a former judge; especially one convicted of a crime that amounted to no less than child rape in the minds of citizens who followed the trial in the newspapers and on television.

So Carter was—and for a long time would be—in great danger of physical harm. A former judge viewed by the prison population as a child molester didn't stand much chance of living out a prison sentence in quiet anonymity. Prison life for child molesters wasn't that pretty. For child molesters who were once a part of the prosecution side of the legal system, it could be downright intolerable.

These thoughts and more ran through the old man's mind as he wiped beads of perspiration from his wrinkled forehead. It was only March, and spring was only beginning. The hot months were still a long way off, but the judge was sweating at the thought of where he may end up and what could and probably would happen to him when not in sight of the prison guards. He'd put enough people in those places, and was more than familiar with the stories of how too many inmates had met their fate inside the prison walls. As the horrid thoughts continued to ricochet inside his head, he suddenly became aware of his son speaking to him in half-whispered tones.

The old man looked up from his folded hands and, for a moment, was only aware of the lips moving in front of him.

"Where will they send you from here?" William was asking.

Caine looked at him in disgust and wondered what the hell his son could be thinking. His own thoughts were running more toward how to get out of this, or how the hell it had come to this.

He wasn't concerned at present with where he was going to end up.

"They'll send me on down to Jackson and process me. From there I don't know where I'll go. I'm sure I'll be fine, for the time being. They'll probably keep me isolated from the rest of the inmates until I get to my final destination, wherever that is." With that, he stood and ended the conversation. "You go on home and get some rest, y'hear? See to it that your mother is holding up. Make sure she isn't killing herself with those damn sleeping pills."

William shrugged and waved his father's suggestion off.

"No, I'll just stay until they tell me it's time to go, if it's alright with you."

The judge looked agitated and responded harshly, "Suit yourself, boy. Stay as long as you like, but I'm going back to the cell to lie down." With that, the old man dropped his head and skulked back toward the guarded exit door.

William watched as his father walked through the doorway and down the hall, escorted by two guards.

"I'll be here to visit you again day after tomorrow!" he shouted to his father as the unlikely convict disappeared into the doorway of the holding cell. The thought never occurred to him that he'd never again see his father alive.

*

When he arrived home, William pulled his BMW into the garage and closed the automatic door behind him. At this hour, his mother would be sleeping, no doubt with the benefit of the sedatives she'd come to rely on since the day her husband was first arrested. The young man walked into the house through the mudroom off the garage and stepped into the family's large kitchen. The breakfast nook was the darkest place in the kitchen, and this is where William chose to sit and work through his shock. He nursed a cold bottle of Bass ale and stared out the window as if looking for answers hidden in the dark panes of glass.

William Jackson Caine was the only child of Judge Carter Roswell Caine and Beatrice Jackson Caine. Bill, as everyone except his father called him, was doted on and pampered by his mother his entire life. At twenty-eight years old he was neither employed nor employable. His indolence and ignorance had gone a long way toward earning him the loathing of his father. The judge had called in more than a few markers to get the boy out of trouble at one time or another. The father had used his influence in the political community to get William accepted at a university. Young William traveled east to Athens and attended the University of Georgia for a short time before being expelled for his involvement in a violent hazing incident.

Without motivation to succeed in any particular arena of life, he spent most of his time playing golf or fishing. William experienced sporadic bouts of enthusiasm that often resulted in employment, only to be dismissed when personality clashes would arise between him and his employer. He'd occasionally run errands for his parents, but even that at times required more energy than he was willing to expend. His mother had been born into money, and his father had fared well over the years practicing law. William was given a generous monthly allowance, and the way he had it figured, that was his income. Handsome but not too bright, William was in all honesty a short order cook in a world of gourmet chefs.

Now with his father being sent to prison, William was worried. He wasn't concerned with the financial position this would put him and his mother in, because Beatrice had plenty of money herself. William was worried about the well-being of his father. The judge hadn't been such a bad father. He really didn't have much time for his son over the years, but that was understandable considering his profession. William felt that his father had been wronged in some way. Granted, the evidence that came out in the trial was quite conclusive and well-presented. He conceded that. But the presiding judge was a friend and colleague, and his defense attorney was his former partner and longtime friend. Surely this had to count for something. This shouldn't happen to people of wealth and power, at least that was the way William saw things. He looked through the window and tried to understand the entire ordeal.

Less than ten weeks had passed since the day his father had been arrested. In that time, the arraignment had taken place, a jury had been chosen, and the trial had resulted in a conviction and a sentence of life. The thing that William found most worrisome was everything taking place right under Ralph Light's nose, and Ralph not taking steps to stall the prosecution's attempts to expedite the process. Ralph Light and Carter Caine had attended Emory Law together and were partners for twenty years before Carter had left the firm for the public sector.

Carter had languished in jail for three days before finally deciding he wanted Ralph to defend him, and even then he had to almost beg his friend to take his case. Ralph was hesitant to accept the challenge and the judge knew why. The climate in the state was changing regarding issues involving children, and Ralph Light knew this case was a loser going in. If the truth was told, Judge Caine knew this as well.

The incident involving Judge Caine and the minor child had taken place on Christmas Eve, 2002. The timing of the incident couldn't have been worse. Across the entire state of Georgia, controversy and bad publicity concerning child welfare had been rampant for more than two years. Several children had died in foster care as a result of abuse or neglect. There were rape accusations inside the Children's Services Department itself. Evidence was beginning to surface indicating children had been placed in the care of private individuals without the benefit of background checks. Several of these individuals were later found to be offenders of one kind or another. Meanwhile, the print and broadcast media missed none of it. Daily doses of the alleged incompetence among State Children's Services Department agents were fed to the public in large quantities. Prior to the allegations of a prominent Atlanta judge raping a fifteen-year-old Louisiana girl known as Jerzy Rabideaux, the most celebrated state case was the tragic death of a young boy named Jerome Mettison.

Jerome was six, and had been abandoned by his parents in the Briarcliff Mall area of DeKalb County. Speech-impaired and severely malnourished when found, Jerome couldn't tell authorities much about his parents except they'd left him, and he was hungry. Most of this information was obtained through a series of questions, with Jerome answering with shakes or nods of his head. No one knew how long the child had wandered the streets before he was found. After tending to the boy's basic needs and putting him in fresh clean clothes, photographs were taken and Jerome had made the evening news. Two days later an anonymous call came in to the Children's Services Department identifying Jerome's parents. That afternoon James and Tabitha Mettison were arrested in the Sandtown area of West Atlanta and charged with child abandonment. James Mettison arrived at the DeKalb County jail with several bruises and bleeding from his face, having fallen down while handcuffed. The arresting officers had tried to help, but James refused.

Less than a week passed and Jerome was placed in the foster home of Matilda Lemming, a 55-year-old former nurse. Lemming had no previous experience with foster children, and there were no other children in the home. Investigators from the Georgia Bureau of Investigation would later learn that Matilda Lemming was the first cousin of Jerome's caseworker. Jerome lived with Lemming less than a month when the first call came into the Children's Services office from one of Lemming's neighbors. The neighbor had heard Jerome screaming the night before and went to Lemming's door to investigate and offer help. Lemming appeared and said no help was needed; that Jerome was having nightmares. The next afternoon when the neighbor arrived home from work, she saw Jerome playing in the back yard and spoke to him. Jerome, happy for the attention, went to the fence and smiled up at the neighbor with split lips not yet scabbed over. This is why, explained the neighbor, she was calling the authorities.

Caseworkers from the Children's Services Department investigated and found no reason to remove Jerome from Lemming's home. A physician never examined Jerome, nor were any attempts made to have Jerome evaluated by mental health professionals. The cuts in Jerome's lips were attributed by the caseworkers to his biting his lips and tongue in the midst of his nightmares. Life with Matilda Lemming was just peachy. Jerome was happy, in good health, and as far as the State was concerned, in good hands.

Five weeks later, Jerome Mettison was dead. The neighbor who made the first call to authorities hadn't seen Jerome or Matilda Lemming in several days. This time when she went to the door to see if everything was all right, the door opened when she knocked. Tentatively looking inside, she called out to Matilda and Jerome. No one answered. Easing the door open, she stepped inside the little two-bedroom house and saw Jerome lying on his side on his bedroom floor. A short nylon rope was tied tightly to Jerome's right ankle. The other end of the rope was tied to an iron bed frame. The boy's fingers had apparently been smashed with something, and one leg was turned outward from his body. When the neighbor tried to attend to Jerome, it was obvious to her that he'd been dead for some time. Matilda Lemming was nowhere to be found. The autopsy on Jerome's small body showed that he'd been repeatedly beaten over a period of several weeks. Broken bones had gone unattended, and several teeth were missing from his tiny mouth. Full disclosure of the autopsy results was never made to the public, and probably for the better.

Some may say that Matilda Lemming's neighbor overreacted. Still others may say she did the right thing. Whatever the case, she first called the police. She then made calls to every media outlet in the Metropolitan Atlanta area, as well as to a cousin of hers in Macon who aspired to be an investigative reporter. Once the lights came on and the cameras started rolling, the story she had to tell became exaggerated and embellished to the point of horror. The media worked the public into a frenzy with little effort. Resignations were called for, and the public demanded that heads roll at the state's Children's Services Department. One semi-prominent local businessman insisted that the Governor himself resign from office, lest he be impeached. Statewide bench warrants were issued for Matilda Lemming, and the search for her continued for months. So the climate in which Judge Carter Caine would be tried wasn't conducive to a fair trial. The public, as everyone in the District Attorney's office was aware, would be watching every single move the prosecution made. Judge Caine's defense team would be watched even closer. Threats would be made, directed at both ends of the legal system as they prepared to adjudicate this case.

Ralph Light knew all these things and more. His first act as legal counsel to Judge Carter Caine was to have the trial judge recuse himself from the case because of his past professional relationship with Judge Caine. Motion denied. The next legal maneuver, to make a motion for a change of venue, was denied as well. Ralph Light knew then that Judge Caine was—as they say—in deep shit. Ralph also realized that his own career in law, one he wasn't yet ready to end, could be in jeopardy depending on how he handled the press and the public. This was, after all, the American South. Down here, folks didn't want their children trifled with, even if they did belong to someone else.

CHAPTER THIRTEEN

William Caine went to the refrigerator for another beer and sat back down at the table. He felt safe in this place, darkened as it was. He remembered doing his homework here in the afternoons while his mother prepared dinner. When Judge Caine and Ralph Light were still partners practicing law, they'd sat at this table for hours, arguing legal points with each other.

William didn't believe Ralph had done all he could to get his father acquitted of the charges against him. He'd never known Ralph Light to lose a case. But he'd lost this one, for some reason not obvious to anyone except William. Of all the criminals Ralph had defended over the years, he must've learned how to recognize when a man was truly innocent. The longer William sat and debated the events, the more certain he became that Ralph Light had more than a little to do with why his father was going to spend the rest of his life in prison. Nothing could've been further from the truth, but William Caine was becoming more convinced, and growing angrier by the minute.

There had to be some level of corruption going on, William thought. Retaliation was in order, and it had to be bad. His father was never going to be a free man again. Someone was responsible for that, and they had to pay. He began to examine all the players in the trial individually. Judge Edward Mason, a native Southerner who had worked with William's father for the past ten years or so. William decided that he had nothing to gain with Carter Caine going to prison. Judge Mason was about to retire and had already made his plans public. Besides, a judge really only rules on what's put in front of him.

So who else could've had it in for his father? The prosecutor, Dean Neeley, the DA's number one ass kisser according to Judge Caine, could've set this up, but why, and for what gain? Other than the fact the DA's office had the most to lose in terms of public opinion if Judge Caine was acquitted, why would they set this up? Neeley was a Yankee and, even worse, a Harvard graduate and known egg sucker, but it really made no sense that he'd benefit in any small way from the judge going to prison.

On and on went the ideas inside William's head; all through the night until he realized the sun was slanting orange rays through the kitchen's side windows, he raged against one person or another. He returned each time to Ralph Light. Maybe it was Ralph who raped the girl. She was supposedly at the DA's Christmas party minutes before the crime had taken place. Maybe Ralph had to see to it his best friend went to jail to save his own ass. That would be like him, uppity bastard that he was. Revenge directed at Ralph Light would be easily accomplished. He'd never suspect that William was up to no good.

William reflected that, even though Ralph and his father were close, never once did Ralph ever bring his daughter around the Caine home. Maybe Ralph thought his daughter was too good to associate with the likes of William. He knew Ralph had only one child. His wife had died years before, when the girl child was very young. William remembered asking his mother once if there were something wrong with the girl that Ralph was ashamed to bring her with him when he came to visit.

His mother told him she hadn't seen the girl in many years, but remembered her as a normal, healthy child. Carney was her name; or something like that. A weird name for a girl, he remembered. William knew she'd worked at the camera store in Lenox Mall until she'd left home to attend Vanderbilt Law. She'd graduated but never sat for the bar exams. Must be a real loser, William thought. He'd run an errand for his mother on one occasion, retrieving some film Beatrice had dropped off for processing, and had actually seen the girl, now that he thought about it. That's right, he thought. She was the fat girl with the bleached blonde hair and big boobs. Kind of a nice girl, too. Very sexy mouth; sweet warm voice. What the hell was her name? Candy or Connie? Something like that.

Nice girl or not, her father had intentionally thrown Judge Caine to the wolves. *To save his own ass at that*, William thought. The only thing to think about now was how to get back at him for what his family had to endure. What was the one thing William could do that would destroy the bastard? William wasn't an evil person by nature, so the thought of directing his revenge at Carney didn't immediately enter his mind. Ralph had money, and had bought some expensive toys over the years. William had overheard numerous conversations between Ralph and Judge Caine concerning the high dollar guns or golf clubs Ralph had purchased. Perhaps some pillaging was in order. Ralph had some very expensive fishing gear as well, as William remembered. *I could profit a little as well*, William thought, *by selling Ralph's shit. That would do it. Steal a few high-value things from him and tear up that fancy house a bit.*

Only Ralph's place wasn't that fancy at all. William remembered hearing his father remark to Beatrice that Ralph chose to live like a man who didn't have much in the way of an income. Conservative and thrifty, Ralph and Carney led a no-frills life at home. But William knew Ralph had spared no expense on his sporting toys. Stealing Ralph's guns would be a good start. Selling the guns would be easy enough, if one knew the right people, and William did know the right people.

With his mother upstairs in bed sedated into a blissful stupor, William's thoughts labored on into the morning. It wasn't until nearly noon, with his body fatigued and his mind off center, that the vicious thought occurred to William. He could steal all the material possessions Ralph Light owned and sell them all right under Ralph's nose. He could ransack his house and set fire to his car. But nothing on earth could possibly hurt Ralph Light more than someone harming his precious little girl. What a perfectly evil thought! Nobody would ever suspect William had anything to do with it. Hell, even Ralph himself was aware the two of them had never met. William was sure he could do it. He was even certain that he could kill the girl without remorse when the time came to do so. How to set it up, how to bait the girl into a situation where no witnesses were involved, that would be the challenge.

William's mind was made up. For years his father had thought him a fool. The old man never missed an opportunity to berate and humiliate young William in regard to the boy's consistent failures and bad decisions. Whenever Judge Caine learned of his son's vengeance against the back-stabbing Ralph, he'd have to feel some pride for his son. William couldn't wait to see the look on his father's face, and hear the praise he'd longed for over the years. Still planning his revenge against Ralph Light, William hummed as he made his way upstairs to his bedroom.

CHAPTER FOURTEEN

William walked through Lenox Mall, looking for the camera store where Carney had once worked. Hopefully someone would remember her and know what she was doing these days. If he was lucky, she may still work there. She'd never met William, so the chances of her recognizing him were nil.

Finding a mall directory near the theaters, he located Wrye Cameras on the second floor. *That's the place,* he thought. *I remember coming here for mother. Seems like it had been on the first floor at the time.* As William stepped onto the escalator for the trip upstairs, Carney stepped onto the escalator going down. At the midway point he glanced over at her and smiled, recognizing her immediately.

Arriving at the bottom, Carney turned and looked back up to see if she could get another glimpse of the handsome man on the escalator. Carney was intrigued, feeling like she'd seen him before or knew him from somewhere. She watched him as he disappeared from view, then she stepped over onto the escalator going back to the second floor. Back upstairs, Carney slowed and discreetly looked in both directions. She didn't see where he'd gone, so she began to walk back toward the camera store to see if he might've walked in that direction. When she stepped into the store, she saw the man standing at the counter. He had his back to her and was holding a digital camera.

Seizing the opportunity to meet him, Carney approached. "May I help you with something?" she asked, smiling.

Startled, William spun around and saw the blonde standing in front of him. "I was loo... Hey, wait a minute. I just saw you on the escalator going down, didn't I?"

"Yes, that was me." Carney giggled sheepishly. "I work here. I had to come back because I forgot something in the back."

"You work here? At this store?"

"Yes, I'm only here a few days a week. Kind of a part-time gig until I can get something better."

"Oh, I see. So, can you help me with this camera?"

"Sure. What is it you want to know? I like these a lot; it's a digital camera. Different than a regular SLR type."

Carney went through all the details of the camera while William listened. He watched her move her hands over the body of the small device, noticing her long nails and the many rings she wore. Her arms were plumpish but well-toned. Nice skin color, like she tanned often. *She must work out*, William thought. He allowed his eyes to venture up from the camera to her ample chest. Realizing she'd caught him staring at her, he quickly diverted his gaze and began stammering.

"I wasn't really... I was looking for a camera that..."

Carney giggled again, sensing his discomfort. She decided to play with him a little. "I do have a face, you know." She feigned a serious look.

"What? A face? What do you mean?" William began fidgeting.

"I do have a face that you can look at when you're speaking. You were talking to my breasts." *This is fun. He's about to turn and bolt*, she thought.

"I was talking to your face. I wasn't talking... Well, maybe I was staring a little."

"A little? You were about to start drooling." *Any second now he'll run out the door. Poor guy. I hate it when I'm so mean.*

"I wasn't about to start drooling. It's not as if I haven't seen big breasts before. I mean, not that yours are big, but..."

"Well, they are big; huge even. But if you can talk to my face and not my chest, it makes it so much easier to understand you. Now, what about the camera? Interested, or would you like to see something else?"

The double entendre was more than William could stand. He'd come here to find a potential victim, not to banter back and forth with someone he intended harm. He quickly pretended to have a pressing engagement elsewhere. He looked at his watch and appeared exasperated.

"Wow, I forgot all about something I need to do. I'll come back when I've got some time. Do you work on commission? I'd like to see to it that you get the sale if, uh, when I come back."

"No, no commission. You come back whenever you're ready. Better yet, come back the day after tomorrow at three and you can buy me a coffee downstairs. That is, if you'd like to."

William looked into her eyes. Big and blue, shaped like almonds. For a half second, he was speechless.

"I, uh, I don't drink coffee," he said.

"Well, that's good, because I said you can buy me a coffee. I didn't say you had to have one. You can drink whatever you want."

"Yes, of course. I can drink whatever I want." *That was a stupid thing to say,* he thought.

This guy is either an idiot or I have him totally baffled, Carney thought as she laughed aloud.

"I'm sorry for laughing. Really I am. I was only messing with you. So, what do you think? Is three good for you? I'd like to talk with you some more. You seem kind of interesting. Like I've met you somewhere before."

This last comment scared William. Maybe they'd met in the past and he didn't remember. It wouldn't be the first time he'd gone brain dead. He couldn't let her know who he was, or he wouldn't stand a chance of getting close to her. Not close enough to accomplish what he wanted to do. He needed to get back to level ground here. So far in the conversation he'd only been able to pass himself off as a bumbling fool.

"I'm sure we've never met. I would've remembered you." *That sounds a little sappy, but maybe she'll bite.*

"Yeah, I'd be a little hard to forget, wouldn't I?"

Her eyes glistened. William could tell she was having fun with him.

"If you're serious about talking, maybe getting to know each other better, why don't we go to dinner tomorrow night? Say around seven?"

He watched as Carney's eyes narrowed while she thought about it. She started counting on her fingers, as if she was doing an unknown arithmetic problem.

"Seven's too early. I have another job that I... Well, I do some volunteer work, and I'll need to go by there to check on someone before I go out. How about eight? I can meet you somewhere, if you'd like."

"Eight will be fine. How about Kobe Steaks in the Prado on Roswell Road? They have great food there and it's relatively close to your..." *Oh shit! Close to your house. Can't say that to her. Damn! Now what?* William began coughing into his hand.

"Close to my what?" Carney asked as her eyes narrowed further until they were only blue slits.

Time to play the idiot again, William thought. *What the hell, she thought it was cute before.*

"Close to your job. The Prado is just up off 285." *Maybe she'll buy it.*

"I know where it is. That's not what I'd call close. Either way, that's fine with me. I look forward to seeing you then, tomorrow night at eight." Carney gave a little wave as she walked into the office at the back of the store.

William breathed a silent sigh of relief as she exited and turned to walk out into the mall. Before he left the store, he heard Carney's voice again.

"Hey!" She started walking toward him with her right hand outstretched. "We didn't even introduce ourselves. My name's Carney."

William sighed again as he smiled embarrassingly.

"I'm so sorry, Carney. It's really nice to meet you. My name's Bill Ammons. I guess the obvious never occurred to me. I'll see you tomorrow night at eight. Bye now."

With that, he turned and left the store. *Damn, I'm really no good at this sort of thing. Better tighten up if I expect to be able to do this. The girl's eyes caught me by surprise. The way she played with me must've fogged my brain.* He replayed their conversation all the way to his car, and then home.

✝

The next day Carney stopped by the center to visit with Myrna. As she entered the front door, she heard Myrna call to her.

"We're in here, darlin'. We were just talking about you."

Carney walked the short distance from the entrance foyer to the family room, where Myrna and Jerzy were sitting. Jerzy seemed to have grown in stature and maturity in the short three months since they'd first met.

"Good morning, ladies." Carney greeted them both as she hugged first Jerzy and then Myrna Blake. "I've got some great news to tell you two. I was leaving work last night when I ran into the most beautiful man…"

"Uh, oh, here we go again," Myrna said teasingly.

"No, this guy doesn't look like the committed type. He's still young, maybe younger than me. Seems to be a little preppy; like a college boy. Good-looking; well-dressed. He's totally able to speak more than two-syllable words. I did have some fun with him at the store though, messing with him a little. He was all nervous and stuttering. It was too funny. I have a date with him tonight."

Myrna's eyes widened as she took in all that Carney had to say in a few short seconds.

"You just met him and he's already asked you out? Seems a bit hasty, doesn't it?

Carney smiled. "Hasty? Not hasty at all actually. I was the one who asked him out."

Jerzy took her turn to jibe the exuberant Carney. "Must be all that, huh? Asked him out right off the bat, didn't you?"

"Yes, I did, young lady. Now you mind your business." She reached and playfully slapped Jerzy on the leg.

Myrna stood and made her way down the hall. "I'll have some lunch ready in a few minutes, if either of you are hungry."

Carney sat and chatted with Jerzy while Myrna busied herself in the kitchen. "Jerzy, have you discussed the Florida plan with Mr. and Mrs. Puckett?"

"Yes. Charlie says since school lets out in May, there's no sense in me going back until the summer break is over. Kim agrees, but wants me to do some home schooling with her. I've worked it out with Danny at the store. He's letting me take the same vacation days as you; except mine won't be paid. So basically, I'm free to go!"

"Hey, that's great. Of course, we'll only be gone a month, so you'll have plenty of time to hang with the Pucketts. Get yourself home-schooled. Kim and Charlie are great people. They've been wonderful to you."

"Yes, I absolutely love them both. I've been able to save almost eight hundred dollars so far. They won't let me pay for a thing. Charlie says he's even going to give me some extra money for helping Kim around the house. So we should be able to have a great time. I can't believe it's only three weeks away!"

"Well, come on," Carney said as she rose from the chair. "We better see if Myrna needs any help in there. Pay for our bread."

CHAPTER FIFTEEN

W illiam pulled into his garage, whistling because he couldn't believe his luck. On his first attempt to find her, Carney Light hadn't just appeared, but had come looking for him. *Left something in the back my ass*, he thought. *You came back up that escalator and into that store looking for me. I saw you walking down the aisle, looking for where I might've gone.*

He ran upstairs to his room and took a shower before returning to the kitchen for a beer. He found his mother at the table in the nook, flipping through the pages of a *Southern Living* magazine.

"Look, William, what would the house look like painted in these colors?" She pointed at the page showing a large home similar to theirs, painted creamy beige with brown shutters.

"Doesn't look right to me, Mom. The beige isn't bad, but the brown is hideous."

Beatrice frowned and squinted at the page again. "Perhaps you're right. I'd really like to make some changes, maybe sell this place and move into something smaller. Earline, from the club, says there's a lovely little bungalow over by the Botanical Gardens."

"I don't know about that, Mom. That area's getting worse every day. It's not like it used to be."

William watched his mother as she became lost once again inside the pages of her magazine, wishing her perfect world were still perfect.

"By the way, Mom, I've got a date with a wonderful girl tomorrow night. I think you'd really like her."

Beatrice looked up from her dream and smiled.

"What's her name? Does she live around here?"

"No, she lives in Jonesboro or somewhere down there. Her name is, uh, Kelly. She's a little older than me, I think, but she's great. I'm taking her to Kobe. She's never been."

Beatrice, still smiling her altered smile, reached for William's hand and patted it as she spoke. "That's great, Son. Maybe you can bring her over one day for lunch on the gazebo. Do you think she'd enjoy that?"

"We'll see, okay? I don't want to rush into anything. We're just going to dinner for the first time."

As the small talk with his mother dwindled, William kissed her on the cheek and bid her goodnight. He walked up to his room and got into bed. He lay awake thinking about Carney, and about his revenge against Ralph Light.

†

William rose early the next morning and dressed in sweat pants and a shirt, tightening his Nike shoes but not tying them. He walked quietly downstairs so as not to disturb his mother, who probably could've slept through the Southern Crescent speeding through her room. Beatrice had become quite dependent on the sedatives since her husband's incarceration, spending most of her waking hours in a tranquil half-stupor.

Rather than risk the motor of the automatic garage door waking Beatrice, William disconnected the drive rail and raised the door manually. He climbed into his car and drove as silently as possible down the driveway. Pulling up to the curb half a block from Ralph Light's house, William looked at the clock on his instrument panel. Six-fifteen. Now all he had to do was wait to see Ralph leave the house. There were no other cars there, and William knew that Carney didn't come home the night before.

Probably has a bunch of guys she services. A girl like that; educated but not working. She has to have a couple of sugar daddies. Played me like I'm an idiot, he thought. *'I have a face,' my ass.* He blushed at the thought of her catching him staring at her breasts.

At seven-fifteen William was awakened from a half-sleep by the sound of a car starting. He rose up enough to look out the window as Ralph Light climbed into a battered Ford and closed the door. Moments later, William watched as Ralph made a left turn at the end of his street.

After waiting several tense moments, William started his car and pulled into Ralph's driveway. He sat in his car in the driveway while he pondered his next move. *Where would Ralph keep his guns?* Part of the beauty of this plan was to hurt the girl with her father's own gun. *Probably a handgun under a mattress somewhere, or in a nightstand. I've heard of people doing that. Maybe he's got a shotgun stashed in the closet. Hell, probably one in Carney's closet, too,* he thought. She didn't look butch though; at least not last night.

As William left his car, he reached under the seat and removed a long screwdriver. He slid it under his sweatshirt and held it there until he stood on the rear deck of the house. Totally hidden from anyone's view, he pulled on a pair of latex gloves he'd removed from Beatrice's kitchen. He forced the screwdriver between the frame of the patio door and the lock and pried the door aside.

With little effort William was inside the house, carefully checking his gloves. He pulled off his shoes, leaving them in the kitchen on the tiled floor. As he made his way toward the back of the house, he inspected everything in his path. The pictures lining the hallway were of Carney and her father throughout the various stages of their lives. Every frame was taken in a different location and portrayed the happy child and her smiling father. His anger flared at the thought of his own father being sold out by this supposed friend. William continued toward the back of the house, finding two small steps leading to a study on the lower level of the home.

Against the wall behind Ralph's tiny desk was a large gun cabinet. William removed a Browning shotgun and two boxes of shells and placed them on the desk. He went through the desk looking for a handgun and found nothing. Picking up the shotgun and the shells, he made his way back to the main floor and found Ralph's bedroom. *A shotgun would work,* he thought. *It couldn't be concealed, but it would work.* On the nightstand to the left of the headboard was an alarm clock and telephone. *That's it,* William thought. *The bastard sleeps on this side of the bed, so there should be a gun in this drawer.* He pulled the drawer open to expose a nickel-plated Colt .357 Python, mounted scope and all. He smiled to himself, finding the perfect weapon. It was big and bulky, but with the scope removed the gun could still be hidden.

William's confidence was building. *I'm inside the house and nobody knows. I knew right where to go to find the guns. I've not left any fingerprints or footprints; no way anyone can link this to me. Even better than all that, when I press this gun against her head, she's going to recognize it. She'll know it's her father's gun.* He wondered what her last thoughts would be as he pulled the trigger. As this last thought crossed his mind, his stomach turned. He still wasn't sure he could pull the trigger. That was something he was going to have to work on.

Having taken what he'd come for, William left the house. He checked the carpet on his way for any marks he may have made and made sure the pictures in the hallway were still hanging straight. He returned to the kitchen where he slipped back into his shoes and went through the patio door, securing it as best he could. *It would be days before Ralph Light even noticed anything missing,* William thought, as he started his car and drove back home.

Back inside his garage, William reattached the drive rail for the automatic door. He walked to the front of his car and removed the stolen guns, wrapping the shotgun in a blanket from his trunk. He laid the pistol in the trunk and put the shotgun down on top of it. Next to these he placed one of the boxes of shells, laying the second box on his workbench. *What a mess,* he thought. *I'm definitely going to need a shower afterwards.* He checked his watch again. Eight-thirty. He'd been able to complete all of his morning errands in less than two and a half hours.

Beatrice was standing in front of the refrigerator when William walked back into the house through the kitchen door.

"Oh, there you are. I wondered where you were. Would you like some breakfast?"

He pulled a chair out for his mother. "I'll make breakfast for you this morning. Come and sit down."

"That's nice of you. Where have you been off to, so early this morning?"

"I had to get the oil changed in my car. The earlier you get there, the quicker they get you finished. I left around seven." He looked back at his mother as he cracked eggs into a stainless steel bowl. She was back in her magazine, mindlessly turning the pages. He heard her speak but didn't turn around. He couldn't believe his ears.

"I'm hiring a company to come in and remodel the house," she said. "I want everything in here changed. I don't want any sign of him left when those people are finished."

William suddenly could take no more. "Mother, what in the hell are you talking about? No sign of whom?"

Beatrice stared at him blankly for a moment. "You know exactly who I'm referring to, William. Your fucking father; the child molester. I won't be able to hold my head up in this town anymore. We were a respectable family, in spite of what some may have thought."

William had never heard Beatrice use a foul word in his entire life. He finished scrambling the eggs he was working on and flipped the pan over onto a plate. He sat the plate in front of his mother and left the room.

†

At seven-thirty William was turning left onto Roswell Road from 285, the giant Interstate that circled Atlanta. He turned sharply into the Prado and parked at the rear of the lot. Carney saw him park his car and watched as he walked toward the entrance to the steakhouse. Allowing him time to get halfway across the parking lot, she left her vehicle and walked quickly enough to catch up with him. She spoke to him as she reached out and squeezed his arm.

"Hi, Bill. I saw you pull up. Nice car. Daddy's money?"

William almost shot out of his skin. He jerked his arm back and let out a muffled grunt. Carney was taken aback by his response.

"Damn, Bill, I didn't mean to startle you. Are you all right? You look like you've seen a ghost."

She reached for his hand and gently took it in her own. He knew she was soft by the feel of her hand. She was sensuous and sexual. He was trembling. Standing in front of him, she allowed him time to gather his wits. William still hadn't spoken.

An eerie silence lingered as the two stood speechless on the sidewalk. After several moments Carney turned to leave.

"Where are you going?" William suddenly spoke.

"Maybe now isn't a good time, Bill. You look like you're not feeling well. Kinda scary, really."

"I'm fine, Carney. I had a terrible argument with my mother; that's all. After thirty years of marriage, she's decided to divorce my dad. I'm a little out of sorts. Please, let's go in and have dinner. This will pass; I'm sure of it."

Carney's voice took on a sympathetic tone, her eyes moistening at the sight of this handsome man and the obvious pain he was experiencing over his parents' marital problems. *He must be full of mixed emotions*, she thought. She reached her arm out to him and lifted his chin, staring into his eyes.

"I'm sorry about your family, Bill. My mom died when I was very young. Sometimes I hurt like crazy for her; even though I never knew her. You must be nearly devastated."

"Well, it is... Hard to understand. She's being very ugly about it. He's taken care of her all her life."

He dropped his chin onto his chest again and tried to act choked up. *Damn again! This isn't good at all. She probably sees right through this act. Damn!* He lifted his head as Carney spoke again, taking his hand and leading him down the steps to the restaurant.

"Come on, maybe you'll feel better after eating. They've got sake here, too, right?"

"Yes, they do. I'm sure I'll feel better after eating. Thanks for being so understanding."

The first few minutes of the meal was spent in idle chatter. The usual awkward silences were broken by the constant stream of waiters and waitresses bringing first one thing and then another. Silk kimonos fanning the smell of the delicious food across their faces. The thin brown soup with bits of ground beef. The green salad with ginger dressing. The shrimp appetizer, fry the tails please. Before long, William was talking as if nothing had ever happened. They ate and laughed as Carney fumbled with her chopsticks, dropping lettuce in her lap. She laughed when William took the chopstick wrapper and a rubber band the waiter brought him, making a pair of one-handed chopsticks for her to use. Carney was relieved he was able to let go of his horrible afternoon and relax in her company. She was infatuated with him, listening eagerly to him as he lied and schemed his way into her trust.

He was an analyst for an offshore trading company. He lived with his parents whenever he was in town. He'd graduated from Notre Dame and had played football, although he'd never gotten to dress on game day. He was taking a three-month hiatus from work, expenses paid. He was only two years younger than her and she loved the way he looked. Carney liked everything about him so far. She thought he was, as Jerzy said, all that.

After dinner, William walked Carney to her car. He made no move to touch her as he took her keys and opened her door.

"I hope I can see you again sometime. You really made me feel much better tonight. I'm glad I didn't have to be alone." He smiled as sincerely as he could.

"I can see you whenever you'd like, Bill. I stay busy most weekdays, but I have the evenings free." She sat behind the wheel of her car and pulled a business card from her console. She took a pen from her purse and wrote her home number on the back.

"If I'm not there, leave a message. My dad will usually answer after six. He's pretty cool, so you can leave a message with him also."

"Thanks again, Carney. I'll be calling you soon." With that he turned and walked to his car.

CHAPTER SIXTEEN

The night shift of the Fulton County Sheriff's Jail staff was just coming on duty. Sometime during the previous shift the decision had been made to move Judge Caine from the county lockup down to the Diagnostic and Classification Center at Jackson Prison. The origin of the instructions were not clear, but Deputy Terry Holtz replied to the night shift supervisor that he and his partner were the crew for tonight and would be making the trip south with the old judge in tow. This was a convenient coincidence for Deputy Holtz. He had a few personal errands to run down in Clayton County and could make his stops on the way back up from Jackson in the morning. It also meant he and his partner would have time to stop at the Dunkin Diner, which was their routine when making prison runs or other duties. Stopping for a moment or two was no big deal, but stopping for breakfast could get the two of them suspended for a time. But the night shift didn't have a lot of brass hanging around, and no one ever knew what they did on their late-night runs.

Judge Caine walked awkwardly down the stairs leading to the enclosed garage of the jail. He looked taller and even more bent in the county prisoner's standard uniform of orange jumpsuit, white socks, and orange plastic shower shoes. His hands were cuffed in front of him and manacled around his waist. The manacles attached to his ankles limited his stride, and made negotiating the stairs difficult. The guards at each of his elbows were pushing him down the stairs as opposed to guiding him. The big guard on his left arm chided him along the way.

"C'mon, lover boy, carry your sexy little ass down them steps."

Judge Caine struggled unsuccessfully to maintain his footing as he fell face first toward the steps below.

Blood flowed into his eyes from a large gash across his forehead as the second guard helped him to his feet. The guard turned back to his partner, who'd already retreated to the top of the stairs.

"Get up there and get a rag, dumb ass, and grab a trustee with a mop on your way back so we can get this mess cleaned up." He looked at Judge Caine. "We'll get you cleaned up and in the car. No one's gotta know about you givin' us a hard time."

This is only the beginning, the judge thought to himself. *The beginning of a series of nightmares that would occur whether he slept or not. The beginning of the end*, he thought to himself, and felt down to his bones that the end was coming sooner rather than later.

As Deputy Holtz opened the door of the patrol car to put Caine inside, the trustee with the mop arrived to clean up his blood. Cordell Anthony was actually a free man trapped for the time being in the custody of the Fulton County Sheriff. Cordell was wanted for a string of petty thefts in New Orleans and Baton Rouge, but neither Louisiana parish wanted to extradite him because of the expense and the red tape involved. Not being guilty of any charges in Atlanta other than vagrancy, the county didn't know what to do with him. So Cordell washed patrol cars and performed custodial duties inside the jail.

Tonight, Cordell was mopping the halls outside the holding tanks when he was called to go to the garage with his mop, Standing on the steps mopping up Judge Caine's blood, Cordell recognized him from the local papers and television news reports.

As the greasy trustee mopped, he spoke to the old man convict style. "So what's next for you, pal?"

Caine regarded Cordell with a look of disgust. Being addressed by such trash offended him. He was about to reply with an air of superiority and disdain when he remembered where and who he was. *Better to start some kind of communication with the likes of this guy*, he thought. With any luck, he'd be living with people like this for a very long time.

Caine spoke for the first time since his earlier conversation with William. "I think they're taking me to Jackson, to begin processing me." Suddenly conscious of his proper speech, the judge lowered his head.

"Damn, gonna do some state time, huh?" Cordell asked. Caine shrugged with his best convict look and nodded his head, afraid to speak again. Cordell tried to keep up the banter. "What'd they tag you with to land you in the big house, pop?"

Judge Caine was about to debut his criminal verbiage— words he'd heard spoken over twenty years on the bench—when Deputy Holtz stepped in.

"All right, fellers, enough chatter. You ready, old bird?" Deputy Holtz put the judge in the rear seat, careful to hold his head down so he wouldn't bump it against the frame of the car. Getting into the driver's seat, he turned to Cordell.

"Hey, Cordell... Uh, Anthony, whatever the hell your name is, take your mop and get back upstairs. Send Deputy Frieze down when you get up there, and tell him to bring one of those field bandages for the judge's head. He's soaked that rag and he's still bleedin'."

Cordell ran back up the stairs. *So it is him,* he thought. He knew it looked like him, and he damn sure sounded like a proper man. But he wasn't really sure until Deputy Holtz called him the judge. Now he was sure it was the man. Cordell had to hurry. He found Deputy Frieze in the men's room, buckling his equipment belt.

"Deputy says to get back down there. He's ready to go. Says to bring a field bandage or somethin'. The old man's still bleedin' all over the place." He let the deputy get almost to the stairs when he called behind him. "Sir, you reckon I can make a phone call before Miller locks me in for the night? I need to call my sister and tell her I'm gettin' out soon."

"Is it a local call?" Frieze asked.

"Yessir, it is. She lives over in Conyers. She said I could stay with her for awhile so ya'll will have an address to release me to."

Deputy Frieze thought for a moment before responding. Feeling like he'd already been a big enough prick for one night, he said, "Go ahead and use the bondsman's phone on the table there, but don't be long. Miller will be right back; he was in the shitter when I was. Tell him I said it was okay."

When the lady at the Urban Shelter of Atlanta answered the phone, Cordell spoke fast. "This Miss Tucker? Over at the shelter?"

She was surprised at the lateness of the call. "Why, yes this is. How can I help you?" the old woman asked.

"Miss Tucker, this is Cordell Anthony. Remember me? I'm the one who fixed the stove at the shelter. I've been staying with my sister for a few weeks," he lied. "I need to see if you have a friend of mine staying there still, a fella named Parlee Rabideaux. Big fella, black hair, and a sorta handsome face."

Miss Tucker thought for a moment and responded. "It's late, Mr. Anthony. Call back tomorrow and I'll see."

Cordell tried to inflect a sense of urgency into his voice. "Oh, no, Miss Tucker, that won't do. I need to speak to him tonight. Right now. His mama died in Louisiana two days ago, and we just found out." For good measure, Cordell continued on. "Parlee'll miss the funeral and the wake and all, Miss Tucker. Tomorrow won't do. He likes to sleep by the window since the weather's been a bit warmer. Could you go see if he's over there? Please, ma'am?"

Several moments later Parlee Rabideaux came to the phone just as Deputy Miller stepped out of the men's room. Cordell pantomimed to Miller that he was allowed to use the phone, at the same time talking to Parlee.

With Miller in hearing range, Cordell was finding it difficult to explain to Parlee why he'd called him at a homeless shelter at such a late hour. "Yeah, I'll be coming home soon," Cordell said. Parlee didn't respond, still half-asleep and agitated. Cordell pressed on. "I saw that guy we talked about a couple months ago. He's gotta go down to Jackson tonight."

Parlee didn't have a clue as to what the hell this near stranger was talking about. "Listen, Cordell, I ain't sure what you're calling me for in the middle of the night, but you're about to piss me off with all of this babblin'."

Frustration and fear enveloped Cordell. Being a garden-variety moron, he didn't know what to do. He knew, however, that he wanted no part of making Parlee Rabideaux mad. He nonchalantly turned his back to Miller and began whispering. "Listen, Parlee. I'm giving you this 'cause I want something from you. Don't hang up. That judge fella that sexed up your daughter is on his way to Jackson, Georgia in the back seat of a Fulton County Sheriff's car. There are two deputies with him, and they gonna be stopping for chow at the diner over on Courtland. You know which one I mean? Got the big donut out front. You been sayin' what you was gonna do, Parlee, so now's your chance. I'll get mine from you later when they let me out."

In one of his drunken brainstorming sessions, Parlee had shared with Cordell an idea he'd been trying to deal to anyone who'd listen. Probably one of the best thought-out plans that Parlee had ever come up with, Cordell knew it was something the faltering man would never pursue. Cordell Anthony, however, knew it was a good scheme when he first heard it, and had acquaintances who'd pay for the idea.

Parlee was awake now; the cheap wine and the sleep all gone from his body. Natural chemicals he couldn't begin to name were delivering him into erect consciousness. The hair on the back of the big man's neck stood up as his nerve endings awakened from their drunken stupor.

"I don't know what you want from me, Cordell, but whatever it is, you can have it," he said. "You still got that little pea shooter stuck in them bushes behind the shelter?" Parlee was with Cordell the night he beat up a local crack head and took it from him.

"It's still there and full of bullets," Cordell answered. "If you leave now and hurry, those cops should still be in the diner when you get there. They usually park at the side of the place, 'cause the front of the building sits right on the street. I've seen 'em there lots of times."

Deputy Miller walked around the desk to face Cordell, speaking to him sarcastically. "Alright, sweetheart, say goodnight now. Time to go. Tell her you'll be out in a month or so."

"Ain't gonna be no month, no sir. Gonna be a day or two." Cordell laughed the words to Miller, and then into the phone, in a normal voice, he told Parlee, "I'll see you soon then. Like I said, won't be but a day or two and I'll call you to come get me. All right. Bye-bye then."

After he returned the phone to its cradle, he turned to walk with Miller back to his cell, asking Miller as he went, "Why'd you wanna go and embarrass me like that, deputy?"

✝

Parlee Rabideaux placed the telephone back on the old wooden desk where Miss Tucker had summoned him. Fully awake now, he thought about what he was going to do. Killing Carter Caine wasn't going to change anything that had happened to his little girl, but it sure would make him feel better. He'd thought about this very thing for weeks now, and had talked about it in generic terms with a few people, including Cordell Anthony. But killing a man, damn, if it wasn't something to think about beforehand.

"Do you need to leave tonight, Mr. Rabideaux?" Miss Tucker's voice seemed to be coming from a mile away.

"What? I mean, I'm sorry, ma'am. What was that?" Parlee asked.

"I said, do you need to leave tonight for your mother's funeral in Louisiana?" Miss Tucker appeared agitated at this late-night activity, but was genuinely concerned.

Parlee hadn't had the benefit of knowing what Cordell had said to get him to the phone, and was confused by this line of questioning. "I'm sorry, Miss Tucker, what are you talking about?"

"The man on the phone said your mother passed away, and he needed to speak to you right this minute. I was wondering if you needed to leave tonight. I could put some fruit in a bag for you, if you'd like." Her voice cracked as she spoke.

Parlee realized what had happened. "Yes, ma'am, I'll need to leave right now and get to the bus station. That fruit sure would be nice of you, Miss Tucker. After I buy a ticket, there won't be much money left for food."

The old woman smiled as she walked toward the serving area of the old building where the perishable food was kept. Content she had fulfilled her role as Southern hostess, she hummed as she put apples, bananas, and oranges into a small paper bag.

Parlee gathered his things from around his sleeping area and met Miss Tucker at the door. "Here you go, Mr. Rabideaux. I'm sorry for your loss, and I hope you make it home in time to see your mother buried." The old woman pressed a ten-dollar bill into Parlee's hand as she gave him the bag of fruit.

Parlee's eyes welled up with tears when he saw the money she was giving him. "I sure do appreciate all your kindness, ma'am. I'll repay you as soon as I make it back to Atlanta and get some work." With this he was gone, out the front door and around the back, to where Cordell had stashed the old revolver. Digging around in the bushes, he found the gun buried under half an inch of dirt. Checking to see that it was still loaded, he slid it into his belt and scampered off toward the diner on Courtland Street.

As Parlee walked, he thought about what had become of Jerzy after she appeared in court. He'd waited outside the courthouse every morning, watching her as she went inside the building. In the afternoons, he'd return and watch again as she left the building with two deputies. Every day they'd escort her to a couple waiting in a big green Ford Expedition with a Gwinnett County tag. He was careful not to be seen by her, and wished that he could've somehow talked to her. She had to be mad at him still, leaving Breaux Bridge, and leaving her with that bitch mother of hers. Marlene beat Jerzy even when Parlee was there, but not as often and nowhere near as severely.

Maybe this is what it will take to get them back together again. Maybe if he killed Judge Caine, and Jerzy somehow found out about it, she'd appreciate him and see how much he loved her. Maybe he could get Cordell to talk to her and let her know what her father had done for her. He was ashamed of his constant failures, and even more ashamed he'd walked away from his daughter knowing what she'd have to go through alone with Marlene. So this had to be it. This was how he was going to get revenge for the family, and get his daughter back.

"Dumb ass," Parlee said aloud to himself. How stupid can a guy be, thinking killing a man would impress a child? Even if the old man hurt her, it was long since over. The man had been sentenced to prison and was going to rot there. *Fact of the matter is,* Parlee thought, *I'm still pissed about it. The girl was only in Atlanta because she was looking for me. If it hadn't been for me leaving her behind, she would've never gotten hurt like that. That's why I'm gonna shoot him; because he's got it coming.*

Before he realized how far he'd walked, Parlee was staring at the police car parked beside the diner. *Dunkin Diner,* he thought to himself. *That's why they have that big fuckin' donut out front. Damn, I coulda thought of that.* He walked to the squad car, looking all around for bystanders as he went. When he got beside the car, the old man inside raised his head up and looked at him. Parlee recognized the face right away. He'd committed the face to memory when he'd first seen the man on television, and was certain he'd never forget it, no matter what happened.

The judge didn't look the same in the orange coveralls. He needed a shave, but it was him for sure. The thin, hawk-like features were sagging under all the mental strain, and the eyes which appeared so bright on the television news seemed to be hollow and blank, as if the man had nothing to look forward to in life. *Well,* Parlee mused, *life in prison ain't much to look forward to, come to think of it. Maybe killing him is the right thing to do. Do him a favor; put him out of his misery.*

Caine sat in the back seat, watching the man with the greasy black hair standing outside staring at him. He ran Parlee's image through his mental file, trying to remember if he'd ever seen the large man before. *Maybe... Wait a minute; you're the fath... Hey! What is that? What is he holding in his hand?* The sweat poured freely in a thin stream down the frightened man's nose. *Is that a... Damn! This moron's holding a gun! What the hell is he doing, staring at me with a gun in his hand?* Caine began to tremble. *So this is it,* he thought. *I know who you are now, you fat bastard. That filthy black hair, those black pie-pan eyes.* Caine began screaming, "I know who you are now! It was an accident! I swear, I thought..."

Parlee watched the head jerk and the lips move inside the car. He saw fear in the hollow-eyed man. He realized the judge was trying to tell him something, yelling through the glass. *He looks pissed,* thought Parlee. *Why the hell is he pissed at me?* He saw the sweat on the man's face and the bulging blue vein snaking across the judge's forehead. *What on earth makes a vein swell up like that?* he wondered. As this last thought occurred to Parlee, he raised the gun and pointed it at Caine's head.

CHAPTER SEVENTEEN

O fficer Louis Friez sat with his friend and usual partner, Officer Terry Holtz at the Dunkin Diner off Courtland Street in downtown Atlanta. Both men had ordered their breakfasts and were discussing their duty for the night. As a matter of course, whenever an inmate in the county lockup had to be transferred to a state facility, whether hospital or prison, Friez and Holtz drew the duty. It didn't seem to matter what shift they were on, they always got paired together, and always drew the shit detail.

The task tonight was to take a convicted child rapist down to the State Prison at Jackson, about sixty-five miles south of Atlanta. While waiting for their meal to arrive, they talked about the convict waiting for them in the squad car, and about the rape that had gotten the old man there. Holtz commented that it probably wouldn't take too long for the old man to wind up being somebody's bitch in prison.

Friez responded that being alive in prison was even too good for the old pervert. Friez was the loudmouth of the two, always talking, always about nothing.

"I say we take him over to Ashby Street and let the brothers have him," Friez said.

"I think you've done enough for one night, big boy," Holtz responded. "That gash in his head may end up getting us both in a ball of shit. And mind you, I ain't going down for your fucking stupidity."

"We can't help it if he fell goin' down them steps, can we?"

"Never mind; eat and shut up. Amy said she wanted us to check something out for her."

Amy was the night shift waitress and had asked them to look around behind the restaurant. She'd heard something back there earlier and was afraid to take the trash out to the dumpster until they had a look.

Although Officer Friez was a big-mouth and an obnoxious prick, he was a fairly good cop. Having grown up in Senoia, Georgia, he served on that little town's police force until he attended the police academy in Clayton County. After graduation, the Fulton County Sheriff's Department hired him. He was the department's best pistol shot, competing and winning every police competition in both Fulton and DeKalb counties. He loved his partnership with Terry Holtz, mostly because Holtz put up with his bullshit.

Friez took one last bite of food and pushed his plate away. "Damn, that was good tonight. Hit the spot," he said as he looked around the diner for Amy. He saw her emerge from the kitchen and motioned her over.

"Ain't gonna finish your breakfast?" Amy asked him as she approached the table.

"No, I'm tight as a damn tick. What'd you say you were having trouble with?"

"I ain't havin' trouble with nothin', Friez. What I said was I heard something going on behind the place a hour or so ago, and I'm afraid to go back there. I got trash piling up in the kitchen 'cause I ain't takin it to the dumpster."

Holtz spoke next. "Just wait, Louis. I'm going to the bathroom. When I get back, we'll check it out." He stood and walked to the men's room on the other side of the diner.

"Aw, hell, he'll be in there for half an hour. I'll go check it out for you, Amy. Tell him he's paying tonight; when he comes out."

Amy walked with Friez through the kitchen to the rear door of the diner. She lifted the metal bar that held the door closed from the inside. "You gotta pull real hard, Louis. Sometimes the damn thing feels like it's bolted shut."

Louis yanked the heavy steel door open with ease and drew his pistol before stepping outside.

"Go ahead and lock it back up, Amy. I'll walk around front when I'm done back here and let you know what I see."

As he walked through the alley, he pulled the hammer back on his service revolver. *That's what I like about a revolver,* he thought as he walked. *Automatics make too damn much noise. You can jack the hammer back on a revolver and nobody ever knows.* He walked the entire length of the alley in both directions, quickly looking into every nook along the way. Nothing stood out as curious or dangerous, so he made his way back around front still holding his revolver out in front of him. *Plenty of cops have been killed coming out of a dark hole like this,* he thought as he turned the corner.

Just as Louis Friez cleared the corner at the rear of the building, he saw a tall, stocky man standing with his back to him about forty yards away. The man was doing something at the side of the patrol car. *Damn, looks like he's... Wait, what is that? Son-of-a-bitch!* The big man was standing at the driver's side of the patrol car, holding a gun and pointing it at the old convict's head. Friez slowly crept toward the man's back. *Thirty yards, the bastard can't even hear me,* Friez thought. *Twenty yards, now to get this guy down.* Looking around to see if his partner was about to exit the front of the building, Friez realized he was going to have to get this guy down by himself.

Very calmly, Friez spoke to the big man's back. "Drop that weapon and put your hands behind your neck."

The big man jumped at being startled, but didn't move.

"I said, drop your weapon, and clasp your hands behind your neck, asshole."

Parlee Rabideaux glanced sideways and looked at the reflection of the cop standing behind him in the driver's side door glass. Parlee was confused. The cops were supposed to be in the diner. He felt fear and excitement; a small tingling of sweat on his back. Nausea overwhelmed him as he turned to face the cop, unaware that he was still holding the gun out in front of him.

Louis Friez panicked. He didn't dive for cover or make any defensive move. He didn't do any number of things a cop in that situation should or would do to disarm a man and avoid a shooting. With his gun already drawn and cocked, he instinctively pulled up a few inches to get off a chest shot and fired. Parlee felt the bullet as it passed through his shirt at the cuff and went through the rear passenger window of the patrol car. He saw the glass implode and explode at once, and watched as the bullet cleaved its way into the forehead of Judge Carter Caine. Parlee, realizing that he hadn't been shot, turned and ran across Courtland Street and into the darkness of the city with Cordell Anthony's gun still in his hand.

From somewhere to his left in front of the diner, Friez heard his partner screaming at him. Exiting the men's room in the diner, Holtz heard the shot and ran outside, toward the sound. When he arrived at the side of the diner, Louis Friez was still standing there, with his pistol aimed at the rear window of the squad car. A quick glance at the shattered glass on the ground and the interior of the car finished telling the story for Holtz.

"Put your weapon down, Lou. It's over now." Holtz sounded like he was pleading with him.

Tears had already begun to stream down Louis's face as he stared at his partner in bewilderment. "I missed the guy, Terry. He was standin' right there and I fuckin' missed the guy." Trembling now, Friez was close to babbling. Spittle formed at the corners of his mouth.

Holtz tried again. "No, Lou, you didn't miss him. His head's all over the interior of the car. You got him, Lou. Now put your gun down."

"You didn't see the guy? He was standing right there, pointing a gun at the con in the car. That's probably what Amy heard earlier. Don't you think, Terry? Where's Amy? She saw him. Damn, somebody had to see him. He was standin' right fuckin' there!"

Quickly, Holtz reached up to the radio transmitter clipped to his epaulette and called for backup. This time he didn't speak calmly to Friez.

"Look, Lou, put the fuckin' gun down now or I'll shoot you my damn self. You've had it in for that old man ever since we got the detail. You pushed him down the stairs and busted his head open. There's no way to prove that now, but there's a witness to that incident. Do you remember the trustee? Lou?"

Slowly, Lou turned to his partner and looked directly into his eyes. *That look on my partner's face is serious*, Lou thought. *My partner thinks I did this thing on purpose.* Louis spoke again, crying his words like a child. He knew then that his career was over, that he'd spend an eternity in prison himself. "What? You think I did this? You think I killed that old bastard on purpose?"

Holtz tried again to get the whimpering officer to drop his gun. "Drop the gun, Lou." Calmer now, smoother, lower tone, gain some of his confidence. "Drop the gun and then we'll talk. I'm sure it won't be that bad."

"That bad?" Friez was frantic. The late-night crowd inside the diner had walked out onto the street to see what all the commotion was about. Friez looked from one person to the other, trying to find one understanding face. This wasn't something he was going to get out of. He was fucked circumstantially, and he knew that for a fact.

"What do you mean, it won't be that bad? I didn't do anything, Terry. I swear it was an accident. There was a guy there, pointing a gun... He was going to shoot into the car..."

"I know, Lou. We've got some backup coming, so just put down your gun." Holtz was pleading again.

In the distance, several sirens could be heard approaching the diner. Friez still held his weapon, refusing to put it down. Fear and panic arrived simultaneously, dressed in the same black that always accompanies tragedy. Friez felt his legs wobble as his body fought the terror. Holtz, still training his weapon on Friez, was reluctant to use force to disarm the man, but was aware of senior officers approaching. How was that going to reflect on him? This was supposed to be his career. Your partner is just a person. If he breaks the law, you take him down just like anyone else. He wasn't about to let this fat-ass redneck make him look bad. He had a job to do, and he was going to do it.

"Friez!" Holtz shouted. "I'm coming for your gun now. I promise, all I want is to take your weapon. I won't hurt you, if you cooperate and give me the gun."

Friez heard the anger and self-righteousness in his partner's voice. He looked to the ground momentarily as Holtz walked slowly toward him. He looked back up at his partner and spoke through the sweat and tears that were beginning to burn into his face.

"OK, Terry, I fucked up. I'll be alright. I just thought... I mean we... Uh..."

Friez let his pistol hand fall to his side. With the gun no longer raised, Holtz moved in to take it from him. "Good man, Lou. It's gonna be all right, man, I swear." Holtz moved closer, still holding his gun on Friez's head.

When Holtz got within three feet of him, Friez dropped his head to his chest and closed his eyes. Taking this as a sign that the loudmouth realized the impasse was resolved, Holtz reached for Friez's gun. As Holtz moved even closer to the big man, Friez reached out with his free hand and grabbed his partner by the wrist of his gun hand and pulled him in close to his body. Without a spoken word, Friez raised his own weapon and shot Holtz in the face, splitting his skull from the bridge of his nose to the top of his head. As Holtz was falling to the ground, Friez lifted his prized revolver to his own temple and pulled the trigger.

CHAPTER EIGHTEEN

The next morning William awakened to the telephone ringing. He heard the answering machine pick up, and then the phone began ringing again. He got out of bed and checked the messages; none from this morning were on the machine. Just as he put the phone back on the cradle, it rang again.

"Hello?"

The voice on the other end was male, high-pitched and nasal.

"Is this Judge Caine's residence?"

William became perturbed. That was no way to address a person when they answer the phone.

"Who is this? Is that you, Mr. Light?"

The voice on the other end realized his mistake.

"I'm terribly sorry. I'm Shannon Hoage from the Fulton County Sheriff's office. May I please speak with Mrs. Caine?"

"She's not able to come to the phone right now. Can I take a message for her?"

"Well… Yes, Sir… I guess you can. Please tell her to call this number and ask for Detective Hoage. This is an urgent matter, so the sooner she gets this message, the better."

William wrote the number on an envelope laying next to the phone.

"I'll have her call you within the next thirty minutes." He hung up the phone, excitement coursing through him at the thought of good news. Maybe the Magistrate Judge had agreed to allow bail for his father. He hurried up the stairs to wake his mother.

Beatrice lay in the large bed naked, the covers kicked askew and her black eyeshade pulled down to her chin. She was snoring loudly when William entered the room. He gently pulled a sheet up to cover her body so she wouldn't be embarrassed when he awakened her. Laying his hand on her shoulder, he shook her gently.

"Mother, wake up. You need to call the Sheriff's office. Mother, do you hear me?"

Beatrice rolled over and muttered something, pulling her eyeshade back over her eyes.

"Come on, Mom, wake up. Come downstairs and I'll make you some coffee. Wake up now. Can you hear me?

Beatrice rolled again; this time William shook her harder and raised his voice.

"Mother, wake up! Come on, this is no joke. You need to get out of bed now."

Beatrice sat up and pulled the eyeshade over her head, flinging it across the room as she did so.

"What is it, William? I'm trying to sleep. What do you want?"

"A detective left a message for you. He needs for you to call him right away. Here's his number."

"What does he want? Couldn't he talk to you?"

"Apparently not. I just got off the phone with him; he wouldn't tell me anything. He wants to speak with you. I'll go put some coffee on, and pour you some juice. Here's the phone."

William handed her the cordless from her nightstand and left the room.

Moments later William stood at the kitchen sink filling the coffee pot with water when he heard Beatrice behind him. "I'll have this ready in a minute or so. Did you...?" He turned to face her as she fell to her knees.

"Mother!" He ran to pick her up, lifting her by her shoulders. As her bathrobe fell open, William could see that she was still naked underneath. He pulled her robe together and tied it with the belt. He half-carried her to a nearby chair.

"What on earth is the matter? You've gone completely white. Are you ill?"

Beatrice stared out the window in front of her, speechless. Her hands trembled as she wiped the corners of her mouth.

"Mother? Talk to me. I can't help you if I don't know what's wrong."

"William..." Her voice was merely a whispered groan. "You have to take me to the coroner's office. There's been an accident."

"What do you mean, an accident? Has Dad had an accident? Is he hurt? How did he have an...? Wait a minute. The coroner's office? Mother, what in the hell has happened? Tell me!"

"I don't know what happened, William. The detective said there's been an accident, and Carter's dead. We have to go down there."

This time William's legs went limp as he reached for a chair and fell into it. Had he heard her right? His father was dead? What kind of an accident can you have in a jail cell? Did somebody hurt him? His head was spinning as he tried to battle the initial nausea. After a moment, he rose from the chair and reached for his mother.

"Come on, I'll help you get dressed. You can't go down there in your bathrobe. Hell, you're not even wearing your pajamas. Come on, Mother, let's go upstairs."

He lifted the feeble woman from her chair and helped her up the stairs. Inside her bedroom, William took a pair of underpants and bra from her dresser. He walked into her large closet and took out a pair of slacks and a top he'd often seen her wear. As he threw the clothing onto the bed, he turned to her.

"Can you get dressed by yourself? Are you all right?"

"Yes, I can manage. You go get the car ready. We'll drive yours, if that's okay."

"That's fine. I'll be waiting for you in the driveway. Hurry, Mother, so we can get down there and find out what happened."

In his car waiting for Beatrice to join him, William's mind was racing. *Fucking Ralph Light. If it's true that my father's dead, you're surely fucked. I'll ruin your life. I'll destroy you and everything you love, you bastard. Something must've gone wrong somewhere. He was supposed to be isolated until they moved him. Somebody fucked up and put him in a cell with a freak or something.*

William continued his silent rant, catching himself talking aloud when he saw Beatrice come out the front door and walk toward him. She was crying now. *That's funny. Yesterday the old bitch hated the judge; now look at her.* Beatrice dabbed at her eyes with the back of her hand as she crawled into William's car.

They drove in silence until William tired of hearing his mother's whimpering. He turned on his radio for background noise; something to fill the void so there would be no need for conversation.

After a few commercials ran, an anonymous newscaster's voice filled the car. "In the local news…"

William was barely listening when he heard the announcer say his father's name. He sat forward and turned the radio volume up.

"…The fifty-five-year-old judge was being transported to the Diagnostic and Classification Center at Jackson to begin his sentence when the shooting took place. We'll continue to bring you up-to-date coverage of this event as we get more information."

"Oh my God," Beatrice said. "This keeps getting worse and worse. What were they saying? Somebody shot him?"

William looked from the road to his mother. Tears rolled down his face as he tried to control his emotions.

"I didn't hear all of it. I wasn't paying attention at first. All I heard was there was a shooting; they didn't say it was him. Maybe the guy who called you didn't have the right information."

William drove faster after hearing the radio announcer. He was anxious to find out what had happened. Beatrice chatted away beside him, but he didn't hear anything she said.

They arrived at the county facility and found someone to direct them to the coroner's office. Walking into the office, William could smell the antiseptic cleaners as soon as he opened the door.

He walked with Beatrice to the counter where a young woman was talking on the telephone. After a moment, the woman put the phone down and acknowledged Beatrice and William.

"Good morning. How can I help you?"

"My name is Beatrice Caine. This is my son, William. We received a phone call from Detective Hoage this morning, asking us to meet him here."

"Yes, Mrs. Caine. That was Detective Hoage on the phone. He said you'd be on your way here. Have a seat and he'll be right over."

Beatrice sat on the wooden bench in the outer office while William paced, mindlessly reading the various posters taped to the institutional brick walls of the room. Several minutes had passed when detective Hoage entered the office. He walked to the counter first and spoke to the receptionist before turning to Beatrice.

"Good morning, Mrs. Caine. Thanks for coming down. I'm Detective Shannon Hoage, the one who called you this morning. Can you come back here with me, please?" The detective opened a door leading to the back of the building.

Beatrice glanced toward William. "What about my son?"

"Oh, I'm sorry." He walked over and shook William's hand. "Yes, absolutely. Both of you, please, right this way."

The detective led them down a corridor to a small office, decorated with several official-looking documents and lists of various procedures to follow. He pulled two folding chairs away from the wall and offered them both a seat.

"Please, sit down. I have some things to tell you, and then we can... Um... We can... Well, let's go over some information first." The detective was obviously uncomfortable.

William refused to take the chair offered him and spoke abruptly to the detective, catching him by surprise.

"Before we go over anything, I need for you to answer one question."

The detective looked first at Beatrice. "Perhaps if we talk..."

"Forget talking for now, detective. Is my father dead? We do have a right to know, don't you think?"

The detective once again looked over at Beatrice before answering William's question.

William could no longer hold his temper. He stepped in front of the young detective and began shouting, spraying spittle on the man's shirt.

"Why in the hell do you keep looking at her before you answer? I'm Judge Caine's son, and I have a right to know what's going on! Look at me when I'm talking to you! My father was in your custody! You people are responsible for anything that happened to him! Now please, answer my question! We're in the coroner's office! You called us down here! Now, is my father dead or not?"

Detective Hoage stared solemnly, first at William and then Beatrice. He searched for the right words before deciding the only way to do this was to be honest with them. *Just do your job*, he told himself. *Be careful what you say, but do your job.*

"Yes, Mr. Caine, your father is dead. He died around two-thirty this morning."

Beatrice lowered her head and fumbled in her purse for tissue. William stepped back and leaned against the wall for support, tears of sorrow and anger rolling from his eyes. He wiped his face with his sleeve and turned his back to the detective.

"How? How did he die? On the way over here we heard something on the radio about a shooting. What happened?"

The detective walked behind the small desk and sat down.

"Two deputies were transporting your father to the State Prison at Jackson. While they were stopped for coffee, an unknown assailant approached their car with a gun. One of the officers came out of the diner in time to see the man and... Look, Mr. Caine, please sit down and let me go over this so that you'll completely understand what happened. You can ask me all the questions you want when I'm finished. There's still a great deal of specula-tion surrounding the shooting. We truly don't have a lot of information yet. Please, Sir." The detective pushed the folding chair closer to where William stood.

William turned around and took the seat. He looked across the small room at his mother. "Are you going to be able to listen to this, Mother? Will you be all right?"

Beatrice had an odd smile on her face. Somewhere in the cold morgue, with its too-clean smell and the ugly yellow brick, was closure. Somewhere behind that glass wall, her problem ceased to exist.

"I'm fine. Go ahead, detective. We're listening." The odd smile remained on her face.

The detective took them through what the police knew about the shooting.

He was careful to explain that there were several people at the scene who wouldn't cooperate with the police, telling them they didn't see anything. Both of the police officers involved were dead, as well as the judge. The unknown assailant, according to one witness, ran away from the scene. The police were trying to determine the credibility of that statement.

When the detective finished describing what the police knew, he asked William if he had any questions. William said he had none.

"How about you, Mrs. Caine? Do you have any questions about what happened I can help you with?"

"No, I don't believe so. Not right now anyway. Is his body here, at the morgue?"

"Yes, it is, Mrs. Caine. Would you like to walk back with me?" He pointed toward the room on the other side of a glass wall. Beatrice looked at William.

"Should we?" she asked. "Do you want to see him?"

"Yes, Mother, I do. But do you really want to go back there?"

"I need to go back there, William. I must. I'll be fine, Son, believe me. I'll be fine."

The detective asked them both to follow him as he opened a rear door in the small office. On the other side of the door was the morgue, where an attendant introduced himself and led them to a long table. When the attendant pulled the sheet from the face of Judge Caine, he did so without warning, taking Beatrice by surprise. She gasped and turned her head in horror. The young detective hurried to her and took her arm to steady her.

"I'm fine, detective. I wasn't prepared for this. My God, there's glass sticking out of his face. That doesn't look at all like my husband."

"It's him," William said. He reached and turned his father's head to face the opposite direction. "See? It's him." William began crying again, then turned around and left the room. He knew now—more than ever—that he had to go through with his plan. The center of Ralph Light's universe was going to collapse when William was finished. He was sure he could do it after seeing his father like this. He was even going to enjoy this. He ran to his car, stopping in the parking lot to vomit.

CHAPTER NINETEEN

William had trouble concentrating during the drive home. He wanted to drive to Ralph Light's office right then and shoot him in front of everyone there. Beatrice didn't speak for the entire trip. She sat in the passenger seat staring out the window, the silly smile still on her face. Once in the driveway of her home, she left William in the garage and went up to her room. She fell into her bed, but didn't take her medication. She wouldn't need it anymore, she thought. The source of the pain was gone.

William checked the guns in the trunk of his car. He'd forgotten about them being there and laughed at the thought of being in the police department parking lot with a car full of weapons. He took Carney's card from his pocket and wondered if she could be reached so early in the day. He was in no mood to talk to her that very minute, but he had to pick up his pace and make his plan work. His father was dead, and Ralph Light was going to pay dearly.

Lying on his bed he dialed her home number first. After several rings, the voice mail answered. He listened to her father's voice on the machine and then hung up the phone. Seconds later, his own phone rang.

"Hello?" He hoped it wasn't the detective again.

A female voice came on the line. In spite of his hurt and anger, he couldn't help smiling at the sound of her.

"Yes, someone just called this number. I was calling back to see who it was."

"Carney?"

"Bill? That's neat. I was hoping it'd be you. Sorry, I hit the call back button."

"Cool… Did my number come up or what?"

"No, we're not that fancy yet. Dad's a little cheap. We just have the call back feature. But I'm glad it's you. I've been thinking about you all morning."

"I've been thinking of you, too. What have you got going on this morning? I'd like to see you."

He heard Carney groan into the receiver. He began thinking of something to say to get her to meet him somewhere.

"What's wrong? Is this a bad time or something?"

"Well, I usually wouldn't be busy, but a friend of mine and I are going to Destin next week. I need to take her around to do some shopping this morning. I wasn't planning to go until the second week in April, but my friend's never been, and we're both a little anxious to get there."

"Well, maybe some other time. When are you leaving to go down there?"

"Monday morning. Early, so we can be on the beach shortly after lunch."

William thought quickly; he needed to come up with something.

"Well, you're not going to believe this. I've got a reservation at Sea Palms beginning Monday. I usually stay for a week when I go down there."

He heard Carney laugh.

"You're kidding, right?" *This is too good to be true*, she thought.

"No, I'm not kidding. I go every year, at almost the same time. I've had next week booked for months."

Carney now regretted Jerzy would be coming along. *This could be a wonderful trip*, she thought, *with the two of us alone*. Too late for that, though. Jerzy would be brokenhearted if Carney bailed on her now.

"I stay for a month when I go, and I usually go alone. But this year, I've met a girl I really have fun with. You know, shopping and girl stuff. I can't get out of taking her with me without hurting her feelings. But I bet we can get together a couple of times while we're there. She wouldn't mind that."

William had been thinking all the time Carney talked. He'd heard most of what she'd said and decided that another person in the picture was fine with him. *The more the fucking merrier*, he thought.

"Honestly, I'd probably bore you both stiff. I like to fish while I'm there, and that's probably the last thing you'd want to do."

Carney's ears perked up at this last statement. This was too good to be true. The shopping trip today was to furnish Jerzy with all the rods and tackle she would need. Carney was looking forward to a couple of hours at Galyon's.

"Bill, I love to fish!" she said excitedly.

"You do? Really? I would've never thought it. You look so... Feminine and all..."

"Yeah right. Feminine and fat. But, really, I do love to fish. I grew up fishing and hunting with my dad."

William smiled. He knew that. He'd done his homework. He remembered his father's conversations with Ralph Light at the kitchen table.

"So, maybe we can get together. Tell you what. I have some work to finish up between now and Friday. What if we plan on seeing each other in Destin next week?"

William had abruptly decided he needed the extra time. He had to put together a plan which included Carney's friend. *Probably lesbians*, he thought. *Fine with me. I'll kill them both.*

"That sounds like a plan to me," Carney replied. "My dad's boat is already in the water at the marina. The folks there usually have it ready to go right about now. Will you call me, or should I call you when I get there?"

"Where are you staying?" William asked.

"Pelican Beach Condos. Right on the Gulf. I should be there early Monday afternoon."

William wrote the telephone number at her condominium on the back of her card and put it in his wallet. After assuring her that he'd call her, he hung up the phone and walked down the hall to his mother's bedroom. He saw Beatrice lying on the bed, eyes closed.

"Mother, are you awake? We need to talk about some things."

"Yes, come in. I'm just resting my eyes. What is it, Son?"

"We need to call Stromann's and make arrangements for Dad's service."

The judge had been adamant about these types of issues in life. He had made it plain to Beatrice and his son over the years that he didn't want any type of funeral. He wanted to be cremated and disposed of; simple as that. No fancy caskets, no crying family members lingering around a hole in the ground. Just a simple cremation ceremony and only his immediate family present for that. Beatrice was more than happy to oblige.

The old woman lay silent for a moment, studying William's face. *He looks more like my side of the family,* she thought. *There's not much of his father in him, no physical reminders of the judge to look at every day.*

"We'll go down in the morning and have it arranged. I'm sorry, but I don't think I can handle any type of service. I don't think your father would mind if I chose not to attend. I think that under the circumstances he'd understand and agree."

"What do you mean, not attend? You can't choose not to be there for the service. That was your husband, for God's sake."

"I realize this may hurt you, William. You weren't there that morning. You don't know what it felt like."

"What morning? What are you talking about? What don't I know? I know my father's dead. I know the only woman he ever loved has bought into the whole scheme to do away with him. I know I did nothing my entire life that pleased him. I also know it's my obligation to see to it he has a proper service. He would've done that for you or me."

"Yes, but I wouldn't have raped a child, William. He would've been burying a faithful wife and mother. I'm not participating in the honoring of a freak. I just will not."

William looked at his mother for a long moment without responding. He hadn't realized the depth of her anger.

"Mother, he did not…"

"Yes, William, he did. He was telling me about it when the police came to the front door. He left out the part about her being only fifteen, but he was confessing to me when he was arrested. Imagine how I felt when the officer said the girl was underage. Think about that for a minute. Think about all the self-righteous bullshit he talked about but couldn't live. No, I will not attend his service. You can hate me if you want to, be mad if you want to. I don't care."

William dropped his head and moved closer to his mother's bed. Sitting down next to her, he began crying again.

"I don't know what to do. How do I arrange something like this? I don't even know where to start."

"William, listen to me. Call the funeral home and tell them you want a simple cremation for your father. Tell them there will be no service; he didn't want any of that. You can go by yourself or get someone to go with you. Maybe Ralph would like to go along. Then be done with it. Go on with your life; that's what I intend to do. I've suffered the embarrassment too long. From last Christmas until now I've suffered the press, the well-intentioned ladies at the club, all of them. I'm finished with the suffering. I'm finished."

The mention of Ralph Light's name triggered the anger in William again. He wanted to tell his mother what he intended to do. He wanted to tell her if she kept talking this way, he'd kill her as well. He needed to do something his father would approve of; perhaps starting right here at home would be appropriate.

"Mother, has the thought ever crossed your mind that this whole thing was set up? I mean, did you ever stop to think of all the people who'd have something to gain if something happened to the judge? Something to discredit him, or have him jailed even? Did you? Only they went too far. They didn't expect the cops getting into an argument outside of the squad car. They didn't foresee anything like that happening. They couldn't. But he was set up, I know he was."

Beatrice sat up in bed, looking at her son as if seeing him for the first time. It appeared William had heard nothing she'd said.

"William, don't be ridiculous. Your father told me he'd tried to help a woman find somebody here in Atlanta. She needed a place to stay, so he rented her a hotel room. He said one thing led to another, and they eventually had sex. He left out the part about her age, and how he'd invited her to the DA's Christmas party. He forgot to mention the fact he let her use his charge cards, apparently to buy lingerie. Even Olivia said in court that the girl had been calling your father for several days. What part of the trial did you miss, Son? What part of all this are you struggling with?"

William stared at his hands. He'd heard all these things in court. He'd read about them in all the local papers. Every station on the radio and television went over the so-called facts again and again. The talk show hosts in Atlanta had topics for weeks. The good his father had done was never mentioned. The causes he championed, the charities he funded; none of the good things made any difference. The whole town was there for his trial. They stood on the steps outside the courthouse. Like Beatrice now, they wanted blood. He lifted his head and stared into his mother's eyes as he rose from the bed with clenched fists. He'd heard enough of this already. Somehow, the words hurt worse coming from Beatrice. Sure she was hurt, but the judge was dead and William sensed Beatrice was content with that fact.

"I didn't miss any of it, you ragged old bitch. I wasn't the one sedated throughout the entire trial. I was there for every second of it. I listened to it on the radio coming and going. But I'm telling you; he wasn't the only person with that girl, if he was there at all. Don't be surprised by what happens next. Just watch and see."

Beatrice shook her head. She could understand the confusion William was experiencing. She herself had lain in bed for weeks trying to work through the perplexity. But she couldn't understand the rage within the boy, or his conclusion her husband might've been innocent. She couldn't fathom how William could've come to that ending.

"You'll do well not to speak to me that way, young man. Be angry if you want to, but don't ever use that tone with me again. I've sat up many nights defending you against your father. I've stood in the way of him cutting off your allowance. I made him get the right people involved in your expulsion from school. He really wanted nothing more to do with you. He only wanted for you to stay as far away from him as possible. He thought you were aimless and lazy. Now here you are, putting him on some sort of pedestal, ready to build a monument to the worthless bastard."

She saw the heat rising in her son's face. She was becoming angry herself that William didn't understand the magnitude of her pain. She continued to chide him, believing she could talk some sense into him.

"I've got an idea, William. Why don't you go to the press with your defense of Judge Carter Caine? Why don't you take your crusade on the road? You can keep the talk shows in fodder for another three months. Doesn't that sound like a good idea? Maybe you can explain this entire mess away. It might take a while, but I'm sure it'd be worth your effort. The worst that could happen is the world will view you as the same sordid fuck your father was. And if…"

"Shut up!" William pounced on her, pushing her back down into the mattress of the large bed. His face was contorted into a fist-like mask of hate as his hands found a grip around her fleshy neck. "Don't talk like that! You never curse. You never talk to me like that! Just shut up!"

Beatrice looked up at him through eyes bulging from intense external pressure. Her vision began to blur as the last of her breath fed oxygen to her brain. She struggled with what strength she had, her body weak from depression and weeks of narcotic dependency. The moment she felt herself slipping into unconsciousness, the needed air began seeping into her lungs.

William loosened his grip on his mother's throat, aware that her eyes had rolled back into their sockets. Beatrice lay perfectly still, the pink-veined whites of her eyes staring up at her demented son. *Oh my God, I've killed her.* He remained on top of her, straddling her waist so as not to impede her breath should it return. He watched her closely for several minutes. Beatrice didn't move. *Oh my God, she's dead. I've killed my mother.* His mind began to race. *This wasn't supposed to happen.*

He'd only wanted to discuss funeral arrangements for his father. Why had she provoked him? Was she a part of the debacle that ended in his father's death? Did she share in the blame? He was getting dizzy at the thought of his mother participating in such treachery. What he'd done was an accident, but he couldn't help wondering if Beatrice was a part of the conspiracy to convict and murder the judge.

He jumped up and ran to his room. *Now I need to accelerate my plan,* he thought. *I can't stay in this house any longer. Not with my mother lying upstairs dead.* He decided then he'd travel to Florida immediately, taking care of loose ends on his way out of town. He could call the funeral home tomorrow morning and make the necessary arrangements. He and Beatrice hadn't been expecting visitors, so the chances of someone coming by anytime soon were slim. It would be days before his mother's body was discovered.

Pulling a large canvas bag from his closet, he began to fill it with the things he'd need. He was trembling as he carried the bag down the steps and through the kitchen to the garage. He walked to the tool cabinet and took out a pair of wire cutters.

He reached inside his car and pressed the remote control for the garage door. When the door opened halfway, William ran under it and around to the back of the house. Finding the wires running from the telephone box, he carefully snipped them and returned to the garage. He thought for a moment about Beatrice's cell phone. His father had insisted she carry one for emergencies, and Beatrice usually had it in her purse. *Damn, I don't want to go back upstairs. I don't want to see her,* he thought. Walking back through the kitchen to the stairway, William found her purse on the kitchen table. Searching the large bag, he found her cell phone and her wallet. He put the cell phone in his pocket and began removing Beatrice's credit cards.

Carefully trying to cover his tracks, he looked around the room. *A robbery,* he thought. *Somebody broke in and robbed them. When Beatrice tried to stop the burglar, he'd strangled her.* William had left for Destin the day before and wasn't home to defend his mother.

He knocked over the chairs at the kitchen table and pulled several cabinet drawers out, dumping the contents on the floor. He threw the remaining contents of his mother's purse on the kitchen table and scattered them about. After smashing the glass doors of his mother's china cabinet, William walked to his father's study. He ransacked the old man's desk, throwing papers across the room as if someone had been looking for something.

The young man was sobbing as he walked toward the door leading to the garage. He looked back at the interior of the house. *This wasn't supposed to happen,* he said to himself. He turned and walked out, locking the door behind him. With a towel wrapped around his hand, William took an iron from his father's golf bag and smashed the glass in the door. He reached his hand inside and opened the lock.

CHAPTER TWENTY

The bright red sunrise over the Gulf of Mexico arrived almost as beautiful as the woman walking briskly through the sugar white sand. Carney Light had awakened early for no particular reason and decided to walk the beach. She was in one of her workout moods, and a fast walk toward the pier would do just fine. At five-feet-seven inches, weighing more than she felt comfortable with, Carney was what most folks referred to as big-boned. The less tactful people simply referred to her outside of her hearing distance as fat. She wasn't really fat. Large, maybe. Plump, sure. But not fat. And she was beautiful.

Huge blue eyes that caught light like a prism. Her bottom lip was larger, puffier than its upper mate, and lent a sensuous poutiness to her overall appearance. The look worked well for Carney, giving her an advantage even thinner women didn't have. Her breasts were large and round. They sat high on her chest and although heavy, didn't sag. Time and its allies had been kind. Carney had curly blonde hair she liked to bleach even blonder; almost white. She kept it a little longer than shoulder-length and liked to let it fall free and air dry after showering. Naturally fair-skinned, she worked hard to gain and maintain a summer tan without burning. She was fond of saying "better brown fat than pink fat," which was a testament to her own sense of self-acceptance and good humor.

The summer sun and a fair amount of skin protection were a part of her summer ritual, along with several trips to Destin. Today Carney wore a one-piece flowered swimsuit, partially covered now by a calf-length purple gauze skirt that split halfway up the side. A lavender fishnet cover fell across her smooth red shoulders. Her thighs were thick and evolved into well-proportioned, shapely calves that were followed by perfect feet, now bare except for a gold ankle bracelet on her left foot. She wore rings on six of her ten fingers, and a large rose quartz on a leather thong around her neck. The pace at which she walked, and the wind from the Gulf, blew her hair and the necklace in a trail behind her. She wasn't often in a mood to exercise or walk, but today it felt good to speed toward the pier, running more than walking toward a place of many warm memories.

Carney was single, not by choice but happenstance. She'd been in love a few times, always to find out the man of the moment was unavailable; either physically or emotionally. After they'd wrung all they could from the relationship, they were gone. Two had been married, she learned after the fact. Another had been wonderful one-on-one, but in the presence of others always seemed on edge. Carney would frequently find herself the butt of his jokes; usually about large people. She wondered if he was embarrassed to be with her because of her weight, and decided to ask him.

The afternoon she discussed the question with him was the last time she'd seen him. His false display of indignation at the question was obvious and Carney had asked him to leave and not bother calling her again. The relationship left her with a sense of insecurity and distrust. So she didn't pursue men, and came to accept the ones who tumbled into her life intimately as accidents, or tourists of the flesh.

Good for a good time, but not for a long time. She didn't mind that a few of the men she encountered belonged to someone else and would be gone before the end of the week, or in some cases before morning. She came to be quite comfortable with being second best. So perfectly imperfect. So beautiful and yet so flawed by some social stigma only human beings are capable of creating and nurturing. Her personality was charming and having been well-educated, she was generally serious-minded and intellectually rounded. Carney was thirty years old and felt certain she'd be alone forever.

Approaching the pier, Carney looked up at the fishermen already in place. The lines trailing from their rods down into the water made long vertical spider webs in the morning sunlight. The webs began to thicken as the line of fishermen grew more crowded toward the end of the pier, and Carney knew this was the place where the biggest and best fish were caught. She'd fished this pier hundreds of times as a little girl with her father. This pier and others like it in Panama City, or Clearwater, or over on St. Simons Island in Georgia.

Whether in a boat, on a pier, or a brushy South Georgia riverbank, Carney fished well, with patience and care. She was deliberate about her line placement, choices of bait, and at what depth she would fish. She'd spent many hours fishing with her father, and loved the memories of the times they'd shared. Ralph Light spent most his free time with Carney, trying to turn her into the son he'd really wanted. In earlier years it was easy, but as she grew up, Ralph knew he'd never succeed. Although her childhood years were spent in tomboyish fashion, Carney eventually developed characteristics and tastes that were definitely feminine in nature.

⸶

Shortly before Carney's 14th birthday, it dawned on her father that he'd raised a beautiful girl who in no way resembled a boy. Funny how this had escaped his attention. She wanted girl things that year for her birthday; Ralph's first clue as to the natural inclinations of his daughter. Prior years' shopping for birthday and Christmas presents had been easy. He simply shopped the same catalogs and stores for Carney as he did for himself.

Cabela's, Gander Mountain, LL Bean. He'd order or purchase smaller versions or sizes, and it had been working fine for them both. But damn, all of a sudden, he had to go to the mall. Ralph had never been to a mall. He wasn't even sure he knew how to get there. It couldn't be that hard to get to, though. Hell, it was right next to the expressway. So having procrastinated until the day before his daughter's birthday, all the while wishing she'd change her mind and ask for new hip waders or a fly rod, Ralph Light found himself smack dab in the middle of the mall.

Somewhere in that cavernous structure, somewhere among the lights and bright banners, the hurried escalators pulling and pushing their human cargo up and down levels, the redneck dad came to tears as the revelation overcame him. As he struggled to remember the names of the stores that stocked his daughter's wishes, he realized how much she looked like her mother. While he fumbled with his feelings there in the middle of the hurrying crowd, he saw the same flip of the bangs, the same single arched brow, and the same pretty smile. A smile damn near identical to the smile that had melted his heart three decades earlier.

He had to find a place to sit for a spell, and looked around until he located a polished wooden bench. He wiped his face and realized his cheeks were wet with tears. *Get it together, Ralph,* he said to himself. *Time goes on and people grow up and out of things; even your little girl. Now, what the hell was that store called? The Gimp or... The Gap or... Aw shit...* He chuckled as he got up and set out to buy birthday gifts for his little girl.

⸙

On this particular morning, Carney was on a mission. She wanted to talk to some of the locals who fished the Destin area regularly to see what was running offshore. The pier was a great place to fish, but she was excited about getting Jerzy out on the boat with her. She tingled at the thought of Bill showing up and going along for the ride as well.

Reaching the steps that led up to the pier, she stopped for a moment and washed the sand from her feet. As she continued toward the end of the long concrete structure, she stopped and spoke to the fishermen along the sides of the pier. Looking into every cooler along the way, she could see the morning catch consisted mostly of sheepshead and flounder. At the end of the pier, she talked with some of the men and women she fished with whenever she was in town. Amberjack and bluefin out here mostly, they said. This time of year, offshore was anybody's guess. Could be a little of everything. All you could do was try, but watch out for the weather; it could really be tricky this time of year.

After promising she'd return to fish with them later in her visit, Carney said goodbye and walked back to her condo. She found Jerzy on the balcony overlooking the Gulf. The young girl smiled, and Carney thought she'd never looked happier in the short time they'd known one another. *Good God*, she thought, *it takes so little to make this child happy. We haven't even done anything yet and she looks like she's having the time of her life.*

"I watched you walk all the way up here from that bridge," Jerzy told her.

Carney laughed at the girl's comment. "That isn't a bridge; it's a pier. It only sticks out into the water a couple hundred yards. It doesn't go anywhere. People fish off it, and there's a small café up on the beach end where people go in the morning for coffee."

Jerzy frowned, truly amazed. She'd never seen anything like this before. "Well, it looks like a bridge from here. Look, you can't see the end of it."

"I can see the end of it. See where all those people are standing? That's the end."

"I guess it's one of those optical illusions or something. I can't see it," Jerzy replied.

"Remember to tell Charlie or Kim you need to get some glasses before school starts this fall. Either that, or you'll have to sit in the front of every class you're in."

They both laughed at Jerzy's nearsightedness, but Carney made a mental note to speak with Kim about getting Jerzy's eyes checked. As Carney opened a package of bagels, Jerzy poured orange juice into glasses and the two sat down for breakfast. They sat in silence; eating and watching the beach come alive with people. Jerzy noticed the rental kiosks opening up for the day and was amazed watching the umbrellas that sprang up along the shore like so many flowers in bloom.

"So what about this new guy you've been talking about? Is he really going to meet you down here?"

Carney smiled and thought for a moment before answering. "He's going to meet both of us down here; not just me. I'm anxious for the two of you to meet so you can tell me what you think about him."

"When is he supposed to be getting in? Sometime today, right?"

Carney thought for a moment, remembering the call from Bill before she and Jerzy left Atlanta.

"He's supposed to already be here. He called me late Wednesday night and said he'd finished up the work he was doing and was headed down then. He called me from a pay phone in Montgomery. Let's get showered and dressed and I'll show you around a little. If he doesn't call before we leave, then he'll leave a message. Either way, I'm sure he'll get in touch with me."

Carney went to her room and got undressed. She walked naked from the bedroom to the shower and was finished in less than ten minutes. She shouted to Jerzy that it was her turn in the shower just as the telephone rang.

Still naked, Carney ran to the living room and picked up the phone.

"Hello?" She smiled when she heard the voice.

"Hi, Carney. It's me, Bill."

"I know who it is, silly. Where are you?"

William wondered if he should be truthful with her. He wasn't sure he wanted her to know where he was staying. Choosing to be honest, he told her.

"I'm supposed to be at Sea Palms, but there was some confusion about the dates I'd be here. It seems they have nothing available for the next two weeks. I'm at the Ramada on the west end of the strip right now. I may stay here; since it's only going to be a week."

Carney toyed with the idea of having him come and stay with her and Jerzy. They had plenty of room, and there would be some measure of convenience as well. She caught herself quickly, traveling backward into her old behavior. Carney was more than aware she was naturally inclined to be sexually aggressive, but this was something she was committed to keeping in check. She'd learned from the young girl that no good could ever come from frivolous promiscuity.

"We were about to go out and do a little shopping. I thought we'd go down to the beach later, after it cools down a little. What are your plans for today?"

"I'm lounging right now. Do you want to get together later and have dinner? I could meet you somewhere, or come by and pick you up."

Again Carney hesitated, selfishly wondering if she wanted to have Jerzy come to dinner with them.

"Tell you what, let's meet at the marina at six. That way, I can show you my dad's boat. We'll take your car to dinner. We can wait until tomorrow to introduce you to my friend. Does that sound like a plan to you?"

William almost laughed at her when she asked this last question. *I have a better plan, bitch,* he thought. *Why don't we skip the niceties and I'll shoot you in the fucking head and throw you in the water.* He had a quick thought about what he really would say to her when the time came. For now, though, some things were better left unsaid.

"Sounds good to me. I'll be in the marina parking lot at six sharp. I can't wait to see the boat. Are you sure your friend won't mind you running off on your first night in town?"

"She'll be fine. She has everything she needs at the house, plus the entire beach to entertain her if she wants to go out."

Hanging up the phone, Carney realized she'd wandered out onto the balcony during her conversation with Bill. Still naked, she hoped the neighboring residents and passersby on the beach didn't look up and see her. She was laughing out loud as she ran back to her room to get dressed.

Jerzy, already showered and dressed, found Carney in the living room.

"I'm ready whenever you are," she said.

"Bill called while you were in the shower. You don't mind if I go by myself to meet him tonight, do you? I told him I'd be at the marina at six."

"No, not at all," Jerzy replied. "I'll spend some time on the beach looking around, and maybe come back up here and watch television."

"I told him we'd all get together tomorrow. I'm going to take him to the marina and show him my dad's boat. Hopefully, he'll want to go fishing with us this week."

"That would be great, Carney, having him along. You already seem so comfortable with him. I bet he's a great guy."

Carney thought about Jerzy's last sentence. She hoped he was a great guy. She was feeling good about him, but she'd been there before. Too many times in her life, the really great guys turned out to be extreme losers. On more than one occasion the ones who appeared to be the most honest and real turned out to be the most deceptive.

"Well, we'll tour the boat and have dinner. I won't be out late. Come on, we've got all day to see the sights. You're going to love this place."

"I think I love it already. I've never seen anything like it." Jerzy smiled as she reached out and took Carney's hand, lacing their fingers together.

As far as many American Southerners are concerned, the Florida Panhandle offers the finest attributes for a beach vacation. Destin, gracefully dressed in pure white beaches and emerald water, is perhaps the gem in the crown of the Panhandle region. With its family-oriented atmosphere and endless lineup of warm weather activities, Carney was sure she could live there a lifetime and never tire of the locale.

CHAPTER TWENTY-ONE

The two women left the large condominium complex, delicately placed on the edge of the beach, and walked west toward the public fishing pier.

"We'll start out by showing you the bridge, as you called it. I have a few friends out here fishing and I promised them I'd bring you down to meet them."

"Will they still be out here? It's getting pretty hot." Jerzy tugged at the top button of her blouse, trying to allow more air to pass over her skin.

"Are you kidding? These people will stay out here all day sometimes, depending on if the fish are biting or not."

They spent the day in and out of the shops on the strip, stopping in between stores when Jerzy insisted on riding the go-carts on the big wooden track. They played a round of miniature golf and taunted each other throughout the course.

It was after five when they arrived back at the condo, both of them spent from the pace of the day and the intense Florida sun. Carney showered again and—without panties or bra—stepped into a pale blue sundress. Jerzy watched as Carney slipped into a pair of thin brown sandals.

"I don't think anyone has ever meant so much to me as you, Carney."

The younger girl was smiling, tears glistening at the corners of her eyes, threatening to build and crest.

"I don't think I've ever seen a woman as beautiful as you, either. I mean, inside and outside. You're just beautiful."

Carney stood and smiled. *Such a sentimental child,* she thought. *She'll probably grow up to be a romantic. Hold that passion, Jerzy,* Carney thought. *Hold it your entire life and never let it go; no matter what happens.*

"I appreciate that, Jerzy. I've only known you since Christmas, but in a way it feels like you've always been there. I don't know about the beautiful thing, though. I'm way too fat."

"I don't think you're fat. There's a lady back in Breaux Bridge that's so fat... Well, she's really fat."

They laughed at Jerzy's inability to describe the fat lady back home. After Carney made sure Jerzy knew where everything was located in the house, she gave her a hug and walked outside. She made sure the girl locked the door, and made her way down to her car. She was on the stairs when she heard Jerzy shouting behind her.

"Carney, come back!" she shouted. "Your daddy's on the phone! Hurry!"

Carney turned and ran back up the stairs to the front door. Jerzy handed her the phone.

"He's got such a dreamy voice. Like a movie star or..."

"Oh hush, give me that. Daddy?" She'd expected him to call much earlier.

"Hey, Carney. How was the drive down?"

"Great, except when you make the turn at San Destin they still haven't finished that road construction. Traffic still backs up a little there."

"Have you been by to check the boat yet? I called Evan yesterday and he said it was ready. They had to do a bottom job on it this year. It should look good."

"We planned on going by there this afternoon, but I got so wrapped up in trying to show Jerzy all the sights and shopping for beach clothes for her that we ran out of time. I have a date tonight, though, and I'm meeting him at the marina. I'll have a chance to go over it then."

"Wait a minute. You just got there and you already have a date with a guy? That's fast." Ralph chuckled into the phone. He didn't worry about Carney or her relationships with men. He knew she could handle her affairs nicely without his interference.

"Oh, aren't we witty today!" the daughter poked back. They were silent for a moment then, each enjoying the sounds of the other. The laughter between them and the playful barbs were all a part of the interaction they'd developed over thirty years of co-nurturing.

"Actually, father dear, he's the same guy I went to Kobe with last week. He happened to be coming down here at the same time. He's only here until Saturday; then he returns to Atlanta. I really like him, and he seems to like me as well." She saw Bill's face as she went on, describing him to her father.

"He sounds like a nice guy. You two have a good time tonight. Will your friend be going along with you?"

"No, she's staying in tonight. I didn't want to overwhelm the poor guy with two beautiful women. She'll probably watch television or walk the beach."

In a serious tone, one in which Carney recognized the sounds of pain and regret, Ralph continued speaking. "I had to go by the Sheriff's Department on Friday and claim Carter's personal belongings. His wife and son couldn't be reached, so they called me. Such a tragedy; the entire mess."

"What are you talking about? What mess?"

She could tell that something was obviously bothering her father. Carney had yet to hear about the shooting of Judge Caine.

"The shooting. You didn't hear about all that?"

"Daddy, I've been so busy trying to get ready for this trip, getting Jerzy some of the things she'd need, that I haven't been paying any attention to the news. What happened?"

"Apparently they were taking him down to the prison late at night; I think last Monday or Tuesday. The officers transporting him stopped for coffee at the Dunkin Diner over on Courtland Street. One of the officers went outside while the other one was in the men's room and shot the judge in the head, right through the rear window of the car."

"Oh my God. Did they arrest the cop who shot him?"

Ralph continued to tell Carney all that had happened. The witness who said he saw a man with a gun outside the police car disappeared. With only a statement from a trustee at the jail about the cop pushing the judge down the stairs, the police could only surmise the rest of the story.

Carney felt bad for her father. He and Judge Caine were friends for many years. She felt herself choking up.

"Daddy, are you going to be all right? Is there anything I can do? Do you need me to come home?"

Out of sight of his daughter, Ralph pushed the tears from his eyes with his fist. "No, baby, don't be silly. You and Jerzy enjoy the beach. Have fun with your new friend and be safe out there on the gulf. Thank you but no, sweetheart, I'm fine."

"If you change your mind, call me. We're not going out on the water until Wednesday morning. Call me if you need me."

They finished the conversation, Carney trying to bring them back to a happier note. When she returned the phone to its stand, she turned to Jerzy, who was lying on the sofa reading.

"You're not going to believe this," Carney said in an excited tone.

"What? Is everything okay at home?"

"The judge is dead, Jerzy. A cop went nuts, it sounds like, and shot him in the head."

Jerzy sprang up from the sofa, throwing her magazine aside.

"The judge? You mean Carter? Somebody…?"

Carney sat down and explained to Jerzy what her father had said. Jerzy showed no emotion. She sat and listened, waiting for Carney to finish the story.

"So now what happens, Carney? Does that mean the police are going to want to talk to me again?"

"No, this only means that it's over. He's dead. It has nothing to do with you. Both of the cops are dead. Daddy said someone told the police there was a man standing outside the squad car with a gun, pointing it at the judge through the window. When they went to talk to the guy, he'd given them a fake address, so they figured he was lying anyway. As far as Daddy knows, the case is already closed. Daddy had to go to the jail and pick up the judge's things because the police couldn't reach his wife or son."

"I remember him," said Jerzy. "He sat in court staring at your dad and me during the entire trial. He was a good-looking guy, but he had this hateful grin on his face; like he wanted to kill us. It was scary. I remember Charlie saying he was going to have him removed if he didn't stop. I don't think Mrs. Caine ever came to the trial. Charlie said she was all drugged up. I guess she took it pretty hard. Poor woman. I hope she finds peace somewhere in all of this."

Carney thought about this last statement, the compassion for Beatrice Caine that Jerzy apparently felt confounded her.

"I can't help thinking that if it were me, I'd be glad the old bastard is dead. That's just me, but what he did to his family wasn't right. Not right at all."

"Did you know them? The wife and son?" Jerzy asked.

"I've met his wife a couple of times at different functions. There was a charity that the judge sponsored, and they had dinners from time to time. I went along with my dad, sort of like his date. But I only met the son once, I think. That was back when we were little kids. I think my dad was a little embarrassed to bring me around the Caines' home. Back then I was probably more boyish than their son. A couple of years ago a guy came into the shop and picked up some pictures for Beatrice; that's the wife's name. I don't think it was her son, though. I can't even remember what the guy looked like, but I didn't get the impression he was their child."

They talked for several more minutes before Carney looked at her watch. "Oh, I'm going to be late. Lock up behind me and have a good time."

"You, too. I'll see you when you get home, if I'm still awake." She smiled at Carney as she closed and locked the door behind her for the second time.

Jerzy sat alone on the sofa, watching the sun going red in the west. *I did all this,* she thought. *It all started because of me. And worse yet, I still don't know where my daddy is. I've caused a man to be jailed and then killed, and all for nothing. Mamma warned me something like this would happen.*

She started crying and stretched out on the sofa, screaming into the pillow. Alone now as she was when she left Breaux Bridge, she cried until she fell asleep. Along with the sleep came the dream; she and her father walking down Peachtree Street, looking up at the tall buildings of the newest city in the South. The New South, where lives could be started fresh and lived long, and a job could be had even if a man wasn't a genius. She and Parlee eating at the Hard Rock Café, listening to James Brown screaming, "I Feel Good" and smiling at one another because they agreed with Mr. Brown.

CHAPTER TWENTY-TWO

As Jerzy dreamed the dream that carried her from Louisiana to Georgia, enduring the painful process of growth and maturity, her foster father was back in Atlanta staring at his watch. No longer a uniformed officer, Charlie Puckett had just this day been promoted to Detective. He turned to his partner—a transplanted Yankee named Giles—and asked him what time he had.

"That's the good part of getting promoted to Detective. You'll be able to afford a fucking watch that works." Giles grinned, thinking he was pretty sharp. He didn't like Charlie Puckett. He didn't like black people at all.

Charlie didn't like being partnered with the likes of Robinson Giles. Charlie didn't like Northerners to begin with, and he liked cocky Northerners even less. He outranked Giles, and could probably make life fairly miserable for him. But Charlie had other things going on right now.

"Listen, dickweed, I have a watch that works. Okay? I'm thinking maybe the battery's going dead. I was…"

"I know, I know. You were waiting on a call that was supposed to come at six o'clock. I've been listening to you whine to your wife on the phone. It's only six-thirty; whoever it is probably got busy. Be patient. I knew a guy like you in Detroit. Up there, we just…"

"Oh shit. Now I get stuck sitting here, listening to you tell me about how ya'll do it so much differently up north, right? All you smart guys, patient guys, fast guys, strong guys. We're so dumb down here, we can't chew fuckin' gum and walk at the same time. Go ahead, Einstein, I'm listening. But when you're finished telling me how great everything is up there, take a little time explaining to me what the hell you're doing down here, you fuckin five-eyed roach."

He looked at his watch again. Giles sat and stared at him, saying nothing. Charlie thought he was going to cry.

The telephone rang and Charlie grabbed it before the first bell was complete.

"Charlie Puckett, Homicide. I mean…Homicide, Charlie Puckett." *Damn,* he thought. *Just… Damn.*

"Mr. Puckett, how are you, Sir. I'm sorry it took so long to get back to you. I had to help with the dinner this evening. We're a couple of volunteers short."

"I understand completely, Miss Tucker. Now, we were talking about a guy who was in your shelter last February; maybe March. A guy named Parlee Rabideaux."

"Yes, I remember him well. He helped out a lot around here when he stayed with us. He left here late one night, saying his mother died in Louisiana and he was going back there. But then, when we opened the new shelter over on Trinity Street, he showed up there. I haven't talked with him any but I did find out he's still there. Is that what you needed to know?"

"Yes, ma'am, it is. I need to know where I can find him."

"What has he done wrong? He seemed like such a nice man. I couldn't imagine him being a law breaker."

"He's done nothing wrong, Miss Tucker. I need to find him for a friend, his daughter actually. Thank you so much for all you've done to help."

Charlie clicked off the phone and called his house to tell Kim he knew where Jerzy's father was. Kim was excited at first and then fell silent.

"What's the matter, honey? Can't you see the look on her face when she gets back and sees her daddy is here? She'll flip out."

"And then we lose her, Charlie. I know it's the right thing to do; that's why she came here to begin with. But she's become my little girl, Charlie. She's become our little girl."

"You're absolutely right, Kim. She is our little girl. And what do we want more than anything in the world for our children, honey?"

Strong men in all colors, Southern style.

Kim knew where Charlie was going with this, but it didn't make it any easier to look ahead to what was coming when Jerzy and Parlee reunited.

"Kim?" He knew she was crying. He knew the bond between the woman and the child was even stronger than the bond between Jerzy and him. He waited before continuing, allowing his wife to grieve a step at a time.

"We want our children to be happy, Kimberly. Healthy and happy; more than anything else. That child has endured something no human should ever suffer, just to be with her daddy. I'm glad I got to be a little part of her life. You should feel the same way. We should both be working toward the same thing."

"You're right, Charlie. I know you're right. Do you think you'll be able to find him tonight?"

"The old woman at the urban shelter said he was over at Trinity. I'm on my way over there in a minute. We can talk about it when I get home."

With that, Charlie hung up the phone and went looking for the Yankee. Giles was dropping quarters in a candy machine when Charlie found him.

"Let's go, Giles," he half-shouted at the man.

Giles followed, walking behind Charlie, eating his candy bar. When they reached the car Giles put his hand on the door handle and looked across the roof at Charlie. Charlie looked up at him, wondering why he hesitated.

"What now?" Charlie asked sarcastically.

"Five-eyed roach?" Giles asked.

"What?" Charlie was confused.

"You called me a five-eyed roach. What is that, some sort of racial thing or what?"

Charlie laughed and climbed into the unmarked car.

"Get in the car, Giles. Shut up and get in the car." He laughed again, wondering how he'd become saddled with this guy.

Pulling up to the curb in front of the shelter on Trinity Street, Charlie turned to Giles.

"These homeless folks sometimes see cops as a threat. Comes from not knowing if what you did was legal or not. Sort of an instinct thing. So you walk around the back, in case one of these yahoos bolts. Don't hurt anybody, and don't get yourself hurt. Simply stop anyone who comes out that door."

"Yeah, I think I can handle that without getting shot or stabbed. You go in the front, come through, and open up for me. I'll make sure nobody runs. Good plan."

Charlie was shaking his head as Giles turned and walked to the back of the shelter. Charlie waited by the car for several moments, making sure his partner had enough time to secure the rear exit. When he felt comfortable enough time had passed, he calmly walked in the front door of the old building.

Walking to the rear of a large open room, Charlie found four men sitting around an old army cot, playing cards. Sitting on a wooden crate watching them was his partner Giles. Charlie leaned over and spoke to him.

"What the hell is going on here?" he asked.

Giles looked up at him; feigning ignorance. "I'm not sure, Charlie, but it looks a lot like Tonk to me."

"That's not what I meant, asshole. Why'd you come in the door? You could've fucked this up."

Giles stood and pointed to the rear of the building. A huge portion of the wall had been knocked out, prepared for some renovation.

"There's no door, Detective Puckett. Matter of fact, there's no wall either. By the way, these are my new friends." Giles began naming them, pointing his finger as he went around the cot.

"This is Mathis. I think that's a last name, unless his parents were weird. This handsome devil here is Parlee, and the fat boy over there…"

Charlie started laughing. Uncontrollably, from deep in his gut the noise filled the three-walled room. He could barely speak as he tried to shut Giles up.

"Shut up, Giles; just shut the fuck up. Damn, man, you talk way too much."

"I just wanted to introduce you guys. Damn, can't even be friendly around you."

"Parlee, is that your name?" Charlie looked at the big black-haired man sitting next to Mathis. He pulled his badge wallet from his pocket and saw the big man tighten.

"No need to try and run, Parlee. You ain't in any trouble…"

Before he could say anything else, Giles chimed in. "Unless you mess with him about his watch…"

"Giles!" Charlie tried to hide his smile, turning and looking at Giles with an angry expression pasted on his face. "I'm trying to conduct business here, Detective Giles. Now would you kindly shut up?" He turned back to Parlee. "Now, like I said. You don't have a problem with the law, Parlee. We're here to try and help you."

Parlee stood up from his card game. Charlie could see Jerzy Rabideaux in his eyes and the coal black hair.

"I don't need any help, officer; unless you come here to give me a job." Parlee towered over Charlie, a foot taller and almost as broad.

"Well, part of what I'm here to talk to you about is just that. A job. A job and a chance to be a father to your daughter."

Parlee squinted his eyes and moved closer to Charlie. Giles put his hand on his gun and moved closer to Parlee, speaking to him as he did. "Easy, big boy. Happy face. Put on a happy face. Don't be scrunching your face up at my partner."

"It's okay, Giles. He's just curious. He's not going to hurt anyone." Charlie had been a cop a long time; most of his career spent in blue on the street. He didn't sense anything to fear from the big man.

"What do you know about my daughter, officer? Is she all right?"

"I know where she is, and I know she's safe and having a good time. She almost died hitchhiking from Louisiana to Atlanta to find you."

Parlee stepped back several feet from Charlie, squinting his eyes as if he was trying to remember whether or not he'd seen him before. His memory was almost washed out, but something about Charlie Puckett seemed very familiar.

"Do I know you?" Parlee asked.

"I don't think so, Mr. Rabideaux. We've never met."

Parlee became more curious when Charlie used his family name. Suddenly, he had a thought. A thought that he knew where he'd seen this face before. He stepped back up to Charlie and, again, Giles bristled.

"Do you drive a Green Ford Expedition?" Parlee looked directly into Charlie's eyes as he asked this question. Charlie laughed, finally relieved of a nagging suspicion.

"I thought that was you. No, Sir, I knew that was you. You stood on those courthouse steps every day and watched that child go to and from court. I wanted to ask you then, but I had more important things at hand. We didn't know then exactly what was going on between you and Jerzy. But I saw you. I saw you every damn day."

"I wanted to see her; I really did. But I don't want to know how bad she hates me. She has all the right in the world, but I don't want to know how much she hates me. I just couldn't... I couldn't take that. I wanted to tell her all the reasons for what I done. I hated her mother; I guess she hated me, too. I wanted to take the girl with me; truly I did. But I didn't have money, and I knew when I got here I'd be living like... Well, like this. This ain't no place for a little girl. She would have... I thought she would have still been there when I got back. You see, I got this idea..."

"Wait, Parlee, just wait. You can tell me all about it later. Right now we have to go."

Parlee didn't understand. "Go? Go where? I'm supposed to..."

"I'll explain later. Right now, let's just go. Like I said, you're not in any trouble, but we need to talk. Just you and me."

The three men walked out into the darkness and got into the car. Charlie waited until they were cruising slowly down Fulton Street before he turned to his partner and spoke.

"I saw your work back there, Giles. I appreciate having someone look out for me like that. You can expect the same from me. Thanks."

"Don't mention it, Charlie. Just don't call me a five..."

"Don't worry, partner, I won't," Charlie interrupted. "That shit with the wall. That was pretty funny, wasn't it? Are all you Yankees fucking comedians?"

Parlee couldn't help being confused by the two bellowing detectives in the front seat.

CHAPTER TWENTY-THREE

William waited patiently in the marina parking lot. He'd arrived an hour early to look around the place. He walked up and down the different docks looking at the boats to see if he could identify Ralph's before Carney pointed it out. Nothing on any particular craft seemed to stand out as a definitive characteristic of the Atlanta attorney or his daughter. His mind raced as he waited on Carney to arrive. He knew what it was he intended to do to her but, even after the long drive down and the previous days spent thinking about it, he wasn't sure how to make it happen. His anger and emotional pain wouldn't allow him to think clearly enough to develop a definite method, causing him to feel frustrated and confused.

Tonight's no good, he thought. *She has a friend here with her, and it wouldn't be long before she reported Carney missing. The police would be looking for her before William even got out of the state. He needed to be patient and he had to get them in one place together, and then he'd kill them both. Maybe the friend has ties to Carney's father.* This thought brought a macabre smile to his face. *Twice the pain, you bastard.*

His face began to melt into a softer facade as he watched Carney pull her car into the space beside him. She smiled as she slammed her door and walked toward his BMW.

William smiled back, thinking she had the most beautiful smile of any woman he'd ever known. *Perfect white teeth surrounded by the most wonderfully shaped lips... Perhaps under different circumstances...*

"Hi! It's good to see you again!"

She interrupted his thoughts with a cheerful greeting as she opened the passenger door and sat down in his car.

"It's good to see you again, too. Isn't it nice down here?"

William was struggling now. He was angry and hurt; being friendly and sociable under these conditions wasn't easy for him. Deception wasn't something he was good at.

"It is nice. This is my favorite place in the world. I'd truly love to live down here."

They sat for a moment in awkward silence. William searched for something to say.

"So where's your dad's boat?" he finally asked.

"Right this way." Carney opened the door and stepped outside. She walked around the back of the car and was standing at the driver's door when William got out. When he closed his door and turned to walk with her, she leaned in and kissed him on the mouth.

William was taken aback. Her lips were warm and moist, naturally puffy. Her tongue found his lips and pried them apart, searching. She playfully bit his bottom lip, causing him to pull away from her grip.

"Ouch! What was that all about?" he asked, fingering his lip as if checking for broken skin.

Carney giggled at his childishness.

"Oh, I'm sorry. I should've warned you," she teased. "I tend to bite a little."

William tried to laugh, feeling the need to participate in the moment's levity.

"Oh, okay. Biting is good, I guess."

He forced another laugh as she took his arm and led him toward the docks. Slowing in front of a long convertible, Carney pointed at the sleek white vessel.

"This is it, the Cheri A Lamore. Daddy gave it my mother's name. Kind of nice, isn't it?"

"Yes, I'd say so. Better than kind of nice," William replied as he walked back and forth on the short dock, looking up and down the boat. "How big is it?"

"It's a thirty-eight-foot Mediterranean, deep-V hull. Twin three hundred horse inboards, a stateroom with a double bed, and a head compartment. You'd be surprised how smooth she is out on the open water. We've even got a kitchen and bar below deck. I've stayed on board for two weeks at a time without ever having to go in. She handles like a dream."

William was truly impressed. For the first time since he'd met Carney, there was no need to force a smile.

"You drive this thing out there by yourself? Out in the Gulf? Alone?"

"Just me and the fishes. It gets a little lonely sometimes. But there's a television and DVD player. Dad has plenty of movies and CDs on board. I bring what I like to read, and do a little fishing. It's really very peaceful out there. Daddy also insisted on GPS and a satellite phone. Very expensive, but it makes him feel better when I'm out there alone. I usually turn the phone off, unless I need to call and check in with him."

"Wow, you sound like you really know the boat. I don't think I could stand it out there. Hell, I don't even know if I could get out there on my own without ending up lost."

"Sure you could. It's really very simple. Navigation charts, or the GPS do most of the work. You couldn't get lost if you tried."

William laughed out loud this time. Genuine laughter, from the gut. "Oh, you don't know me. I'm sure I could find a way to get lost."

"Were you serious about going fishing with Jerzy and me?"

This caught William by surprise, both the question and the name Jerzy. He'd heard the name before, but where? Maybe Carney had told him over the phone.

"You and who?" he asked.

"Jerzy, my friend who's here with me. Are you serious about going out there with us? It'll be an all-day trip. If you want to, we can stay overnight. We'll have a blast. I've caught some pretty big fish out there."

"Yeah, I was serious. When did you want to go?"

Carney thought about it for a moment before she answered. She realized his time was more limited than hers.

"Whatever day works best for you. We're here for a month. You're only staying a week, so you tell me. Any day is fine. The boat's loaded, except for food and drinks, and I can get all that the day before. So pick a day."

William didn't respond right away. At the moment, he was trying to cope with the feelings of hate and contempt for her father and his obviously increasing attraction to her. This woman was an enigma. He felt compelled to just hold her, pull her in close and not let go. But *I'm here for my father,* he thought. *The revenge, my motivation for seeking her out to begin with.* He hadn't expected to be so taken with this woman. She wasn't the type of woman he'd normally pursue. She was larger than his tastes preferred, and a little forward. But she seemed so in touch with everything around her. Somehow it seemed like they were both tuned to the same frequency or something. He wondered why she couldn't see through his façade, be aware of his deceptiveness.

"Let me think about it over dinner," he finally said.

"That will work," Carney responded. "Any day is good for me."

They drove east on 98 toward Panama City. The restaurant was on the opposite end of the strip and the drive was made in silence, each of them preoccupied with their own thoughts. William continued to marvel at the fact that this woman was having such an emotional impact on him. This was going to be harder than he had thought. He could probably still kill her and her friend but it wasn't going to be as easy as he'd anticipated. He wondered if he'd live a lifetime of regret over this.

Just her presence softened him a little. She seemed to find small, almost imperceptible ways to get close to him. She'd taken the opportunity on the dock to press herself against him, letting him feel the warmth of her body. He was aware she wore nothing under her cotton dress; he could smell the musky sweetness of her as the heat rose from her skin. She wasn't flashy or flamboyant. Plain would be a better description, he thought. No part of Carney Light was lost on him. What he didn't observe of her with his eyes, he felt with some weird sense he didn't know he possessed... His radar was fixed on every womanly signal she sent; intentional or not.

Dinner was at Lagniappe, a Cajun affair situated directly over the Gulf. Carney sat with her back to the water, while William sat to her right across the table from her. The sun sinking in the west caused the water to ripple orange red, creating a dramatic background which perfectly suited the blonde-haired Carney.

William was once again entranced by her magnificence. He tried to shake the encroaching melancholy. He struggled to stay committed to his plan and not cave in to whatever it was devouring his darker feelings. He needed the hatred and disgust to be the driving force behind his intended actions. He tried returning his thoughts to the logistics of murder.

The thought of killing them on the boat had crossed his mind as he and Carney were leaving the marina. *That would be a triple hit*, he thought. *The boat must've cost a small fortune, and was probably under-insured.* He began to play the scene in his head. They'd be out on the open water where there would be no interference. He tried to picture the three of them alone on the boat, nothing around them for miles. *Throw them overboard? Shoot them and then throw them overboard? There were sharks out there; the bodies would probably never be recovered. Then I'd set fire to the boat after I've hoisted the dingy over the rail. I'd have to get within sight of the shore though; I'd be afraid out there by myself if I couldn't see the shoreline.*

As he considered his options he began gaining back his confidence in his ability to kill the two women. The dark adrenaline began flowing once again. *I can do this*, he thought as he finished the last of his meal. *I must do this; I owe it to the judge.*

"You must've been famished." Carney spoke for the first time since their dinner arrived.

William looked up from his empty plate and smiled.

"I was. I've been eating fast food since I came in last week, so the change of pace probably made me hungrier than I thought I was."

Carney took a sip of her tea and spoke to him over the rim of her glass. The orange light of the sunset began to stroke the edges of her hair, accentuating the natural curl and adding orange-red highlights to her fascinating blonde hue.

"What would you like to do after dinner?" she asked.

William stuttered, but didn't speak. Embarrassed by his tongue-tied attempt, he covered his face with both hands. The regained confidence spiraled into the rough-hewn floor beneath his chair. The emerging tough guy was again overwhelmed by the look of her.

"Walking the beach at night is nice, if that's something that would interest you. I really don't want to be out late. I've been under a terrible amount of stress lately and I'm rather exhausted."

Carney smiled and remembered he'd been grieving over his parents' marriage dissolving after so many years. His apparent sensitivity to such issues was one of the things she liked about him. Too many men these days were afraid to care.

"A walk on the beach is fine with me. That's one of the things I enjoy most down here; especially at night."

They left the restaurant and began walking westward in the sand. When they reached the hard-packed sand at the water's edge, Carney pulled her sandals off and stepped into the water. Taking William's hand, she turned it up to her lips and kissed his fingers.

"We'll walk to that row of hotels and then back to the restaurant." She pointed ahead to a stretch of buildings a half-mile in the distance.

"That's fine. How does the day after tomorrow sound for the fishing trip?" he asked her.

"Let's see; that's Wednesday. Do you want to stay out overnight, or make it a day trip?"

She watched as William pondered this question. She wondered what he was thinking about. Most other guys would've jumped at the chance of being out there with her all night. *Well, maybe not most guys,* she thought.

William realized overnight would be better. He may be able to get back to shore in the dingy before daylight and not chance being seen.

"I think overnight would be fun," he said. "What about your friend? Will she mind? I wouldn't want her to not go because of me."

"Oh, no, she'll want to go because you're there. She's anxious to meet you. It's a date then. We'll leave Wednesday morning around eight."

Carney squeezed his hand and they continued their walk with minimal conversation. When they returned to William's car, he opened her door to let her in. Carney approached as if to enter the car, but instead pulled William to her and began kissing him. She felt him struggle at first and then relax, as if yielding to her strength. After another several seconds, he put his hands on her shoulders and gently eased her away from him.

"Whoa... I, uh, I wasn't expecting that."

Carney moved forward again, speaking softly. Words he couldn't hear, but knew were words of passion.

Again William took her shoulders, holding her at arm's length.

Frustrated and confused, Carney lifted her hands.

"What's the matter, Bill?"

He sensed genuine concern in her voice, thinking hard to develop a rational answer.

"Carney, I..."

"I know you've got a lot on your mind, but let it go, Bill. Please let it go. It's their life; not yours. Just relax and enjoy this time. You're not responsible for your parents' lives; they are. You must accept that you can't fix either of them."

"It's not that, Carney. We need to be a little more... Cautious. I really don't want to rush into anything with you. I mean, you're absolutely beautiful. I really love everything about you, but..."

Carney needed to hear the rest of his comment. She needed to know right now what this guy was about. She wasn't angry, but it wouldn't take much to get her there.

"But what. Bill? But I'm too fat, or I'm too pushy? But what?"

"It's nothing like that. I can't even look at you without smiling inside. It's not about being fat or pushy. I don't even know what you're talking about. It's about me. I can't figure out how to explain it to you."

"I'd like to see you more, Bill. I didn't realize you were taking things so personally. My timing could probably be better, but I thought... Well, I guess I wasn't thinking. Take me back to my car, please. This will all work out."

It wasn't until Carney had left William's car and unlocked her own when he finally spoke again. He stepped out of his BMW and walked over to her, speaking to her back.

"I'd like to see you again, Carney. I hope you still want me along on the fishing trip Wednesday. We can still be friends, don't you think? Can't we still see each other while I'm sorting this all out?"

Carney thought for a moment before turning to face him. The handsomeness of his features were changed now by something Carney thought she recognized. She felt a pity for him that almost made her cry. She made an effort to soften her voice as she answered.

"We can still be friends, Bill. I'd love to have you join us on the boat, if you still want to, but you're different today. I've sensed all along some unwillingness to be closer, or more affectionate. I thought it was nerves or first date kind of stuff."

She hesitated now, feeling the need to choose her words carefully. Even the right words, taken the wrong way, would send him away forever. Carney didn't want him to go away.

"You're struggling with something in your heart. I don't know if you're in some kind of emotional pain, or if you're in some kind of trouble or what. But you're definitely fighting with yourself about something. Maybe it's 'the should I or shouldn't I?' kind of struggle, but I don't think so. Something seems to be eating at you, something substantial."

William could only look at her. No words came to mind that would have any intelligent meaning at that point. The thoughts of murder and revenge were absent as he stood puzzled over her ability to read him. The noise of the marsh behind the parking lot filled the air as he struggled to find some reply.

Carney stood watching him, finally becoming uncomfortable with his lack of a response. She opened her car and sat inside, looking straight ahead at the boats rocking in their slips. William stepped to her car and knocked on the window, motioning for her to lower the glass.

"I need to think about some things, that's all. I do have some things to work through in my personal life, and it's not about my parents. I'm struggling with myself and I may be in trouble. I don't know yet. I don't even want to think about the problem yet; I've just been letting it kick my ass. But I want you to know that my hesitation isn't about how I feel for you. That's about all I feel comfortable telling you right now. I hope you understand."

Carney smiled and started her car. She lowered her head to stifle the urge to burst into tears. Composing herself, she looked up at him. William had stepped closer to her car.

"That's possibly the only thing you could've said to convince me that you're not full of shit, Bill. Thank you for being honest with me. I don't care what you are struggling with; knowing that you recognize the problem is good enough for me. I only hope you can find a solution quickly, so you can end the suffering you're going through. Call me sometime tomorrow, if you want to. Otherwise be here at the boat Wednesday around eight."

They said their goodbyes and went their separate ways for the night. Carney to her condo on the water and William to the humid cement walls of the Ramada. Somehow, William felt a sense of transformation, from violent hatred and revenge to total bewilderment and confusion. He stepped into his hotel room still wondering what had just happened to him.

CHAPTER TWENTY-FOUR

William rolled over in his sleep and picked up the telephone. He looked at the clock as a voice cracked loudly in his ear.

"Mr. Caine?"

"Who is this?"

"It's the front desk, Mr. Caine. I apologize, Sir, but a message came in yesterday I'm afraid you didn't get. We were short of..."

"Whatever! What was the message?" He looked again at the clock; not yet fully awake.

"A Mr. Stromann called, Sir. He left a number for you to call him back. He said he has a few questions for you."

William had called Stromann's on the drive down and asked them to go ahead with the cremation. He told them that he and his mother wanted to avoid any more publicity, and he would claim the remains when he returned from Florida next week. Writing the number down on the desk pad, he thanked the operator and hung up the phone.

The receptionist at Stromann's answered the telephone on the first ring.

"Hello, this is William Caine. I've just received a message this morning I think I was supposed to get yesterday. May I speak to Mr. Stromann, please?"

His call was quickly transferred to the funeral director's office.

"Garrett Stromann, how can I help you?"

"Mr. Stromann, this is William Caine. I understand you have some questions about my father's arrangements."

"Oh, Mr. Caine. Thank you for returning the call, Sir. We couldn't get in touch with you yesterday, and the phone at your house seemed to be out of service. We tried there after you didn't return our call to your hotel. We figured you might've just come back home."

"Well, what's the problem, Mr. Stromann?" William was becoming impatient with all the babbling that was going on this morning.

"No problem now at all, Mr. Caine. We tried your house this morning and were able to get in touch with your mother. The yardman had apparently sliced through the telephone line with a weed eater. She said BellSouth was leaving when I called her. We've already got everything straightened away."

William asked incredulously, "You spoke to my mother?"

"Yes, Sir. I really felt bad about that. I know you wanted to take care of everything yourself, considering all she's been through. But we needed to know exactly what receptacle you'd chosen for your father's remains. We thought we had it in the computer, but it wasn't there. I assured her that it was our mistake; not yours. Your mother was really gracious about it all. She's taking this very well."

William placed the receiver back on the cradle, his mind in a whirl. Was this some kind of a joke? Was Beatrice alive? He rubbed the sleep out of his eyes and turned on the television. He'd been keeping up with the news, both on television and on his car stereo. He wanted to know when and if they'd found his mother's body in her bed, strangled and robbed.

Picking up the phone once again, William began to dial the number to his mother's home. Three digits into the number, he quickly put the phone down and began to pace the small room. The bristling heat of fear brought beads of perspiration to his forehead as he searched the room for his clothes.

⸙

"Large coffee, black," William told the woman at the café across the street from the hotel. He laid two one-dollar bills on the counter as he took his cup and walked back to his room. He checked carefully up and down the street as he crossed for any sign of someone watching him.

The only way to be sure, he thought, was to call the house himself and see if Beatrice answered the telephone. That was the easy part; the ensuing conversation was what worried William about the most. Whatever was going to happen was something he couldn't control, but he had to call. He had to know if his mother was alive. He sat down on the bed once more and reached for the phone.

As he placed his hand on the receiver, the silence in the room was shattered as the phone rang. William jumped at the sudden sound. He picked up the phone and shouted. "What is it now?" he asked loudly.

"I'm sorry. I called Stromann's to find out where you were. They gave me this number. Are you all right?"

Fear gripped William's stomach from deep inside. He felt his bowels begin to loosen as the voice came through the wire. An accumulation of fear, relief, and confusion blended together to dry his throat. Not able to speak, he croaked unintelligibly into the phone.

"I'm sorry, Son. I can't understand what you're saying. Are you all right down there?"

He swallowed air, no fluid in his mouth to moisten the inner flesh. He picked up the coffee cup and drank the last few drops.

"Mother?" This seemed to be all he could manage. He had no idea what to say or how to say it.

"Yes, William. Answer me, Son. Is everything okay down there?"

"I'm fine, Mother. Everything's fine. I need to talk to you, Mother. I realize I've done something terrible. I was so afraid I'd hurt you. What do you want me to do? I'm so sorry. I'll do anything you tell me to."

Beatrice heard the panic and fear in her son's voice. *Nothing much has changed about him since he was a small boy,* she thought. Back then, whenever he was in trouble for some stupid prank, he'd run to her. He knew it was pointless to go to his father, who had no sympathy for ignorance. She'd always been the one to care for him. From bandaged knees to bail bonds, Beatrice was the one who kept the boy afloat.

"I don't want you to do anything, William. I'm fine. I provoked you into a rage, but you must understand the humiliation and degradation I've been exposed to. Yes, you did something terrible, but I feel partly responsible for everything that happened. I don't know what else to say."

William felt a bit of relief, hearing this from his mother. He was more relieved she was indeed alive. He'd spent the past several nights in fitful sleep, laced with dreams too horrible to recollect. *Mother's alive*, he thought, *and I'm not a criminal. At least not yet.* He felt another pang of guilt as this last thought crossed his mind.

"I hear what you're saying, Mother, but I'll spend the rest of my life making amends to you for my behavior. I don't know how a person forgets that sort of incident."

Beatrice smiled into the phone. He was growing; she could hear the maturity in the tone of his voice. He somehow seemed older and wiser than the last time they'd talked.

"I do want something from you, William," Beatrice said. "I want you to come home when you're ready and help me tear this place apart. I want you to help me turn it into something that says Beatrice Caine lives here. I've lived in this stuffy judicial palace for too long, and I can't stand it anymore. Can you understand that, Son? I want to see you be successful at something as well. I never cared if you went to college. You have my family's genes in you. You'll survive well without all the formal education. I just want us both to be happy."

"We can do that, Mother. I'll help you with anything you want. I'm sorry I felt so strongly about the wrong thing. We'll burn the house down, if that's what you want, and we'll be happy. I've already been thinking of some options as far as a career goes. I'm too old to go back to school now, but I've got some ideas."

The two of them spoke for another hour, Beatrice assuring William he was in no trouble with the law for trying to hurt her. He told Beatrice about his involvement with the girl he'd taken to dinner in Atlanta. They got on well, and were in Destin together, at different hotels of course. He shared with her that he was going on a fishing trip with her and her girlfriend, and that he'd probably be home by Sunday night.

When William was finished telling his mother about the girl, Beatrice asked her name. He quickly changed the subject, pretending not to hear her question. He'd done enough to his mother so far and didn't want to tell her a lie. Beatrice realized he was avoiding her question, and didn't push him for an answer. *I'll know soon enough*, she thought. *He'll either come to me with his broken heart, or I'll hear him bragging about breaking hers.* Such was the nature of her boy.

CHAPTER TWENTY-FIVE

Tuesday morning, Carney and Jerzy sat in the back booth of the Donut Hole on the north side of the strip near the marina. Carney had shared with Jerzy the events of the previous night. They sat now talking about the handsome man who seemed to be so troubled. For the first time since their dinner at Kobe, Carney had begun to question her involvement with the mysterious Bill Ammons.

"So, I really like him but I think he has some issues," Carney continued the conversation they'd paused as the waitress served their breakfast.

"What do you mean by issues?" Jerzy asked.

"When we met for dinner that night in Atlanta, he seemed really shook up about something. He calmed down after a while but when I tried to get close to him, he kept backing off. Then last night I tried to kiss him twice and he froze. One time he even put his hands on my shoulders and pushed me away. No one has ever done that. I wasn't being fresh or anything; I just wanted him to know I really like him."

Jerzy smiled at Carney as if she knew something the older girl did not.

"Do you think he might be... Uh... Well, do you think he might be gay?"

Carney looked out the window at the traffic passing by the restaurant. She looked as if she was close to resigning herself to that fact.

"I thought about that all night, Jerzy. Like, maybe he just wants to be friends or something. Maybe he is gay. He admitted to me that he had something going on, like he was in trouble or something. He did say he was in trouble. I don't know what he meant; he didn't go on about it. But I don't think he's gay. I think he's afraid of something that's happening to him right now and he has no one to reach out to. It's really sad."

"So did he ever answer you about going fishing with us tomorrow?" Jerzy asked.

"I won't know until he calls, or until he shows up at the marina. I told him, either way, we are leaving around eight tomorrow morning. I guess we'll know then for sure."

They finished their breakfast and left the restaurant. They drove across the street to the marina and parked. Moments later they were standing in the small galley of Ralph Light's boat. Jerzy's mouth fell open as she looked around her. "Wow, a real kitchen. You have everything in here; it's just like a little house. Is it hard to cook when the boat is rocking back and forth?"

Carney laughed, remembering a time that pots and pans were thrown all over inside the galley as Ralph and Carney were trying to get back to shore in a sudden storm.

"We try to make sure everything's calm before we cook anything. I remember a long time ago, when my dad and I got hung up in a trough... That's a big ditch between two big waves... Anyway, we were pitched sideways and all the cabinets popped open. Everything flew out into the galley floor. It sounded terrible, and made the entire incident really scary. My dad still talks about that."

Jerzy noticed the look on Carney's face as she spoke of Ralph. As Judge Caine's defense attorney, Ralph had reluctantly questioned Jerzy in the courtroom. She remembered him as courteous and polite, handing her tissues when she broke into tears. She got the opportunity to meet him one afternoon at his house and thought he was really sweet. It was obvious he loved his daughter.

"Your whole face lights up when you talk about your dad. That's so cool. You two must be really close."

Carney nodded, looking at Jerzy across the galley.

"He raised me. I was his fishing buddy, his hunting partner, and his little girl. He hated it when I grew up, but he accepted it and respected that I didn't want to be a tomboy anymore. I still love to hunt and fish with him, whenever our schedules allow it."

Jerzy's head was down now, tears rolling from her eyes. Carney reached out to pull her up to face her but Jerzy resisted, trying to turn her face away.

"What is it, Jerzy? Are you crying?" Realizing what had happened; she pulled the young girl close.

"Don't cry, Jerzy. We'll find your father. Let's hang out here for a month and enjoy this vacation. You know you deserve it. You've been through so much for a girl your age, or any age for that matter. We'll start looking for your dad when we get back to Atlanta." She rubbed the girl's heaving back as she tried to console her.

"He's probably long gone by now, Carney. He's probably heard everything about the trial and all... There's no telling what he thinks. He knows a little about how I used to go around doing things. He probably thinks I got what I had coming to me."

"Not your dad, Jerzy. Daddies don't think like that. Mine doesn't, and yours doesn't either. Don't be silly. Come on. Now that we know the fridge is working, let's go get some groceries to put in it." Carney jumped up and walked to the back of the boat. Jerzy sat for a moment and then followed, head still down.

⚡

Approaching noon, the girls walked through Winn-Dixie, throwing anything and everything into their cart. They went up and down every aisle, making sure they didn't forget anything they might need.

Walking past the bakery, Jerzy slowed to look at the cakes. Carney walked ahead of her, taking two loaves of bread from a shelf. When she turned to put them in the cart, she noticed Jerzy had lagged behind and was now standing still, an odd look on her face.

"Hey, girl, bring that cart up here. We're not finished yet." Carney walked back to meet Jerzy halfway and tossed the bread into the cart; looking to see what had caught her attention.

"Got a sweet tooth, have you?" she asked jokingly.

"Birthday cakes," Jerzy said. "I was looking at the birthday cakes and I realized yesterday was my birthday. I'm sixteen now, Carney, and I didn't even know it until now." She started laughing, the high-pitched giggle of a little girl.

"You're kidding me, Jerzy. Yesterday was your birthday? What in … What is your birthdate?"

"I'm not kidding, Carney. I was born on April 8th, 1986. I turned sixteen years old yesterday. Isn't that cool?"

"I should've known. I've read your paperwork at the center; at least twice that I can remember. I'm so sorry, Jerzy. Come on, let's get a cake!" Carney was more excited than Jerzy, picking out a cake and having the decorator print Jerzy's name and "Happy Birthday" across the pink frosting.

They loaded their groceries into Carney's car and began to drive back toward the condo. Half way there, Carney turned to Jerzy.

"One more stop before we go back to the house. It's kind of personal so I need for you to wait outside. I promise I won't be long, okay?"

"Sure, but hurry. Remember we have cake and ice cream in the back seat."

Carney made a sharp right turn into an L-shaped strip mall and parked in front of a dentist's office. She smiled at Jerzy and pointed at her mouth as she left her car and went inside. The receptionist greeted Carney as she walked in.

"Do you have a back door in this office?" she asked the woman.

"Yes, but…"

"Thanks," Carney said as she went down the hall and found the door herself, exiting the rear of the building.

The next building over, now out of sight of the car, was a jewelry store Carney had visited several times. She walked inside and was immediately greeted by the owner.

"Carney!" he shouted, startling his other customers. "I haven't seen you in months, young lady. I'm going broke here." He came from around the jewelry cases and grabbed her in a bear hug.

"I wasn't able to make my September trip, Huey. I snuck down to Tampa to take my bar exam and ended up staying a week. That cut into my budget with the hotel and all."

"So did you pass? Are you a real lawyer yet?" Huey smiled big and real,

Southern style. He liked Carney, had fished with her often, and sold her some jewelry from time to time. She was a no-nonsense kind of girl and he liked that. He had watched her pull a twenty-pound king mackerel straight up from the bottom of the Destin pier without any help. So in Huey's book, Carney was good people, and he liked to look out for the few good people he knew.

"Yes, of course, I'm a real lawyer now, you big oaf. I'm just not licensed to practice law yet. When I figure out where I want to live, I'll get my license and start seeing clients."

"That's good, Carney. That's really good, girl. Now what is it that brings you in here today?"

She told Huey about Jerzy Rabideaux as quickly as she could. He was dabbing moisture from his eyes as she told him what had happened at Winn-Dixie.

"So, I want to get her something really nice, like a necklace of some kind. Or whatever you suggest. Sweet sixteen, you know? A girl only gets there once, Huey."

From behind the glass, under the shelves out of view, he removed a small board with a gold chain and a diamond pendant. The stone glistened in the artificial light mounted over the counter.

"It looks even better in the sunlight, Carney," he said as he passed her the board. "It's a three-quarter carat, with fourteen-carat white gold chain. I can let you have it for four hundred even. I've got two of them, if you start getting jealous down the road." He smiled as she handed the board and the necklace back to him.

"Put it in a box and put the other one away. Charge them both to my account, if you don't mind. I'll come by on my way out and pay them off."

As Huey arranged the gift in a presentation box, Carney continued with her small talk. She liked Huey a lot. When she was in town, she looked forward to the few days he could sneak away from his shop to join her and the others on the pier.

"So what's the scoop on 'Bama?" She liked to get him going on college football. His team, the Crimson Tide from the University of Alabama, had coach problems. Carney was one of the rare people who could jibe Huey about this and get away with it.

Huey faked a serious glance at her over the top of his glasses. The customers still in the store froze.

"Don't start no shit, young lady, and there won't be none. 'Bama's going to be fine. Better than that damn sissy school up there in Nashville."

They both laughed as Carney grabbed the box and ran back to her car. Buried in a tourist pamphlet, Jerzy didn't notice her return until she opened the door and climbed in.

"How's that for time?" Carney asked.

"Pretty good, I guess. The ice cream's a little soft; that's all."

They drove back to the condo, each in their own thoughts. Carney was excited for her friend; she was going to love her new necklace.

Carney grilled two steaks outside while Jerzy prepared the salad and set the table for dinner. Two tall candles stood in holders on the fireplace, and Jerzy arranged them in the middle of the spread. She touched a match to each and was turning the lights off when Carney came back in with the steaks.

"That's a nice touch," Carney said as she handed Jerzy her dinner and placed her own on the table.

"I know it's not much of a party, but happy birthday, Jerzy."

Jerzy smiled, she couldn't remember when she had ever felt this loved by a woman; with the exception of her foster mother, Kim Puckett. This was somehow different. Where Kim had wanted a daughter, Carney wanted nothing. It took some time for Jerzy to realize this, but she knew it now.

The cake and ice cream portion of the meal was taken to the balcony. Carney tried to sing "Happy Birthday" but the two of them started laughing so hard she finally gave up. She walked to the kitchen drawer and brought the box from Huey's and sat it on the table in front of Jerzy.

"I hope you like this, Jerzy. I wanted to get you something that would always make you remember our vacation here and your 16th birthday."

Jerzy opened the box and held the necklace up to the light. "Oh my God!" she exclaimed. "I've never seen a more beautiful stone. What is it?"

"Well, if my friend Huey isn't lying to me, it's a diamond." She smiled at the thought of Huey lying to anyone.

"You mean a real diamond? Like in carats and all that?"

Carney smiled at the way Jerzy spoke. The child had a way about her that flowed with innocence.

"Yes, like carats and all that. It's actually only three-quarters of a carat, but it's still a pretty big stone for a girl your age. You'll have to be very careful with it."

"Oh, I will, Carney. I think I... Thank you so much. You shouldn't have done this."

"You're very welcome, Jerzy. I wish we could've done this yesterday on your real birthday."

"I don't care, Carney. This was worth the wait. Really, I could've waited until next year. This is really great."

⸸

The dishes were washed and the girls were seated in front of the television when the telephone rang.

Carney picked it up, grinning at Jerzy as she did.

"Hello?"

"Hi, Carney, it's Bill."

"You've got to be shitting me!" she replied, trying to be funny.

"Well, no I... It's really... I mean, yes it's me, Bill."

Carney couldn't speak. She pressed the phone into the sofa to keep him from hearing her roar. She was laughing so hard, she handed the phone to Jerzy and stepped out onto the balcony.

"Hello? Hello? Carney?" Jerzy decided she better speak or he was going to hang up.

"No, this isn't Carney. This is Jerzy. Carney had to run to the bathroom. She's soiled herself."

Hearing this, Carney pulled the sliding door closed. Jerzy could still hear her howling laughter out on the balcony. William persisted, trying to get through to this girl that he wanted to speak to Carney.

"Do you think I could hold a moment until she can come to the phone? You almost sound like her, you know? Tell her Bill Ammons would like to

175

speak to her." Jerzy shot Carney a scolding glance and held the phone against the glass door. Carney tried to regain her composure and took the phone.

"Hello?" She tried not to laugh by blowing out short puffs of air.

"Hi, Carney, it's Bill..."

The entire scene could've been replayed had Carney wanted it to. She already decided she liked Bill a lot, but he was definitely still a rotary dialer.

"Oh, Bill. I'm sorry I couldn't come to the phone right away."

"I understand, your friend said you..."

"Yeah, Bill, I know what she said. So, what's up? Going fishing in the morning?"

"Yes, I'd like that, if the offer is still good. I've been thinking a lot about what you said the other night. You've helped me to make sense of some things. So, is eight o'clock still good for you?"

"Yes, we'll be on the boat when you get there. Bring a lightweight jacket if you have one."

After she hung up the phone, she and Jerzy collapsed on the couch, laughing until their sides hurt. Jerzy scolded Carney for giving Bill such a hard time.

"What do you mean, I gave him a hard time? You're the one who told him I soiled myself. He'll probably never want to date me now. That is, if he ever really did."

"I think he still wants to date you, Carney. He keeps calling you back; that means something."

The two of them replayed the conversation between themselves and again fell into the couch, laughing. Within the hour, they were both asleep.

While Carney and Jerzy slept, across town William pondered his next move. Tomorrow night he'd be out on the gulf with Ralph Light's boat and his daughter. He tried to think; he had to have a plan when he got on that boat.

CHAPTER TWENTY-SIX

William stood in front of the window in his room, staring out at the parking lot. He'd purchased a small canvas duffle bag the day before, and at six o'clock that morning he already had it packed and ready. In the bag he'd stuffed an extra pair of shorts and a long-sleeved shirt. He'd fished on charter boats out of Destin more than a few times. He knew the horror of prolonged exposure to the intense Florida sun on bare skin.

Also in the bag was the jacket Carney had suggested and a white hand towel he'd taken from the hotel bathroom. Wrapped up in the cheap towel was the heavy Colt Python stolen from Ralph Light's home. Lifting the bag from the bed, William walked out to his car and put it in the passenger seat.

Driving west toward the marina, he thought about the day in front of him. Without realizing it, he pulled into the parking lot at the pier. He sat for several minutes, sweating profusely in spite of the air conditioner raging from the dash. *Damn, it's hot,* he thought. He looked at the clock in his car and saw it was only seven o'clock. He climbed out of the car and began walking toward the pier.

The sun over the water to his left turned the small waves into floating diamonds, but William didn't notice. The people on the pier were busy casting or retrieving their lines as William passed them by, but he couldn't see them. His mind was full of thoughts, whirling and crashing into a thought-depriving mass. As quickly as he tried to focus on specific details, his mind would venture off on its own tangent as if it were trying to steer him away from harming Carney.

He stood at the very end of the long concrete structure, oblivious to the activity surrounding him. *What does Carney really have to do with all this anyway?* he asked himself. *What the hell could I have been thinking? She's innocent of any involvement with all that had happened to my father.* He tried to shake whatever it was he was feeling; this emotion of no known origin.

He looked to his left and saw an older man, forty something, William thought, and graying. The man was pressing the body of a live shrimp onto a hook. Turning, he handed the baited rod to a little girl. *Maybe that's it,* William thought. *Maybe I should just go after her father. That was the original thought, before I dredged up this current ugly plan. Then she would still be here, and we could try to be more than friends.* William smiled, confident that he'd found the solution to his dilemma. *I'll be there for her, too,* he thought. *She can lean on me as she mourns her loss. I'll take care of her and...*

Why would that be a good idea? he asked himself. *If I'm not going to use her for revenge against her father, why would I kill him? I know enough about her to know anything bad happening to her father would devastate her. She never had a mother; Ralph's the only parent she's ever known. They're close, much closer than I've ever been with either of my parents. So killing Ralph to avenge Father's death wouldn't be such a good idea, if I'm truly interested in Carney.*

The anger and hatred, the murderous ideas and plotting of them, were slowly disappearing from William's heart. He thought of his own father, and flinched at the idea that Judge Caine was in fact the originator of this misery. Had he not put himself in a position to be thought a child rapist, William wouldn't be here now. *What is my motivation after all? I'm risking my freedom and my life to avenge the imprisonment and subsequent death of a... Pedophile? Was that the word Mother used?* He remembered and was at once ashamed. He wondered if the word would always be associated with the Caine name. He looked at his watch; seven forty-five. *I should just not show up. Carney and her friend will wait for a while, and then leave without me. I can call her when I get back to Atlanta and explain somehow.*

He began walking back toward his car. He pushed his palms against his temples, hoping the pressure would stop this self-reflection. *I've told her so many lies; sooner or later she's going to realize I haven't been honest with her. My*

God! Embarrassment overwhelmed him as he remembered their conversation at dinner back in Atlanta. *Did I really tell her I graduated from Notre Dame? My God, what was I thinking? What was it I said I did for a living? Oh shit. What was it? I remember saying I was staying with my parents. But what did I say I did for work?*

He was on the brink of speaking out loud; people walking by on the pier looked back laughing at the young man banging his hand against his forehead; zigzagging his way along the pier.

Finally, William gave up trying to remember all of his lies. *I'm just not going to meet her. I'm going back to the hotel to get my stuff and go home. She's better off if I never call her again. She's bound to find out who I am, sooner or later. Damn! I even lied about my name. Oh God… What did I say my name was? Bill, I remember that. Bill what? How could I have forgotten that?* He was almost ready to scream; his heart pounding inside his chest. *I must be losing my mind,* he thought. *All this… I'm just not meant to be a killer. I've told little lies before and they never bothered me, but I usually remembered what I lied about. This isn't me; no, no, no. This isn't me at all. I'm supposed to be better than this.*

✝

William found himself sitting in his car; he was soaked with sweat from his head to his shoes. The motor off and the windows up, he was suffocating. He immediately patted his pockets and found his keys. He started the car and turned on the air conditioning. He turned his head away from the initial blast of hot air. He noticed the clock on the dash; nine-thirty. He wondered how long he'd been sitting in the car as he shifted into first and pulled out of the lot.

Continuing west toward the marina, William started to cool down. *She should be gone by now,* he thought. *At least she had a friend with her to keep her company. That's scary, a girl going out there all alone. Hell, a girl could get hurt that way; anything could happen.*

He slowed as he passed the marina parking lot, looking for Carney's car. *Have to be careful here,* he thought. Carney drove a blue Escape, like a couple million other people. He would know hers by the big Vanderbilt Law decal across the back glass. He drove past the marina and down to the light, making a U-turn on the green signal. He approached the marina and slowed again, looking carefully. *This doesn't make any sense*, he thought. *If she and her friend are on the boat, her car should be at the marina.*

Carefully making sure her car wasn't there, he pulled in and parked. William was disappointed. Surely she wouldn't have cancelled the trip because he didn't show up. Quickly, he pulled out of the parking lot and drove to Pelican Bay. *Maybe she had someone bring her car back here, or maybe she hasn't left the house yet.* He searched the lot at the high-rise condominium; still no sign of Carney. Another thought suddenly occurred to him. *I'll go back to the boat and leave her a message.* He found a pen and an envelope in his glove compartment and scribbled a note, circling his cell phone number. When he arrived back at the marina lot, her car still wasn't there. He turned off his car and got out, slinging his bag over his shoulder and stuffing the note in his pocket. Looking around him, he hoped she wouldn't be pulling into the lot behind him. He patted his pocket for his keys and the note to Carney, and then made sure his doors were locked before starting toward the docks.

CHAPTER TWENTY-SEVEN

Beatrice heard the phone ringing while she was in the bathroom, peeling wallpaper from over the vanity. She was breathing heavily when she finally picked up the receiver in her bedroom.

"Hello?"

"Good afternoon, Beatrice. Ralph Light here. How are you?"

"Good, Ralph, wonderful even. How have you been?"

Ralph heard something he couldn't quite place in Beatrice's voice. Something so different he was immediately aware he'd never heard it from her before.

"I've been better, Beatrice, to be real honest with you. I, uh… Have some things to bring over to you, if you're going to be home."

"I'll be here all day, getting the house straightened out. Is there something else?"

"No, nothing else, Beatrice. Just a few items that need to be returned to you and William. I'll be there in about an hour, if that's alright with you."

Beatrice knew what he was talking about. He'd been called to retrieve the judge's belongings.

"An hour is fine, Ralph. See you then."

Beatrice ran back to the bathroom, humming as she continued peeling wallpaper. There were major changes underway in her home. She'd driven her own car for the first time in months. She knew where the day laborers gathered in the parking lot of an abandoned strip mall. Coming home with two of them in the back seat of her long Mercedes, she'd taken them to the judge's study and instructed them to put everything outside on the curb for the garbage man.

When the men finished that chore she'd had them clean the garage, leaving only what belonged to William behind. The large bed in her room was taken to the curb, as was the entire suite of living room furniture. At the end of the day, she'd taken the men back to their spot at the old mall and had given them each five hundred dollars.

Ralph Light pulled into the driveway at the Caine home, looking at the chaos in the front yard. He jumped from his car; walking over to look at the disarray that included the golf clubs he'd watched his friend use for years. Other things were familiar to him as well. He walked to the front door, realizing the sound he heard in Beatrice's voice was the sound of freedom. *Happiness; that's what it was,* Ralph said to himself. He smiled and rang the bell.

Beatrice greeted him at the door dressed in blue jeans and one of William's tee shirts. Her long hair was no longer graying, but colored an attractive reddish-brown. She was wearing it pulled back into a ponytail, with a baseball cap holding back the stray hairs. He remembered what she'd looked like years earlier and, at this moment, she was just as beautiful as ever.

"Ralph! Come in, hon. Excuse the mess. How are you?"

"I'm good, Bea. I tried to call you the other day; the people at the jail were trying to return Carter's things to you. No big deal, but they thought you might want them." He sat the large paper bag on the floor in the foyer.

"Well, that was nice of them, Ralph. Say, come in and have a drink. I'm taking a break and I'd like to talk to you for a bit." She led him into the living room, where she had only her kitchen chairs to sit on. "I'm sorry for the lack of comfortable seating. My furniture isn't arriving until next week."

She seated Ralph in the living room and walked to the corner where the bar was still intact. "Still drinking Cutty?" she asked as she poured two fingers of scotch into a glass.

"Yes, no sense changing something I like so much." He grinned as he spoke. The two of them hadn't shared words alone since the early days of his partnership with her husband. Back then, Beatrice would bring lunch to the men while they worked. Sometimes she arrived at the office to find

Carter had been called back to court. She and Ralph would eat in the tiny conference room and talk about their children.

Beatrice handed Ralph his drink and sat down in the hard wooden chair next to him. The chair being too uncomfortable, she rose and walked over to the outer wall and sat on the carpet, leaning back against the paneling.

"That's better. I apologize again for the chairs, Ralph. You can sit here, too, if you want."

Ralph almost laughed. She was like a youngster again, crawling down on the floor like that. Hell, she was making him look old, sitting up in the stiff kitchen chair.

"Were you having trouble with your phone last week? No one could get through."

Beatrice sat up a little, leaning forward. "No, the wires were cut. I'll tell you about it later. First, I want to know about the will. Surely, you'll be the executor. Then, I want to know about everything else. Don't bullshit me either, Ralph. I'm serious. I'd like for you to remain a part of my life. I've known you over thirty-five years, so don't bullshit me. I can take whatever you have to tell me, but I have to know. All of it; no matter what you may be tempted to hold back."

"Well, I guess we can do without a formal hearing then. But are you sure you want to be the one telling William? It's not good, Beatrice. I'd been talking to Carter about this for some time, trying to get him to ease up a little and change his mind. You know better than anyone else how headstrong he was."

Beatrice looked at the amber liquid in her glass. "I'll handle William; don't worry about that. I'll tell you about that later, too."

"The will leaves everything to you, Bea. Up until William left UGA, Carter had him in for better than half, considering your ability to liquidate family assets that were apart from his. After the hazing incident, Carter called me in a fury and had me remove the boy completely. I was never able to get him to change his mind."

"Exactly what is everything, Ralph?" She knew there was money everywhere.

"Well, including the real estate, and after funding the scholarship he set up when he discontinued the Marathon Charity, it looks to be close to two and a half million dollars. He invested wisely and, as you well know, he never spent a damn dime; except for those golf clubs out there in the trash, and his car."

"And his little girls," Beatrice added while choking back her anger. She jumped up from the floor. "I can't believe it. He poor-mouthed so often, I thought we'd be getting into Daddy's money any day."

Ralph watched as she paced back and forth in front of him. For a woman fifty-two years old and not wearing a bra at the moment, her breasts looked high and firm. He diverted his gaze before he spoke again.

"I'll get the paperwork to probate within the next few days. You'll be set for the rest of your life. You'll have to decide for yourself how to handle this; as far as William is concerned."

Beatrice continued to pace, swirling her scotch in her glass as she walked. "Now tell me about the trial. Who was the girl and how old was she? I know what I've heard, which hasn't been much. I slept through most of it, and I refused to listen to the radio or television. What was the evidence presented? You know what I'm talking about. I want you to tell me everything."

Ralph felt uncomfortable, shifting in the stiff wooden chair. Finally he rose, walked over to the spot near the wall and sat on the carpet. He handed his glass up to Beatrice and asked her to refresh his drink. She went to the bar and poured four fingers of Cutty into his glass, returning to sit next to him on the floor. Ralph looked over at her as he began to speak.

"First off, Bea, understand that I wanted no part of this case. I went to the DA and the judge and asked them to recuse me after Carter talked me into representing him. I only told him I'd do it in the first place because I was certain they'd remove me. When they didn't, I was stuck with it. I hate to put it that way, but it was bad going in and continued to get worse."

Beatrice patted him on the leg. She knew this was true. Ralph Light had many opportunities as a defense attorney over the years to represent rich people he knew were guilty. He could've gotten most of them off, and become rich in the process.

"I did everything I could; legally speaking. There was an overwhelming amount of evidence supporting that everything happened just the way the girl said. Hell, Bea, she even said she seduced him. She said she took his credit card and bought herself some clothes. I…"

Beatrice cut him off before he could continue. "She bought underwear; that's what I heard. She bought lingerie with his credit card at the hotel mall, is that right?"

"The receipts the DA subpoenaed listed underwear, yes. She also purchased two or three dresses and some men's clothing she said she bought for her father."

"Her father?" Beatrice hadn't heard this before.

"Yes, he was somewhere here in Atlanta. That's why she came here to begin with. She met Carter when he caught her breaking into parking meters. She was…"

Again Beatrice interrupted him. "Breaking into parking meters? He caught her breaking into parking meters? Where?"

"Right in front of the building, near where he parks his car."

"Why, Ralph? Why was she breaking into parking meters? Is she some kind of nut or something?"

Ralph had no idea he'd be going into this much detail with her. Jerzy Rabideaux was a minor at the trial. Much of what Beatrice wanted was protected information. But he knew she needed to have it. He knew it was the last piece of the puzzle that if never found, would haunt her forever. He only knew of one way to ensure the conversation they were having would never leave the room.

"Bea, listen to me. The kid's a minor. The information is protected. I want to tell you but if it ever got out that I did, I would… Well, it wouldn't be good."

Beatrice already knew this, and was prepared for it. She didn't shock Ralph when she brought it up either.

"You're my lawyer, Ralph. My husband just died and you're my fucking lawyer. Now talk to me."

Ralph leaned forward and began to explain. "First off, the girl isn't a freak, or a nut, or anything like that. She was a mixed-up little girl who never had anything. A drunken mother that beat the hell out of her just for being a pretty girl, and a dad who isn't worth two dead flies. I'm telling you, Bea, the more I heard, the sicker I got. Anyway, she watched her mother whoring around their little town, men buying her drinks and what not. Taking them out behind the bar for a minute and returning all disheveled with money for more drinks. She learned how to…"

Ralph stopped, hands shaking as he lifted his glass and drained it. Beatrice took the empty glass from his hand and set it on the carpet next to her.

"Go on, Ralph, please."

"Well, hell, Bea, she learned how to start milking the men herself. It wasn't long before she had what the other girls in town had; nice clothes and things like that. Simple things; like a few dollars to buy groceries. Then her father left them. He wasn't much of a father, but he treated her with love, and at least tried to be a parent. He decided one day that he'd had enough of his wife, who by this time was openly promiscuous. So he left and came here to Atlanta. He's not real bright, Bea. He came here to sell an idea about a bean sower."

Beatrice laughed. She'd never heard Ralph speak so animated about anything.

"A bean what?"

"A bean sower, some machine that was supposed to help plant beans. Problem is, it was invented about a century ago."

They both burst into laughter, leaning into one another until they became aware of the closeness.

Ralph sat up and continued his story. "So he's here in Atlanta trying to sell his idea, and his daughter hitchhikes all the way from Louisiana to find him. She was hungry, Bea, and too proud to beg. Thus, she was breaking into parking meters. Carter found her and you know the rest."

"He put her up in the Westin. Is that true?"

"Yes, that's true. He told her to come to the DA's Christmas party. Hell, I saw her there. She came up to us at the bar and Carter volunteered to give her a ride. I even made a joke about it."

"How old was she, Ralph?"

Ralph put his head down and didn't look at her.

"She was fifteen, Bea. She'll be sixteen sometime this spring, as I recall."

Beatrice thought for a moment about all she'd been told. *Certainly Carter could tell she was a child,* she thought. She asked Ralph what he thought.

"Did she look fifteen to you, Ralph?"

"Not at first, Bea. Not when I saw her at the party. She was wearing this Jean Harlow kind of dress; she wore a lot of makeup and had her hair done up real nice. I tried that angle in court. I tried to make the point that she'd made herself up to look like a woman. But the day Carter met her, he took her into a satellite police precinct. She said she wasn't stealing the meter money, but wanted to return it. He ran into the cop who arrested William with the pot. Name's Dan something. Anyway, he testified when he first saw her, he knew she was a kid. Then when I saw her again, it was even obvious to me. She's built kind of full-figured, so to speak. But it's all baby fat that gives her that shape. Hell, Carney didn't lose the baby fat until she was seventeen."

Beatrice had heard most of everything she wanted to hear. She knew Ralph was holding something back, something he was too embarrassed to talk to her about. She figured if she talked about it, all Ralph would have to do was agree or disagree.

"They found his semen inside her, didn't they, Ralph?"

"Yes, Bea, they did."

"They combed her and found his pubic hair as well, didn't they?"

"Yes, that was the nail in the coffin. That and his credit card bill with the Westin charges on it. All that pretty well cinched it for the state. Plus, it didn't help any that all the government agencies in town are being rearranged because of child abuse and neglect allegations. That boy who died while in state care; all that controversy fanned the fire. The entire community wanted him lynched."

"So what happened to the girl? Did she ever find her father?"

"No, he hasn't turned up yet that I know of. But the girl lives with foster parents here in town. A cop and his wife; good people. They're the ones who found her running away from the hotel that night."

Beatrice hoped Ralph wouldn't take her next question the wrong way.

She didn't quite know how to ask. *Well, she thought, he's been honest about all this, and he seems like he'd understand. All I can do is ask; what the hell.*

"Is there any way… I mean, would it be considered appropriate if I met this child?" She looked at Ralph hopefully.

"For what reason, Beatrice? Please tell me it's not to satisfy your own curiosity. That kid's been through enough already."

"Nothing like that, Ralph. I'd like to offer her an apology on behalf of the decent people in our family. I'd like to think I could help her get on her feet; maybe with her education or in another area. She's turning sixteen, you said; she might need a car soon. I'm not sick, Ralph. You should know that after all these years. Look outside on the lawn. I've cleaned the disease from my home. I want to tell her everything will be all right. Is that a bad thing, Ralph?"

"Listen, Bea, the girl came into the center where Carney volunteers. Carney didn't tell me this until after Carter was convicted. She made sure the girl didn't know me; even though she told her I was Carter's friend. She stayed in the background and let the authorities do their jobs. Yes, I think I can arrange a meeting between the two of you, if it's kept strictly confidential, and if you assure me it's for noble reasons."

"I assure you it is, Ralph. I can't tell you how much better I'd be able to function if I knew I helped ease some of the pain my husband caused. Thank you, Ralph."

"So, you were going to tell me about some things. I've sat here spilling my guts; now it's your turn. I can see you're taking measures to clean the place out."

"You're my lawyer now, right?"

"Absolutely, for as long as you'll have me." He smiled and puffed up his chest.

"You can't say anything about what's said in this room, right?"

"Oh shit. I thought we cleared that up already, Bea."

"Just making sure, Ralph. There's someone I love at stake here."

Ralph assured her anything she told him was strictly between them. Not just as a lawyer, but as a friend.

Beatrice told him everything that happened between her and William, from the time the detective called to tell her the judge was dead. Ralph listened, interrupting at different junctures to clarify what she'd said. He was in complete shock.

"Are you sure you don't need to go to the police?" he asked her.

"No, I have all the money now. I can cut him off whenever I choose. I'm past the point of not being strong enough to do it, if that's what you are thinking. I'm certain he wouldn't have been so violent had I not provoked him. I said some evil things to him, Ralph, and the boy's been hurting anyway. I should've kept my mouth shut until all this passed."

"So where is he at now, running? Does he even know he didn't kill you?"

Beatrice smiled at this, the best part. She replayed in her head the fear in William's voice the morning she called him.

"Oh, yes, he knows he didn't kill me. Stromann's called me for some information they didn't have. They thought William had returned from Florida already. They said they'd left a message at his hotel and he didn't return the call, so they called here. I got the hotel number from them and called. I honestly think I heard him wetting himself when he heard my voice."

"So he ran to Florida. Where, to Disney World? Kill Mom and go see Mickey?"

"No, he ran to Destin. He met a girl up here and they went to dinner over at Mr. Taki's place in Sandy Springs. I can't ever remember the name of that place. Anyway, they met up down in Destin. He's supposed to be home on Sunday."

Ralph shrugged off the coincidence of Carney and Jerzy being in Destin at the same time as the disturbed William.

"Don't hesitate to call me if you need anything, Bea. If you need me to sit down and talk with William, all you have to do is call. I'm serious, anytime you need me, day or night, just call."

Beatrice smiled and pulled Ralph into a hug. He was thinner than her husband had been, but he felt tight and strong. She missed tight and strong; she'd been missing it for years. Ralph felt a pang of discomfort as she released him and looked into his eyes.

"Thank you, Ralph, for both talking and listening. I think I'm going to be okay now. I know I am."

Ralph turned to leave, stopping at the door to remind her about the bag he left in the foyer.

"Ralph?"

He turned back to her. "Yeah, Bea?"

"Day or night, is that what you said?"

"Yes, Bea, day or night. Why?" He was chuckling to himself.

"Because I need you right now. That's why."

Oh shit, he thought. He felt his stomach tighten.

"What is it you need, Bea?"

"Well, I need you to pick up that bag and put it out front with the other garbage. Then I wonder if you could leave through the garage so I won't have to go out there by myself to close the door."

"You scared me for a minute there, Bea."

"I figured I would, but it's not so scary a thought, is it, Ralph?"

He didn't answer. He walked past her into the garage and winked at her as he closed the door. Walking to the driveway, he turned to release the automated lever so he could close the door manually from outside. A box on the workbench caught his eye. Shotgun shells, good ones. Remington, the same kind he used. *William must be the shooter*, he thought. He knew Carter had never even held a shotgun. He left the garage and closed the door. Before getting in his car he walked to the trash heap and threw the paper bag containing the judge's personal effects into it. The fact that the shell box had RL written on it almost came to the surface in his conscious mind.

Pulling out of the driveway and into the street, he thought about Beatrice Caine and wondered why the old broad chose tonight to go without her bra.

CHAPTER TWENTY-EIGHT

At two o'clock Wednesday morning, Ralph sprang up in his bed. Half-asleep, he searched his mind for the thought that had interrupted his dream. "Letters," he said aloud. The sound of his own voice startled him and he reached to turn on the light to see if there was someone else in the room.

Letters? He wondered if he'd forgotten something at the office that day as he lay back down and pushed his face into his pillow. Damn Cutty Sark; too much, too late at night. He drifted back into a sound sleep. The dream came again, this time different than the first. A bull elk in his crosshairs, looking directly at him and not moving. He enjoyed waking after these dreams. He sometimes joked with Carney about free hunting.

At eight o'clock he was awakened again by the same thought, interrupting his hunt. He sat up in the bed and turned on the light, looking at the clock. *Damn, I'm late.* Making a mental note to call his office and let his secretary know he'd be in later than usual, he crawled out of bed, feeling the beginning of a headache creeping up on him. In the bathroom, he opened the medicine cabinet and found a box of Goody Powders.

While filling a cup with tap water, he glanced at the Goody's box and froze. *Letters,* he thought. The box of shells in the Caine garage had letters written on them. He walked to his study and opened the drawer in his gun cabinet. His twelve-gauge shells were gone. Two boxes of them. He searched the second drawer. His twenty-gauge shells were still there, with RL written on them in black marker. He always put his initials on his shell boxes. A result of growing up poor; take care of your stuff and it will last longer.

Identify what is yours. He looked at his guns, and saw that his twelve-gauge Browning was missing from its nook. Starting to panic, he ran to his bedroom and opened the drawer in his nightstand to get his revolver. It was gone as well. *What the hell? Who would've come in here? Would Carney have taken my guns with her? Stupid question*, he thought. *Carney never would take anything of mine without telling me. But the box of shells in the Caines' garage, they had my initials on them.*

Ralph was beginning to fear something terrible was about to happen. He couldn't place it, but there was something he wasn't getting. Something not right. *What the hell is it?* he asked himself. He looked at the clock on his nightstand again. By now, Carney would already be at the boat.

He picked up the phone and dialed the Caines' home number. It rang several times before the answering machine picked it up. He clicked off and pressed redial on his phone. Same thing. *Damn, Beatrice. Wake up, woman.* Three more times he pressed the redial button and Beatrice finally picked up.

"Hello?" Her voice was shallow; she'd been getting the best sleep ever these past few days.

"Beatrice, this is Ralph. Are you awake?"

Damn, that was a stupid question, he thought.

"Yes, I am now, Ralph. What is it? Everything alright?"

She was awake now. He could tell.

"I don't know yet, Bea. Can you walk down to your garage for me? I need you to look at something."

Beatrice was already getting out of bed, pulling her eyeshade high up onto her forehead. She carried the cordless with her down the stairs.

"Okay, Ralph, I'm in the garage. I hate this place; it's so scary."

"Beatrice, do you see a box of shotgun shells over on the workbench, under those cabinets?"

"I see a box of something. It has your initials on it, whatever it is. Did you forget something?"

"No, Bea, it was there already. I noticed it when I was closing the door for you. It didn't register right away."

The shells being in the garage still don't mean anything, he thought. Then the coincidence of William being in Destin hit Ralph full force. *Oh my God. Oh God, no.*

"Beatrice, what was the girl's name William went to dinner with? The one you were telling me he's in Florida with? What's her name, Bea?"

She was wide-awake now, searching her mind for an answer. She heard the panic in Ralph's voice. She was becoming frightened.

"He said I wouldn't know her, Ralph. He only said that she was from the south side; almost like he was avoiding telling me. But I do remember asking him."

Ralph was half-listening to her as his mind started thinking about how to contact Carney. He remembered she said they were leaving Wednesday morning. *I'm sure she said nine o'clock. Maybe she'd put it off a day.*

"Hang up right now, Bea, but stay by the phone. I'll call you right back."

He clicked off from Beatrice and dialed the number to the condo in Destin. No answer. *Oh God, no. Please let her be okay. Please.* He tried the redial as he'd done with Beatrice earlier. No answer. He left a message, then tried redial again. He finally hung up and called Beatrice back.

"I can't get her to answer the phone, Bea. I'm really worried that William may be up to something. I'm missing two guns, and a box of my shells is in your garage. It doesn't make any sense."

"I see what you mean, Ralph. What do you want me to do?"

"Can you call William at his hotel? See if he's there at least?"

"Give me ten minutes. I'll call you right back."

Beatrice found the number to the Ramada that Garrett Stromann had given her. She dialed the number and got the desk clerk. Seconds later, the phone was ringing next to William's bed.

"Beatrice?"

"Yes, Ralph, I called and there's no answer. What do you think is going on?"

"I don't know, Bea. They don't know each other, do they?"

"I don't think so, Ralph. He asked about her a while back, but I don't think they've ever met."

Ralph thought hard, trying to churn up every possible conversation or thought that had passed by his lobes in the past forty-eight hours.

"What was the name of the restaurant, Beatrice? Where William took the girl to dinner?"

"Oh God, Ralph, I tried to remember it after you left last evening. I've always called it Mr. Taki's place. I think he's the maître d' or something. I'm not sure."

"Is it Kobe? Is that the name?"

He was getting desperate.

"That's it! That's what it's called."

She was excited; thinking a major piece of the puzzle was solved.

"Well, that's the same restaurant where Carney's date took her. She told me the guy's name, though, so that doesn't work. She said she went to dinner with Bill Ammons."

Beatrice was silent. Her hands trembled as she tried to hold onto the phone. She wanted to speak, but couldn't. Finally, Ralph's voice brought her out of the trance.

"Bea? Are you still there? Bea!" he was shouting into the phone.

"I'm here, Ralph. I'm sorry; what did you say?"

"I was asking you if you've ever heard of the guy, the one Carney went to dinner with. Bill Ammons. Ever heard that name?"

Beatrice swallowed hard, wishing she'd never answered the telephone.

"Ralph, Bill Ammons was my sister's husband."

She started crying, holding the mouthpiece away from her.

"I thought your sister passed away ten years ago or so."

"She did, Ralph. She and Bill both were killed in a plane crash."

Ralph couldn't understand. Why would William have anything to do with Carney now? He'd never known her, didn't go to the same places or have mutual friends. This is something Carney would've told her father. Why now? She's not like the skinny little girls he dated over the years; she's not even close. She's smart and ambitious. Why would she enjoy the company of such a loser as William Caine? He scoured his mind, looking for some answer that made sense.

CHAPTER TWENTY-NINE

K im Puckett was watering the hanging ferns on her front porch when Charlie's car pulled into the driveway. She smiled at the thought of her husband being promoted to detective. She marveled at how good he looked in his pressed jeans and button-down shirt, climbing out of the big black LTD.

Charlie came around the front of his car as Parlee Rabideaux opened the passenger door and got out. Kim looked to the street as a rusty Dodge van pulled up to the curb.

"Who is that?" Kim asked as Charlie approached her and kissed her cheek.

Charlie smiled at his wife and hesitated, waiting for the man to come closer before he spoke. "Kim, this is my new partner, Robinson Giles. Giles, this is my wife, Kimberly."

The two shook hands and smiled, exchanging greetings as they watched Parlee Rabideaux walk toward them.

"And this is Parlee Rabideaux, Jerzy's father." Charlie smiled proudly as he introduced the big man.

Kim walked up to him and extended her hand. She stared into his face for a long moment before finally speaking. Parlee shifted where he stood, uncomfortable at the silence as the woman peered into him.

"I'm sorry, Mr. Rabideaux. I just, well, I've spent so many hours trying to picture what you might look like. I should've known already, having listened to Jerzy go on about you. Your eyes; the two of you have the same eyes. She has your hair, too. Oh, you should see it now. It's almost past her waist and..."

Kim burst into tears and hurled herself into the big man, the top of her head barely reaching his middle. She squeezed him hard and he felt her chest heaving into his stomach as she sobbed in joy and relief. His arms still hanging at his sides, he looked at Charlie as if for some direction.

Charlie rubbed tears from his own eyes as he looked up at Parlee.

"Hug her back, big man. The lady's been waiting for you to show up for a long time."

Parlee lifted his big arms and wrapped them around Kim Puckett. *She's a tiny woman*, he thought, as the bulk of his arms nearly swallowed her whole.

Kim held on for a moment longer and then stood up straight. She turned to look at Charlie's new partner.

"I'm sorry, Mr. Giles. We're usually not this emotional. This must be some spectacle, out here on the lawn bawling in front of all my neighbors."

"It's not all that bad, Mrs. Puckett. No tears, no heart. I heard that somewhere once. Seems like you folks have a lot of heart. Charlie's told me about what's been going on with the little girl and all. I'm glad we finally found this guy." He smiled at Parlee.

"Come inside and have a seat. I've made some tea, if you'd like some."

Parlee stood still, looking to Charlie again. Giles reached out to shake Charlie's hand.

"I'm going to leave you folks alone for now, if that's alright with you, Charlie. Looks like the three of you have a lot to talk about. I'll see you tomorrow."

Charlie tightened his grip on Giles' hand. "Thank you, Giles. Thanks for following me home, too. We're going to be a good team out there. The bad guys don't have a chance."

Giles nodded at his partner and then looked at Kim, still dabbing at the tears in her eyes with her fingers.

"It was truly nice to meet you, Kimberly. I look forward to seeing you again. Take care of the big guy. Well, both of the big guys."

He turned and walked across the lawn to his van.

†

At the Pucketts' kitchen table, both hands wrapped around a tall glass of sweet tea, Parlee Rabideaux had the Pucketts rolling with laughter. Kim was holding her sides, feeling the muscles rippling as she tried to draw a breath.

"...So then I said no, I'm not a crawfish salesman..."

Parlee rushed toward the end of one of his endless array of tales, dangling the punch line like the proverbial carrot. When the story was told and the laughter subsided, Charlie Puckett turned the conversation to a more serious note.

"Kim and I were wondering, Parlee, what it is you're good at. We'd like to help you get on your feet. You know... Be better able to take care of yourself and Jerzy. What kind of work have you done in the past?"

Parlee rolled his eyes upward, searching the kitchen ceiling for bits of his past. After thinking about it, he leaned back in his chair and spoke in a serious tone.

"Well, Chuck, I've done a bunch of stuff. I worked on cars for a while there, until all that computer stuff made it too hard to fix 'em. I worked at a gas station, too. Let's see. Oh, yeah, I worked as a carpenter almost a whole year. Building houses; I did what they call tees and corners. Framing work, you know? Then, I plucked chickens for a guy over in Geneva, Alabama right before I came to Atlanta. Just for travelin' money. Pluckin' chickens ain't no kind of work for a man though; nasty job. Stinks to high heaven. Made me sick to my stomach."

Kim and Charlie looked at each other. Kim was surprised Charlie didn't respond to Parlee calling him Chuck. He hated to be called Chuck. She smiled at her husband, knowing he had a plan for Parlee that would keep him and Jerzy in Atlanta. She hoped the big man would go along with the plan. She looked at Parlee as Charlie asked his next question.

"Parlee, I have an idea I want to run by you. I've taken the liberty of running your name through the police department computers, and you don't have any wants or warrants. You've never been convicted of any crime, and there aren't any creditors looking for you. Kim and I have a friend who is a supervisor at Atlanta Gas Light, the gas company. They have an opening for a route person. Someone who replaces the regular meter readers when they take vacation, or travels to a customer's home to investigate a problem or complaint. That kind of thing. Does this sound like something that would interest you?"

Parlee thought for a minute, again consulting the ceiling for an answer to Charlie's question.

"That all depends, Chuck. What does the job pay, and how do I get around to these places? I ain't got a car, as you know."

"Yes, I know. That's another good thing about the job. You get to keep the company truck at all times. You may have to address an issue late at night or something, you know? And as far as wages, the job starts at twelve dollars an hour with full benefits. That means you and Jerzy would both have health and dental insurance. A lot of jobs don't even offer that these days. Your pay would go up as you get better at the job, until you top out at something like fifteen an hour. What do you think?"

Parlee was thinking. He frowned and looked at first Kim and then Charlie.

"I don't have to wear a suit and tie, do I? I mean, them..."

"No suits, no ties. They provide you with uniforms; pants and shirts. All you have to do is keep them clean and pressed."

"Shoot, I can do that. I like to put them four creases in the back of my shirts, like the army does. Yeah, Charlie, that sounds good to me. But how do I go about getting the job?"

"That's not a problem at all. We've talked to the supervisor, a woman named Jill Johnson. She and Kim went to school together over at Tech, way back when." He smiled and reached across the table for Kim's hand. He pinched her fingers one by one as he continued with Parlee.

"Jill says if you can pass a basic aptitude test, since we've already done a background check, you've got the job. I have to bring you in there to handle all the paperwork."

Parlee thought about the aptitude test. *They want to make sure I'm not a dummy,* he thought. *I can read and write, and I can add numbers, too.*

"I can do that, Chuck. The aptitude test won't be a problem. I ain't as dumb as I let on sometimes, you know what I mean?" He squinted his eyes as he held Charlie's gaze.

"I know exactly what you mean, Parlee. I really do."

He squeezed his wife's hand, knowing how happy it made Kim that Jerzy wouldn't be forced to walk out of their lives. Now all he had to do was let Kim do her part and bring Parlee up to speed on the living arrangements he and Kim had secured for them.

She pulled in her breath and looked at Parlee. This was the hard part; hence the decision between them to let her handle it. Most folks didn't like for others to plan this much of their lives out for them. A job was one thing; people needed money to survive and choose where they wanted to live. Kim and Charlie had gone a step further; a step they hoped wasn't going too far. They'd found a place nearby where Parlee and Jerzy could reside, provided Parlee would go along.

"Parlee, do you know anything about home maintenance?" Kim asked innocently.

"You mean like a leaky faucet or somethin'?"

"Yes, that's exactly what I mean. That and maybe lawn care?"

Parlee squinted again, once more seeking the advice of his seer in the ceiling of the Puckett home.

"I can do anything around the house. Say, Charlie, that's another thing I did for a while. I forgot. See, there was this old lady who had a few duplexes in Lafayette. This was back when I still had my old Ford. I'd go down there every two weeks and take care of things. Like sometimes she had yard work, or maybe a pipe leakin'. Paid good, too. Real good. Sometimes people would run off without paying the rent and leave some pretty good stuff behind. The old woman didn't have no use for it, so she'd let me cart it off. She up and died of a heart attack and her family sold out."

Kim decided to cut in before Parlee had a chance to go on. Once he got started on something, he could go on forever.

"I see. Well, that's something else we've tried to get set up for you, considering you need to get a head start on things. A job doesn't do much good without a place to live, now does it?"

"No, ma'am. So you know about a place we might be able to live in? Here in Atlanta?"

She saw that he was getting excited. The tone and inflection in his voice seemed to say he wanted to stay in town. This was almost too good to be true.

"It's better than you could ever imagine, Parlee. It's a two-bedroom apartment, right over here on Seabreeze; just two blocks from us. It's exactly like you told Charlie about. My friend at the gas company, Jill's mother, is almost eighty-five years old. She has six apartments she's been renting for almost forty years. She recently caught her maintenance man stealing things from her renters so she fired him and made him move out. She needs someone who can live there and do the maintenance work for the cost of the rent. Does that sound like it would work for you?"

Parlee was overcome with emotion. He put his elbows on the table and covered his face with his massive hands. He tried hard not to let the Pucketts see the tears he knew were on the way.

He tried to speak, to let them know he was happy to have any help they could give. Only muffled croaks came through his hands until Kim reached up and pulled them away from his face.

"Are you alright, Parlee? Did I say something to hurt you?" Kim leaned down, looking at him.

"I'm fine, Mrs. Puckett. I'm really, really fine. I've never met anybody as nice as you and Chuck here. I'll take the job, sure. And I'll do a jam-up job for the old woman, too. I'm so glad ya'll been keepin' Jerzy."

He was babbling now. He tried to bring his hands back to his face but Kim still held them in her own. She patted them, thinking they were more like huge paws than hands. After sitting silently at the table for several more minutes, Kim spoke to Charlie.

"Well?" she asked, eyebrows raised.

Charlie looked at her. He thought she was handling the rest of the conversation; especially this, the best part.

"Okay, then. Say, Parlee, have you ever been to the beach?"

"Lake beaches, Charlie. I took Jerzy to the community pool for swimmin' mostly. Why's that?"

"Well, Jerzy's in Destin, Florida with her friend, Carney Light. You'll love this girl. Anyway, we've called Carney and asked her if she thought it would be a good idea if we all came down there for a couple of days. Sort of a little reunion; so to speak. Would you like to do that? Go down there with us, I mean?"

"What about the job? Is there a time I'm supposed to start?"

"Anytime, I guess."

Charlie looked to Kim for help. She winced, thinking about this before she spoke.

"They really want you right away, Parlee, but we may be able to..."

Parlee interrupted her, straightening up in his chair and speaking firmly.

"I sure do appreciate the offer of the vacation, ya'll. But you folks have gone to some kind of trouble to get me and the girl all set up. I think it's best I go on and get to work, then check out that apartment deal. I'd feel a whole lot better seeing Jerzy Jane with a few dollars in my pocket and a roof over my head. I mean, look what I got to offer her now. Ain't much changed since the last time she saw me. And a couple warm meals would fatten me up some, make her recognize me better, if you know what I mean."

Charlie and Kim sat staring. From all that Jerzy had told them about her father, they'd envisioned him as perhaps lazy for the most part. They knew they were going out on a limb, getting him connected with Jill Johnson at the gas company. Here he was, insisting he not take a beach vacation so he could build at least a small semblance of a life for his daughter. Kim was flabbergasted. She jumped from her chair and again pulled the human paradox into a hug.

Parlee was taken aback. He hadn't been hugged this much since he was a baby, he'd bet. All at once, he was aware of Kim laughing. She loosened her grip on him and stood back to face him.

"Jerzy Jane? Is that what you call her? Jerzy Jane?" She was grinning from ear to ear.

"That's her name," Parlee said, indignantly.

"Her name is Jerzy Jane? That's her given name, or is it a Southern thing?"

Kim stifled any sign of laughter; afraid she would hurt Parlee's feelings.

"No, ma'am, Kim. My daddy was in the army up at Fort Dix, New Jersey, back World War II. He fell in love with a girl named Jane Griffin. He called her Jerzy Jane. I always liked the stories he'd sit and tell me about his time in the service; especially when he talked about that girl, Jerzy Jane. So when the little girl came out, that's the name I gave her. Almost had to fight her mamma, right there in the hospital. Only I found out a few years later that I spelled it wrong. But yes, ma'am, that's the little girl's name. Jerzy Jane Rabideaux. Prettiest girl in the whole world. I'm sure of it. Prettiest girl in the whole world."

CHAPTER THIRTY

Ralph considered his options. The conversation with Beatrice had been revealing enough for him to have some concern for Carney's safety, but he wasn't sure how concerned he should be at this point. There was no rational reason for the two of them to be together. Especially not in Florida, and especially not with... *Oh, fuck me... Jerzy Rabideaux is in Destin with Carney. If William didn't know it then, he knew it now.*

At once Ralph's mind went back to the trial when, on more than one occasion, he caught William staring at Jerzy with a hateful gaze. He was targeted with a few of those stares as well, now that he thought about it. Beatrice said it when she talked about what happened when William almost strangled her to death. 'Watch what happens next,' he told his mother. *Oh God, no. Not Carney, and not that little girl.*

His next call was to the Destin Marina. The owner was a friend of Ralph's and Carney's, and Ralph was sure he'd help him with this.

"Destin Marina, this is David."

"Yes, uh... May I speak with Evan, please?"

"Sorry, Evan's out sick today. Can I help you?"

I'll take whatever help I can get, Ralph thought.

"Yes, I'm looking for a girl named Carney Light. She's got blonde hair. She should be getting ready to board the Cheri A Lamore. Slip number thirty-three. This is an emergency. I need to speak to her badly."

"Yes, Sir, she's been in and out already this morning. She's been gone about fifteen minutes, I'd say."

Ralph looked at the clock; eight-forty. *Damn, she's almost never on time.*
"How far do you think she's gone by now?" He could've figured this out
by himself, if he was thinking straight.

"Reckon I don't know, Sir. Does she drive fast?"

"No, not in the harbor area. Hell, it's all no wake."

David started laughing into the phone, snorting on the up pitch.

"I'm sorry, Sir. Let's start over again. I saw the blonde-haired girl standing
on the deck of the boat in thirty-three about eight o'clock. A few minutes
later I went out to hose the pier tubs out and I heard her cussing, down
below deck. Next thing I know, she gets off the boat, stomps across the dock
to her car, and drives off. Kind of a chubby girl, right?"

Ralph let out a breath he'd been holding since the conversation began.
She noticed something wrong with the boat that she didn't see before, he thought.
She decided not to go out. Remembering he still had the marina on the line,
he turned his attention back to the phone.

"Thanks for your time, young man. Say, if you see her come back, tell her
to call her dad. Tell her it's very urgent."

"Yes, Sir. Thanks for calling."

Ralph hung up the phone and called Beatrice back.

"Hello?"

"Hi, Bea, it's me again. I got in touch with the people at the marina. The
guy said Carney boarded, but then he heard her cussing and she left. He
said she stomped off, so she must've been pissed. Apparently something's
wrong with the boat; otherwise she would've been gone by now."

"So there's no reason to worry; is that what you're saying?" Beatrice wasn't
so sure.

"There still is a possibility of something happening, isn't there?"

"I would think that. Yes. I remembered after you hung up a while ago
that William said something like, 'Just you wait and see what happens,' or
something like that. I simply don't know, Ralph."

Ralph decided then to tell her. *It may help us both shed some light on this
situation,* he thought.

"Beatrice, the girl is in Destin with Carney."

As soon as he said it out loud, it was obvious what William Caine had been up to.

"The girl Carter raped? Jerzy? Ralph, someone needs to find William. That's what he was talking about. He intends to harm that child; perhaps your daughter, too."

They ended the conversation quickly. Ralph agreed to call her back with any information he was able to dig up. He found his briefcase on the living room floor and pulled out his personal planner. Finding the number he was searching for, he picked up the phone.

"Ingram Air, where do you want to go today?"

Ralph was short with the man at the charter service. Time was running out.

"Where's Eric?" he asked sharply.

"Hold for a sec."

Ralph paced his kitchen floor, thinking of all the things he'd do to William Caine if his daughter were harmed.

"This is Eric, how can I help you?"

"Eric, Ralph Light. I need some help with a flight right away."

"Hey, Ralph, where to?"

"I need to be in Destin two hours ago. Can you help me with that?"

"I can get you close, but you better hurry. I can't fly it. I'm going on a long one, but I got a guy here that's up for it."

"Thanks, Eric. I'll be there in about forty-five minutes."

From Atlanta proper to the Peachtree DeKalb Airport is forty-five minutes on a good day. Wednesday morning at nine o'clock isn't even close to being a good day. Ralph grabbed a pair of jeans and a golf shirt from his closet and threw them in a bag. He found his cell phone and wallet and threw them in. He was in his car parked at PDK in forty minutes.

The pilot Eric had taking him down looked like he was a kid. The plane wasn't ready, and the traffic was heavy in front of him. Eric was nowhere to be found. Ralph sat in the plane, nervously watching the comings and goings of airport personnel and other passengers until the boy announced they were ready to taxi out. When the wheels finally came up, Ralph looked at his watch. It was eleven-fifteen.

He opened his bag and took out his cell phone, dialing the number to the condo. When the answering machine picked up, he left another message. *Damn! Where could she be?* He dialed the number to the marina, listening to several rings before hanging up. *Maybe the kid's giving her the message.* He dialed his home number and checked his messages. Just one; from Beatrice.

He called her number, almost wishing he'd brought her along. *She might have been able to talk some sense into the boy. That is, if she had gotten the chance.*

"Hello? Ralph?"

"Yes, Bea. I'm in the air. I've decided to go down there. I didn't know what else to do."

"That's a good idea, Ralph. I'll keep trying his room. If I reach him, I'll call you back. Otherwise, you call me when you find Carney and the girl, okay?"

"Sure, Bea. I'll call you either way. Bye."

His last call went to a rental car agency in Panama City. Hopefully, a car would be waiting for him at the airport and he could be in Destin before two-thirty. He hoped he was overreacting to the entire situation.

CHAPTER THIRTY-ONE

Willam was convinced he couldn't hurt Carney Light. She'd threaded a part of her soul into the fabric of his own in such a very short time; he knew there existed mysticism between them that allowed no anger. The option of taking his hatred out on her father seemed out of the question as well, if he ever wanted to have a wholesome relationship with her. *Her father was the center of her universe,* he'd told himself. *I need to explain some things to her; that's all. I need to explain my reasons for not being honest with her. She'll understand the pain and the sense of hope lost.*

He walked slower now, engaged in a silent conversation with himself. He stopped and took the note from his pocket, reading it over again. *She'll understand,* he told himself. *We can get back together in Atlanta when she returns. I can meet her friend then.*

When he approached the Cheri A Lamore, he smiled, knowing he was right. She must've either cancelled the trip or packed up and went home. *I hope she isn't too mad at me for standing her up,* he thought. There was no one around as he boarded the boat in slip number thirty-three.

He stood on the deck, looking for a place to put the note. He walked forward to the small wheel and thought about folding the paper tight and wedging it between the spokes. *No, out here the wind might catch it.* He shaded his eyes from the sun with his left hand and looked up to the flybridge. The motion of raising his head upward while standing on the deck made him feel unsteady. *Don't want to climb up there,* he thought.

He turned aft, walking to the side cushions and tried prying the note into the space between the vinyl. *Too much wind here, too,* he thought. He suddenly laughed at himself, wondering why he didn't just call the condo and leave her a message. *That would be rude,* he thought, *as if a piece of paper stuck to her boat was better. Damn, there's bound to be somewhere I can put this thing where she's sure to find it.*

He walked back to the cabin doors. French-style mahogany swinging panels, joined in the middle by a stainless steel latch. He reached to flip the latch and found it already open. He pushed the doors forward with both hands and was greeted by a high-pitched scream. Startled, he jumped backward through the doors and tripped, falling onto his back. He looked up from the floor and into the ashen face of a horrified Jerzy Rabideaux.

Unable to rise from the floor, he looked up at her. His mouth moved, but at first no words came out. He recognized her immediately and remembered at once where he'd heard the name Jerzy.

He pointed at her, trying to speak until words finally came. His voice squeaked, like an adolescent in puberty. If she weren't so terrified, Jerzy would've laughed.

"You!" he shouted, not knowing where the sound of his voice was coming from. "What are you doing here?"

He still lay prone, the gears of his mind grinding persistently into silt. Her presence on Carney's boat was beyond his comprehension. Any friendship between the two women stank of conspiracy.

Jerzy hadn't traveled this far in life without learning a little about fear. Mostly she knew when to be afraid and when not to be. Something in William Caine's face as he stared up at her told her that she needed to be very afraid.

William screamed again, his voice not improved. He wished he sounded manlier.

"You're the girl. Aren't you? Don't you lie to me, don't you dare. My father's dead, you know. You killed him. You and... Damn it!"

He drove his elbows into the flooring of the deck, trying to push himself up. His shoes wouldn't allow him to dig his heels into the slick floor for additional leverage. He screamed at Jerzy again, reaching out to her.

"Help me up, you stupid little bitch! Here, take my hands."

Jerzy saw an opportunity. She thought she could make him think she wanted to help him. She stepped toward him and took his hands in hers.

"Here's some help," she said, stomping on his groin and launching her body over his toward the cabin doors.

Her feet landed right beyond his head, still moving as she made contact with the deck. William rolled over quickly and grabbed her foot as she tried to jump to the back of the boat. Jerzy screamed out as he pulled her down and clamped his hand over her mouth.

She bit the inside of his hand, forcing him to release his grip on her face. Jerzy screamed again and he hit her. A hard, dizzying forceful slap that produced more surprise than pain and sent Jerzy a clear message. He leaned close to her face and spat his words through clenched teeth.

"I'm not giving you any breaks here, sugar. You scream again and I'll bust your face. Am I making myself clear?"

The words were more frightening to him, perhaps, than Jerzy. He didn't know where they'd come from.

"I won't scream. I promise. Just don't hurt me, please."

Her hair was in her face. She tried blowing it away but it was too thick to be moved by the thin air of her increasingly shallow breath.

He pulled her up by her blouse, tearing the material at the shoulder as he did. The thin cover fell open, exposing the top strapped underneath. She wore a pink swimsuit in anticipation of a day on the water. She saw William looking at her and reached up to pull the material back over her.

He pushed her toward the cabin, where he slung her down on the small stateroom mattress.

Looking around for his bag, he found it and picked it up, searching through his clothing for the gun.

"Where's Carney?" he asked.

"She went to get film." Then she thought of another tact; one that might scare a coward like this guy. "She and her new boyfriend. They went to Winn Dixie, but they'll be right back."

She watched his face as he received this new information. William turned from his search and looked at the girl. She saw tiny white curls of spittle at the corners of his mouth as he spoke to her.

"Her new boyfriend. Have you met the guy?"

He was tiptoeing across the line of sanity as the hammer of the gun lodged in the seam at the bottom of his bag.

"Yes, I've met him. Of course, I have, and you better be gone when they show up, 'cause he's huge. He'll break you in half." She curled her wonderful lips at him, trying to snarl her words.

William screamed and threw his bag on the floor. He stomped his right foot in a frustrated attempt at a tantrum. Another step closer to the line, teetering ever so slightly. Gingerly going down to one knee, he tried to slow his breathing, struggling to compose himself.

He finally freed the gun from the seam and removed it from the bag. Lifting it in front of Jerzy, he turned to face her and smiled as the white curls began to trickle down from the corners of his mouth.

"What are you going to do with that?" She was crying now, beginning to panic.

"What do you think I'm going to do with it? I'm going to…" He stopped mid-sentence, considering his next words. "I'm not going to do anything just yet. Say, that boyfriend of Carney's, has he got a name?"

"Yes, he has a name. Why? You don't know him. He ain't like you. I'm telling you, he's going to beat you blind if you're on this boat when they get back."

William grinned; realizing he was the boyfriend Jerzy was talking about.

"You think I'm stupid, don't you? You think I'm as dumb as my father was, don't you? Well, don't make that mistake, you little whore! Don't think you can play me for a fool! I'm not who you think I am; not today! No way! Today, I'm Bill Ammons! Ever heard of me? Have you?"

He was screaming now, spraying rank drops of mist from his mouth as he pushed fear deeper into Jerzy's heart.

He saw the fear in her eyes then and it fed him. Like sugar in a rat, he got a rush from it. He moved forward and leaned over her small body, screaming his infected breath into her face. The spittle was dripping from his angular chin, bristled from not shaving.

"I asked you a question, bitch! Answer me! Have you ever heard of me? Carney and I went to dinner Monday night! We've been dating since before she left Atlanta! Sound like anything you might've heard before?"

Jerzy drew herself up into a ball on the mattress, afraid anything she said would be the wrong thing. She realized what had happened. The stares at court; those hateful stares. He'd been stalking Carney to get to her. He really was the guy Carney was dating, and this was what he was after. She knew for sure now he was insane and didn't want to upset him further. She looked at him, trying hard not to make eye contact. She squeezed her eyes shut as he approached her, reaching.

Grabbing her again by her blouse, he pulled her up and slapped her across the face. Jerzy pulled away quickly to avoid getting hit again. He lost his grip and she slid to the corner of the mattress, against the side of the boat. He stretched across and grabbed her again, threading his fingers through the strap of her top.

Resisting the force of being dragged to him, Jerzy pulled until the strap broke and she fell free; scurrying back to the safety of the corner, both breasts naked and exposed to him. She raised her arms, covering her breasts. William again stretched across the mattress, twisting the fingers of his left hand in her hair and pulling her to face him. He pressed the nose of the revolver into her cheek, the iron sight cutting her olive skin. She closed her eyes and held herself tightly, determined to keep her breasts covered.

"You know who I am now. I didn't come here for this, honestly. But I swear, I..."

His sentence was broken by the sound of Carney's voice. He dragged Jerzy by the hair, back to the cabin doors where he stepped up and looked down the dock. Carney was approaching, shopping bag in hand. He hurried back to the rear of the cabin, taking Jerzy with him. He pushed the gun into her forehead now.

"Be very still and don't say a word. If you move, I'll shoot you first and then kill your friend. Nod your head if you understand me."

He let go of her hair as she nodded. Carney called out again.

"Don't try and hide from me, Bill. I saw your car in the parking lot."

Jerzy heard the happiness in Carney's voice as she came closer to the boat. William peered over the doors again. She was standing at the back of the boat, talking to a teenage boy.

"She really likes you. She likes Bill Ammons anyway. I don't think she had any idea who you really are. This is going to hurt her bad. Please don't do this. Please don't." Jerzy tried to appeal to him.

"I told you I didn't come for this. I didn't even know you were here. I knew she had a friend with her, but I didn't have any idea it was you. I was coming today to tell her the... Well, I was going to leave her a note and tell her why I wasn't going to show up. I thought you two had left or something."

Carney stepped through the transom door and onto the deck. Her voice was happy and light.

"Come out, come out, wherever you are."

William put a finger to his mouth, telling Jerzy to stay quiet. Carney was rummaging through a compartment under the wheel.

"Jerzy, come on up, darlin'. Help me find the satellite phone. I need to call my dad." She continued to throw things around, mumbling. "Come on, Jerzy. Stop fooling around, you little mutt. Dad called the marina and left a message for me to call him. He told them it was urgent. I hope nothing's wrong."

Finally, she gave up and started toward the cabin. Jerzy watched William's face. His eyes darted from side to side, wondering what to do next.

Carney walked through the cabin door. She was wearing beach clothes as well; a one-piece, light-green swimsuit that exposed most of her breasts. A white mesh sarong was tied loosely at her waist. The bottom cut of the suit was French, riding high on ample thighs already tanned. She wore a tattered white baseball cap to keep her hair in a bundle on top of her head.

She gasped as she looked at Jerzy, the muzzle of a shiny pistol pressed against her cheek. As if it were a great distance to the holder of the gun, she turned her head slowly until her eyes rested on William Caine.

At first she thought it was a joke. A pirate on board; that makes sense. Maybe this because she didn't want to think it was real. Perhaps because she once thought she might be able to fall in love with Bill Ammons. Then, she looked back at Jerzy and knew the scene was real.

Like her first days in the Midtown Women's Center, Jerzy's eyes were black balls of fear, no longer wide and seeking as Carney had become accustomed to seeing them lately. Tight and narrowed, closed to the next event. Eyes that had no interest in what was coming next. Sightless black orbs with nothing but misery to look forward to.

She was startled out of her thoughts by the sound of William's voice.

"Carney, listen to me. We're all going to walk upstairs together. You're going to start the engines and get us underway. Do you understand me?"

"Bill..."

"Don't try and talk to me, Carney; not until we're out on the water. Nod your head if you understand me."

Carney nodded her head and started to turn around, lifting her hand to the cabin doors.

"I didn't tell you to go yet, Carney. Don't fuck with me. Turn around here and look at your little friend. Ask her if I'm serious."

Carney turned and looked beyond the frightened eyes at the small arms, tightly hugging her breasts to keep them from the monster's view. Her hair in a tangle around her face, Carney knew she'd been roughed up.

She looked at William without speaking, shaking her head.

"Good, Carney. Now I'm going to get the girl here to walk right behind you. It's really very simple. Up the stairs, start the boat, and get out of here fast. Now go."

He grabbed Jerzy tightly by the hair and pushed her against Carney's back, forcing them both up the stairs.

William stood directly behind Jerzy as they watched Carney pilot the boat out of the harbor. As soon as she'd traveled past the no-wake zone, William leaned over and pushed forward on the throttle. The big boat picked up speed quickly, impressing William with its performance. Carney turned to William and shook her head, lowering her gaze as she did so.

"Why are you doing this, Bill? Does it have something to do with the trouble you said you were in?"

"I'm not in trouble anymore. No, this has nothing to do with that. This entire thing was never supposed to happen."

Carney wanted answers. This was someone who had occupied her thoughts for several days now; as well as several nights.

"Then what's going on? Please tell me there's a reason, Bill. I'm really scared, you know?"

She started crying, looking away from him. Jerzy, with the pistol still in her face, turned to William.

"Tell her who you are. Don't let her suffer like this. Tell her who you really are and get this over with."

William didn't know how to do that. He didn't know how to deliver that much hurt to someone who'd been hell bent on creeping into his heart against his will.

Carney turned back to look at Jerzy. The girl seemed to be trying to speak with her eyes; afraid if she said any more the gun in her face would end her life on the spot.

"Please, Bill, put the gun down. Don't keep it in her face like that. I promise, we'll do whatever you ask. Just take that gun out of her face."

William obliged her and lowered the gun to his side. As he did this, Carney noticed the gun had a silver loop screwed into the bottom of the butt. A remnant of cowboy days, Ralph had told her, when she'd asked about the same loop in the butt of his gun. It dawned on her that the Colt Python was missing its scope. She looked at William, searching his face for any sign of the man she thought she knew.

"Are you going to tell me anything? What did Jerzy mean when she said to tell me who you are? Are you someone I should know? I thought…"

"Just shut the fuck up, alright? Just shut your mouth and I won't shoot you."

He moved quickly, pushing the gun in front of her. He aimed at a spot between her eyes, twelve inches from her face.

Carney saw it then and trapped laughter in her throat. She turned away quickly; facing the water, hoping the wind would aid her in stifling the urge. Unable to hold back, she burst into a fit of low-pitched laughter. William stuttered at first and then grabbed her by the hair, pushing the baseball cap off her head and into the wind.

"What the fuck are you laughing about, fat ass? Do you see anything funny here? Do you?"

He pressed the gun into her throat as he tightened his grip on her hair. Carney continued the laughter, low and grunting; the huge chest heaving in a near-perfect rhythm with the pace of the boat as they skipped across the gulf.

"It's just too funny, Bill! It never fails. I thought I was falling in love with you. I wanted you to fall in love with me. But I'm a loser magnet. I can't believe it. You were great; a regular fucking Oscar winner. I thought you had a problem because your parents were ending a long marriage. Maybe you were stuck in another relationship. I had no idea you were just another fucking schmuck. What is it about me? What is it that makes me so attractive to men who are so emotionally crippled? Is there a sign on my head? Do I look like someone who's dying to be tortured by scum like you?"

William didn't like what he was hearing. She said so many things so fast, he didn't know whether they were directed at him or not. *The language coming from her mouth was foul,* he thought. *Women shouldn't talk like that.*

"Shut up, Carney. I'm war..."

"Do you want to know what it was about you that really threw me? Do you, Bill? You didn't even want to kiss me. I thought that was so fucking quaint. So fifties, you know? I wanted to fuck your brains out. I wanted you to ask me to go to your hotel room. You know, most guys want it on the first date. Not you, no. Not on the second or the third. Hell, I thought you were gay for a minute. Jerzy and I even talked about it. I kept saying no, he's just a gentleman, Jerzy, but he's definitely not gay. Do you still need to know why I'm laughing? Do you? Isn't it obvious? I'm such a dumb ass, letting someone like you..."

Jerzy couldn't stand it anymore. She couldn't stand by and watch Carney take the blame for what she thought was her fault. She couldn't let Carney go on beating herself up over all of this. *He might hurt me, but I have to tell her,* she thought.

"Carney, he's the judge's son. He's William Caine."

All that could be heard was the sound of the engines below and the wind being sliced by thirty-eight feet of fiberglass. The three of them looked back and forth at one another, neither of them knowing what to say. The youngest spoke first, to Carney.

"He's here for me, Carney. He thinks I did something bad to his dad. He's right, too. I know he's right."

She turned to face William, still holding the gun at Carney's throat.

"Please don't hurt her, please. I'll do whatever you tell me to. Just don't hurt her. Let her turn the boat around and go back to the marina. I'll go wherever you want to go. Do you hear me? You and I can go wherever you want. I don't care what you do to me."

"Shut up. I didn't come here for you. You're wrong. I came here for Carney. I came here to leave this note." He pulled the paper from his pocket and handed it to Carney as he stared into her eyes. "It was you all along. I found you at the mall, and let you think you found me. I lied about who I was. I wanted revenge against Ralph for letting them convict my dad. He was supposed to help my dad. Then after he got killed, I decided the only way to hurt Ralph was to hurt you. I started calling you and going out with you. I was looking for a way to kill you. All that time, waiting for a chance. Then we started talking more, and I started seeing you in a different light. You seemed to really like me, and that felt good. Then I started seeing everything about the case differently. I think the night we met at the marina, your first night here, I decided I wanted to spend more time with you. I wasn't coming fishing today. I was bailing out until I found a good way to explain all my lies."

"Is there a good way one explains their lies? I'm sorry, William, but had I known who you really were, I probably would've still felt the same way. I know now that it was all a lie, but nothing you lied about made me feel anything for you. You made me feel for you. Did you really graduate from Notre Dame? I don't care. I graduated from Vandy. Are you really a broker? I don't care, babe. I've saved over a hundred thousand since high school and I work in a damn camera store. Were you really a football player? A big, agile athletic-type guy? Whatever. I can fuck like a French whore, and most times I don't care who it's with. That's all just biography, William. I was becoming more and more attracted to a man; not a story. Not a list of shit that means absolutely nothing to me."

William began to turn red. Beatrice's voice as she sat on the bed screaming at him came back into his head. The more Carney talked, the more agitated he became. He barely heard the last of her sentence as his mind snapped.

Drawing the gun back, he swung the weapon hard and landed the steel against the side of her head. The rib atop the barrel hit her where the cartilage of her ear made contact with the creamy softness of her face, tearing a wide gap in her flesh.

Carney brought her hand to her face, feeling the gaping slice in her skin. She screamed and tackled the surprised man, knocking him to the deck. Jerzy jumped and ran to assist, kicking him in the head. Both women screamed at him as he writhed on the deck, still gripping tightly to the gun. William rolled onto his front and struggled to bring himself up to his knees. Jerzy moved slightly left and began kicking him in the stomach. Mustering what strength he could, he raised himself up, shoving the lightest woman away from him first. Jerzy fell backwards and landed on the rear deck of the boat.

William absorbed all Carney continued to pummel him with as he reached his hand into the belt around her waist and pulled her forward. She tumbled over him, staggering until she fell. As Carney rolled to the deck, William stood up. His nostrils flared and clear liquid sprayed as he breathed hard through his nose. He pointed the gun at Carney and pulled the hammer back.

Jerzy watched him aim the gun at Carney and again she moved forward to jump him. She couldn't let him harm Carney. Within three feet of him, the youngster pulled up and stopped. He pivoted abruptly and pointed the gun at her. With William now preoccupied with Jerzy, Carney slowly inched backward to the control panel. *Any minute now. As soon as you pull the trigger, dumb ass.* She placed her right hand on the throttle, already at half-speed. She moved her left hand deftly up to the wheel, careful not to be seen in his peripheral vision.

She listened as William shouted violently at Jerzy. "You first, you stinking whore!"

He laughed loudly, madly screaming like some animal cornered. He carefully aimed at her fully exposed breasts and pulled the trigger.

Click. William looked at the gun; puzzled. He aimed again; pulled the trigger again. Another *click.* Carney pushed the throttle forward with a hard thrust, at the same time spinning the wheel hard to the right. The sudden burst sent the madman flying backward to the rear of the boat, the gun leaving his hand as he flailed in the wind in search of balance. Carney spun the wheel further right and pressed her weight on the throttle. William was screaming as he flipped over the transom door and into the blue-green water of the gulf.

Jerzy ran forward to Carney and pulled her into a hug. Carney slowed the boat and righted the wheel. Pulling the tattered remains of her shirt from her shoulders, Jerzy pushed it against Carney's face to stop the bleeding. The women held each other for several minutes before either was able to speak.

"He shot me, Carney. He really shot me. If the gun was working he would've killed me."

Carney shut the engines down and eased herself from the grip of the still terrified teenager. She walked to the rear of the boat and picked up the gun, bringing it back to show Jerzy.

"The gun's working, Jerzy. It doesn't have any bullets in it. This is my dad's gun. Look right here."

Carney swung the cylinder out, exposing her father's initials etched into the weapon's frame.

"I saw the empty cylinders when he put it in my face. Then when he lowered it to his side, I saw this little loop and I knew then it was my dad's gun. It's never loaded. Dad keeps it in his bedroom drawer. William must've taken the scope off, so I didn't recognize it at first, but the loop gave it away."

"He really was going to shoot me, wasn't he, Carney? I mean, he didn't know the gun wasn't loaded, did he?"

"No, he didn't bother to check it. I doubt he even knew how, dumb ass."

The two sat on the rear deck cushions without talking for several minutes as they drifted on the open water. Carney walked down to the cabin and searched a small chest until she located the satellite phone. While she was gone, Jerzy removed her top and lay back in the seat behind the Captain's chair; her long black hair falling over the transom. Carney returned to find the half-naked girl sunning herself as if nothing had happened.

"Girl, get down there and get some clothes on."

She was smiling, thinking she'd join Jerzy as soon as she talked to her father. Dialing her home number first and getting no answer, she tried his cell. Ralph answered on the second ring, still high up in the sky en route to Destin. He listened as Carney relived the past few hours. Ralph then told her all that had taken place between him and Beatrice which led him to fly to Florida.

Carney was proud of her dad, having put the puzzle together before she realized William's intentions. She teased him, relieved that she was alive to do so.

"So you knew already? I guess you were just going to let that freak kill Jerzy and me? Is that it?"

"No, of course not, Carney. I just couldn't get down there fast enough. I called down there and told the people at the marina to tell you to call me if you came back. I told them to tell you it was an emergency."

"I went to buy film. A man named David caught me when I got back; he said it was urgent. Trouble is, William was already on the boat by then. When I boarded, I went down to the cab..."

"Carney!"

She heard Jerzy scream. Her father could hear the terror through the phone. She turned in time to see William kneeling on the swim platform, using Jerzy's long hair to pull himself into the boat. Carney screamed into the phone.

"Daddy! He's back. He must've grabbed the ladder on his way down. He's got Jerzy."

Carney was terrified, babbling into the phone without regard to what Ralph was saying. Ralph shouted, trying to get Carney to calm down. The sound of her father's voice loud in her ear finally caused her to calm down and listen to him.

"Carney, can you still hear me?"

"Yes, Daddy."

"Go below now."

"Daddy, I can't leave Jerzy up here with him. I have to..."

"Carney! Be still and listen to me. You said you have my gun, right?"

"Yes, but he knows it's empty. That's no good, Daddy."

"Baby, go below and listen to Daddy, okay? Jerzy will be fine. He has to be weak by now, baby. He can't hurt her too badly. Just go below now and do as I say."

Carney followed her father's instructions and walked below, closing the cabin doors behind her. William watched her go and leaned into Jerzy, whispering in her ear.

"Your friend left, you bitch. She's locked herself below deck. See that? Do you see that? She abandoned you, just like her old man abandoned my dad. Both of them are fucking cowardly, two-faced pieces of shit. Help me get her. How about it, sugar? She's left you for dead, bitch; think about that."

Jerzy only trembled, the clutch of fear evident in the puddle forming on the cushion she sat on.

"Are you in the cabin now?"

"Yes, Daddy. What can I do? He'll kill her out there."

"Look in the locker to your right, the one with the mirror on it. Is it open yet?"

"Yes, it's open."

"Look inside the Coast Guard kit. There should be six hollow points in there."

"I see them."

"Put them in the gun, Carney. Shoot the bastard now. Just like at the range, baby. You shoot that crazy bastard."

"Oh, Daddy, I can't..."

"Yes, you can, Carney. You don't have any choice. He'll kill both of you. I'm still forty minutes away, so I'm no good to you yet. But you can shoot him, Carney; you know you can. Go now, baby. Don't hang up the phone; just lay it down and go now. "

William managed to climb to his feet. Walking toward the cabin doors with Jerzy in a headlock, choking her hard. His left hand was hanging free, the forearm mangled by the propeller. Blood dripped onto the deck from his fingertips.

Carney came through the cabin doors holding the gun on him.

"Let her go and back up, William. I'm serious. Let her go and back up. I'm going to give you a chance to live. Maybe not much of a chance, but a chance. Don't fucking think about it; just let her go now."

"You'll give me a chance to live? What the fuck are you talking about? You can't kill me with an empty gun."

"I'm not as stupid as you are, asshole. The gun isn't empty anymore. Now let her go and back up. I won't shoot you, if you jump off the boat."

"Jump off the boat? Are you fucking crazy? I did jump off the boat, bitch, and I paid hell getting back on. Look what the prop did to my arm." He held his wounded limb up for her inspection. "Jump off the boat, my ass. I'll fucking kill you."

He tossed Jerzy to the side and lunged at Carney. She quickly took aim and pulled the trigger. The shot missed, but the sound of the gun going off stopped William in his tracks. He dove for cover under the wheel, grabbing Jerzy as he did so.

"Let her go, William. Let her go now."

She eased the hammer back this time. Carney knew why she'd missed the shot. Pulling the trigger with the hammer down took additional force, and her fingers were weaker than her dad's. But with the hammer back, the shot would be true.

William stood now, grabbing Jerzy as she tried to crawl toward the safety of the cabin steps. He pulled her up from the deck, holding her closely against his body. Only the left side of his face was exposed as he shouted at Carney.

"Put the gun down! You're not going to shoot me with this little slut in front of me! You've missed once already! Hell, you'll kill her; you know you will!"

He pushed Jerzy along as he forced his way toward Carney and the cabin doors.

"Don't come any closer, William. I don't want to kill you, but I will. Let her go and leave, please. At least that way you have a chance of surviving. Now, William! Go now!"

William took another step closer, pushing Jerzy in front of him. Carney heard him mumbling into Jerzy's ear as he advanced.

"Fucking fat ass bitch. See if she shoots. Not with you here. No fucking way. I ain't that stupid. Fucking fat ass bitch."

Still hiding behind the trembling Jerzy with only half of his face exposed, Carney took aim and allowed him two more steps. *I can't hit that narrow of a target*, she thought. William was opening his mouth to speak again when Carney screamed at Jerzy to drop to the deck. Jerzy responded quickly, making her body go limp and collapsing in William's grasp. Surprised, he reached down to catch the melting girl. For an instant, he looked up at Carney as she pulled the trigger and blew off the left side of his face, spraying her friend with blood and bits of matter.

Jerzy collapsed, unconscious from sheer terror. Carney lifted the small girl and placed her on a side cushion as a gray Coast Guard helicopter suddenly showed up off the starboard bow. Carney saw movement from the corner of her eye as she looked up at the helicopter. Although William was dead, his right eye continued to circulate the boat looking for her. His mutilated hand reached up to explore the cavity created by the hollow point bullet as he convulsed once and became still.

Carney ran below to call her father back on the satellite phone. When she picked the device up, she could hear Ralph calling her name.

"Daddy?"

"I heard most of what happened," Ralph told her. "Is he dead?"

Carney exploded into tears, struggling to answer her father.

"Calm down, Carney. I had the pilot radio the Coast Guard. They should've picked up the sat phone signal and have your location by now."

"They're already here, Daddy. Are you coming out here, or should I take us back in now?"

"Turn the boat to shore. I'll be there by the time you get to the marina. The helicopter should follow you in. There's nothing to worry about, Carney. You did the right thing."

CHAPTER THIRTY-TWO

Parlee turned the faucet on and off quickly and watched the water swirl down the drain in the tiny sink. Fascinated, he turned to speak.

"Damn, Charlie, this here sink ain't much smaller than the one in me and Jerzy's apartment. And look here."

He bent to open the small refrigerator under the three-burner range.

"They even got a refrigerator. Got beer in it, too. A whole twelve-pack."

Charlie laughed, watching the face of the big man as he explored the galley on board the Cheri A Lamore.

"I'm glad we were able to make it down here, Parlee. I'm really glad we all got together. This is going to be fun."

"Are you sure all six of us are gonna fit on this thing. I mean, sleepin' and all?"

"Mr. Light said we'd have room to spare. Besides, we're only going out overnight. We shouldn't be too cramped."

Parlee stayed below, opening the door to the head to explore further while Charlie made his way through the cabin doors to the rear deck. He stepped out onto the dock to put the remaining supplies on board.

On the flybridge, Carney and Jerzy were huddled in the white-cushioned settee, listening to Kim Puckett explain all that had taken place since finding Parlee Rabideaux.

"He didn't want to come down here," Kim said. "Jill kept telling him the job would be there when he got back, but he insisted he work at least a week. It turned out for the best, though. He's got the apartment looking pretty good. I went over and helped him finish the painting so we could get the curtains up before we left. Jerzy's room is beautiful. He even managed to come up with a few things to make it look more feminine."

She smiled as she turned and watched her husband place the last suitcase aboard the boat. When she sensed enough time had passed, she looked at Carney and spoke again.

"What was Mrs. Caine's reaction when she was told about all that happened? I mean, was she angry?"

"She wanted to come on the boat," Carney said. "She wanted to meet Jerzy and have both of us explain what had taken place. Daddy said she called him on his cell phone as he was flying down here, and she was already in her car heading this way. She didn't find out William was dead until Thursday morning after she arrived. Jerzy and I met Daddy at the marina, and the police took the boat over. That was Wednesday night. Daddy stayed until the police were finished. On Thursday morning, he came down and made sure Evan, the owner of the marina, had the boat pressure-washed and the mess cleaned up. By the time she got on the boat Thursday afternoon, everything was pretty normal. She walked around with us while we explained everything the way it happened. She was great about it. She said nothing he did surprised her."

Kim looked shocked, turning from Carney to look over at Jerzy.

"You mean, it didn't surprise her that he tried to kill the two of you? If she knew he was so disturbed, why didn't she tell someone?"

"She did. She told Daddy. They talked for a long time the night before, but neither one of them put it together until Wednesday morning after we were already gone. That's when Daddy flew down here and found out Beatrice was on her way in her car. She told us William strangled her. He thought she was dead, so he left town right away. He tore up her house to make it look like someone had robbed them and killed Mrs. Caine. I really feel sorry for her, having to go through all that."

The three women continued to talk, waiting for the boat to be loaded and the rest of the passengers to arrive. Parlee finished exploring the boat and climbed the stainless steel ladder to the flybridge.

"This sure is somethin' else," he said. "This thing has everything a house has; just smaller."

He walked over and wedged his large body into a seat next to Jerzy, pulling her close and squeezing her with one massive arm. He looked at Carney.

"So what time do we set sail, missy?"

Carney laughed and shook her head. She'd grown fond of Parlee in the short time since they'd met. His arrival in Destin the previous week brought healing to both her and Jerzy. The turnaround in the young girl's attitude became more obvious when reunited with her father. She seemed to sense it was all right to be a teenage girl, now that her daddy was there to look after her. Carney remembered her own youth; how it seemed to shock her father when she began wearing dresses and makeup. Ralph was resentful at first, she thought. It took some time before he realized even though she was growing more feminine, she was still his little girl.

She was anxious to share her plans with him. Her path in life had become more clearly defined as a result of Jerzy Rabideaux. Her perception of everything changed, as did her focus. She'd taken the bar exams and passed. She'd discussed a law practice in Destin with friends, all of them supportive. Her friend, Huey, committed to providing any financial assistance she might need, as well as a promise to send her some business. The tiny resort town had enough year round residents to support another lawyer. She knew Ralph would be proud. He may struggle with the idea of her leaving home, but he was looking at retirement within a few years, and who knew what might happen?

Carney awakened from her daydream to voices on the dock directly behind the boat.

"What time are we sailing, Skipper?" Ralph shouted up at her.

"Where have you been? You two were supposed to be here an hour ago. We were getting ready to leave without you."

Carney laughed as she slid down the ladder to the main deck. She walked to the transom door and took two large shopping bags from her father's hands.

"Beatrice wanted to stop and pick up a few things. I thought we'd never get out of that store."

Carney walked to the cabin door and handed the bags down to Charlie. She turned and watched as her father held gently to Beatrice's hand and guided her aboard the boat. She thought there was a new look about her father, something that was never there before. She smiled, switching on the blower as she prepared to get them underway. Moments later as Carney steered the boat into open water, Jerzy and Beatrice appeared in the small cockpit, each holding a small bag. Beatrice pulled herself up onto the cushioned bench next to Carney and placed the bag she carried on the seat between them.

"I had to stop and get these little trinkets for the two of you. Ralph said Jerzy recently had a birthday, and I thought that... Well, as a *thank you* for taking me along on this fishing trip... I wanted to give you both a small gift. They're little shell necklaces; another beach fad. I hope you like them."

Carney looked at Jerzy. She already had her necklace out of the bag, fingering the glossy shells.

"It is all right to bring you a gift, isn't it, Carney? I mean, you're not..."

Carney looked at Beatrice. *Such a pretty woman*, she thought. *So kind and thoughtful; even under these conditions.*

"Oh, I'm sorry, Beatrice. I was watching Jerzy. She's grown so much these past few months, but she's still like a little kid with a new toy."

"She has a good role model in you, Carney. You've learned something from her as well. Your father says he can see change in both of you, so you're obviously good for each other. I'm glad to have an opportunity to get closer to you both."

Carney blushed, embarrassed by the compliment.

"Thank you, Beatrice. And yes, it's fine to bring us a gift." She took her necklace from the bag and put it on, Jerzy reaching up to help her with the clasp.

"There we go. We look like twins, yes?"

They all laughed at the thought; all tension gone.

Carney stood and reached for Beatrice's hands.

"How would you like to learn to drive this old girl, Bea?"

Beatrice smiled at Carney's use of her nickname. She slid across the seat into the driver's position, and took the helm.

⸸

Kim and Charlie Puckett sat on the flybridge with Ralph, the wind gently smoothing their faces as they watched Beatrice steer the boat through two-foot waves. Carney was still busy giving her a crash course in boating while Parlee asked endless questions about the boat in general.

On the rear seat where she had ten days earlier resolved to die, Jerzy watched her shipmates watching each other. She remembered how nervous she was when Ralph Light first mentioned Beatrice Caine wanted to meet her. She couldn't fathom why the wife and mother of the two dead men would want to meet the person most responsible for their deaths. Ralph and Carney reminded her the judge was the one responsible for the tragedy; not her. She tried her best to imagine what Beatrice Caine would look like, and didn't even come close. She wasn't a frigid old witch; she wasn't unfriendly and uncaring either. The things the judge had told her about Beatrice were nothing close to the woman Jerzy knew today.

She was younger than Jerzy envisioned her, very high-spirited. The widow was thin, rather pretty and still firm. The young girl looked into the cockpit where Beatrice sat with her white cap pulled down over her head and the long red hair blowing in the wind, smiling as Carney playfully chided Parlee for asking dumb questions. *Beatrice never belonged to the Caine family,* Jerzy thought. *She's been looking for the same thing I have; probably for a lot longer.* On the flybridge holding hands and looking out at the Gulf of Mexico were her foster parents. Although she'd live with her father, she'd never leave Charlie and Kim. She'd grown to love them too much. She remembered how safe she'd felt in Kim's arms the night they'd found her in the parking deck. Jerzy knew that was how a child was supposed to feel in the arms of their mother. Safe, and without fear. They loved her also, and Jerzy knew that. Ralph sat on the flybridge across the table from Charlie and Kim. When Jerzy and Carney finally arrived back at the Destin Marina that terrible day, Ralph jumped into the boat and grabbed the young women as if they were both his daughters. The three of them were huddled on the deck, crying in joy and relief until the police arrived and pulled them apart so the investigation could begin.

Jerzy remembered Ralph telling them to get William's body off his boat, that he needed a few minutes with his girls. He shouted at the officers until they turned them both loose and busied themselves with the task of lifting the dead man onto a board. His girls; Jerzy liked that. Back at the Light condo, after the police released them and the initial shock had subsided, the three of them discussed Jerzy's plans for the future. Ralph offered her a job for the remainder of the summer, and encouraged her to graduate; something Jerzy thought she'd never accomplish. When the Pucketts arrived the following week with her father, Jerzy was almost sure it was a dream. *She loved her family just fine*, she thought, as the Cheri A Lamore slid gracefully across the waves, the shoreline disappearing behind her.

AUTHOR BIO

Jimmy Hurd began writing stories, poetry, and prose over thirty years ago. Born in Monroe, Michigan, the author has spent most of his life in the Southern and Western United States, with the exception of an extended tour in Korea while serving in the U.S. Army. He describes his early years as his "Migrant" years.

"My stepdad was a carpenter and he would take us with him to wherever he found work. We lived in Ohio, Indiana, West Virginia, Texas, and Florida. On my own, I've added Tennessee and Georgia to that list."

Jimmy began writing to amuse his maternal grandmother, who eventually succumbed to complications associated with Alzheimer's disease in 1993 while convalescing at her home in Clearwater, Florida.

"She was always a little ditzy, and I mean that in a good way. At over seventy years old she liked to wear her bikini and sun herself outdoors, walking the beach as if she were still a young girl. She was the positive I so desperately needed as a child; to her, anything was possible and she never let me forget that. She just always made me feel like she loved me best."

Jimmy has been employed in the auto industry for twenty-seven years, going to work for Ford Motor Company in 1978. After an extended layoff, he transferred to Atlanta, Georgia in 1984.

The author currently lives in Fayetteville, Georgia with his wife, Patricia. Jimmy has three children, Vaughn, Sarah, and Madison.